DARK SERVICE

LINDA COLES

Blue Banana

Introduction

As this is a story set in the United Kingdom with English characters, I have opted for UK spelling rather than USA. Therefore, there will be what seem like typos to some readers, and perhaps words you may not be familiar with, but they are in keeping with the British way and terminology.

Linda

Chapter One

HER EYES FLICKERED BRIEFLY, like an almost-gone candle, and then slowly opened. Her eyelids were heavy, and she struggled with the desire to keep them closed. Heavy from what, she'd no idea. With an effort, she wrenched them open, and now another problem presented itself. Where the hell was she?

The glow in the room was dusky orange, the lamp in the corner the only thing giving light; the world outside the window was dull and dark grey. Her hand reached out and felt where she was lying. The satiny fabric of the sofa told her she wasn't at home; her own sofa didn't feel this way. And there was a soft, pale green blanket draped over her. She didn't have one of those. Sitting up, she licked her lips; her mouth was parched dry as a biscuit and her head buzzed with a sound like a drone hovering around her ears. She looked around the room and noticed the tea tray set out on the table in front of her, a single empty cup and a plate of uneaten tiny triangles of delicate sandwiches without crusts. A slight curl at the edge told her they'd been there a while; the day was warm and no match for soft, fresh bread.

So, where was she? And more importantly, how had she gotten there? And even more importantly, *why* was she there, wherever 'there' was? With no immediate answers to her questions, she took in the rest of the dimly lit room. It gave her no clues. Orienting herself, she stood on wobbly legs and walked to the door. She turned the handle, which opened easily, and, holding the door carefully open, looked out into an empty though somewhat familiar space. The corridor looked like any other hotel corridor in London: thickly carpeted, traditional styled art adorning the walls at sporadic intervals. She stepped back inside and shut the door again, deep in thought. The room was quiet, save for the hum of distant traffic and the odd car horn blaring, more or less a constant in London.

A quick scrutiny of herself told her she felt fine, apart from her dusty mouth and the drone stuck inside her head. Her clothes were all still in place, and she seemed not to have been harmed in any way. But something felt different, lost almost, and she couldn't place what it was. It was weird. Had she fallen ill and someone taken her in, looked after her? Why was the blanket covering her when she woke, and where had the food come from? Where were these people? Closing the door, she wandered around the room a little, taking in the large undisturbed king bed, the luxury unused bathroom and the sitting area where she'd woken up only moments ago. An envelope propped up on the ornate desk caught her eye. There was one word written on it – Taylor. So, somebody knew her name – that was obvious. Picking it up, she slid the expensive-feeling embossed card out and read the message.

Your debt has been settled. I'd advise you to tell no one. It wouldn't be wise.

It was beautifully handwritten in a fancy, styled font. Sliding her finger over the words, she guessed quite rightly it had been written with ink. Not from a cheap plastic pen, but from a fountain pen; that in itself was quite uncommon, and something she knew a little about. Confusion still clouded her head: what *had* happened, exactly, and what debt was the sender talking about? She caught her own reflection in the gilt mirror over the desk and gave an involuntary scream. In place of her long, wavy cognac locks was one short stump, still secured by a hair tie. Panicked, she raised her hand and tentatively touched her head.

Someone had stolen her glorious hair.

Chapter Two

TWENTY-FOUR HOURS earlier

Taylor stood patiently at the check-in desk, surrounded by a long snaking queue of other travellers. Newark airport was just like any other – the noise of chatter in languages from across the globe, the hugs and tears of loved ones leaving, the excited cries of children off on the trip of a lifetime.

But for Taylor, the trip ahead signified the end of an era, an era of twelve months in New York working for one of the best galleries in the world, dealing with some of the most sought-after antiques money could buy. And money did buy them, in obscene amounts, but that was the very wealthy for you. When they were willing to spend hundreds of dollars on a glass of the finest champagne available, millions was small change for the purchase of whatever they desired. She'd enjoyed her time living in the city, though her tiny flat was nothing spectacular, unlike the items she worked with, but it had suited her and the location was perfect. Going back home to London would mean a huge adjustment but she eyed it as another chapter in her life, another story to be written, another adventure all her own. She'd make it work; she always did. She shuffled forward, her two large bags on a trolley in front, passport at the ready. The desk in front became free and the attendant beckoned her over. Taylor gave her name and handed her passport over.

"Good morning, Miss. Palmer." Her east coast accent rolled over Taylor in a way she knew she was going to miss.

"Morning."

"I have good news for you: you have been upgraded to First Class, no less."

Taylor stuttered a little as she replied, "Pardon? Are you sure? How come?"

"It doesn't tell me. I'm sorry, but you definitely have been issued with a First Class ticket. There is no mistake. Is that alright, Miss Palmer?"

Taylor didn't need to think long, and the smile that broke out on her face confirmed to the attendant it was, indeed, okay.

The attendant carried on. "Today is your lucky day – perhaps I might suggest you buy a lottery ticket?" Her smile was sincere. She handed Taylor her boarding pass for the trip back to London – in First Class. "Enjoy your flight."

"Oh, I think I will. Thank you." With her luggage handed over, Taylor carried on towards security and passport control, a smile on her beautiful young face at the stroke of good luck. Never in all her times of travelling throughout the world had she ever been upgraded, but there was a first time for everything, and right then, she really didn't care. It was a shame the journey back wasn't even longer so she could enjoy the full experience, though; she'd always wanted a glass of the real McCoy in a crystal flute. Now she might just get one.

Behind her and well out of sight, a tall, dapper-looking silver fox of a man stood watching her delighted smile. The corners of his eyes wrinkled slightly as he strained to catch odd words of her conversation with the check-in attendant, gauge her reaction in full, but her body language gave him the verification he needed, nay, hoped for. Her hair gently flowed over her shoulders as she moved, mesmerizing him with its shimmer, and he hoped he wasn't staring too much; otherwise he'd get caught. All around him the hustle of the airport carried on, but he was lost in his thoughts as long as she stood there, fixed to the spot as though his feet had been glued to the tiles beneath them. He was glad he'd been able to get her a place in First Class, give her the gift, and all without her knowing it had been he. This was as he'd wanted it to be: he'd asked the check-in attendant not to tell a soul he'd been the one to upgrade her. He'd said it would be a nice surprise; she was a friend of his daughter's and hadn't seen her for some time. She'd be thrilled, he'd said.

The attendant had smiled at his generosity. "What a lovely thing to do," she'd said. And so it had all been organized; the young woman was none the wiser. When she finally took her seat later, they'd sit next to one another in comfortable silence, perhaps even make small talk, he safe in the knowledge he'd given her something nice, something she'd enjoy, look back on with delight. Then he could be repaid in full, at a time that suited him. And suited his needs. That, he knew, would be quite soon.

She had just what he desired. Watching her move away towards the gate, her Louis Vuitton bag balancing in the crook of her elbow, he pulled his phone out and activated an app, knowing the rest would happen seamlessly while he was in the air. Seated next to her.

Chapter Three

TAYLOR RELAXED BACK in her reclining chair, her legs stretched out in front, and marvelled at the soft leather and how the other half travelled. She'd only been on board a few minutes and already the attendant had served her a glass of champagne at her seat – and they hadn't even taken off yet. Glancing around the small private cabin, she took in the surroundings. The large leather seats, the state of the art personal screens, the space each passenger could enjoy in their own capsule-like environment, the smart bag containing toiletries and pyjamas to slip into later. It was unlike anything she had ever experienced, and her delight was obvious.

"It's a beautiful way to travel, don't you think?" A male voice to her left caught her attention. She jumped slightly.

"I'm so sorry. I didn't mean to startle you."

"You didn't. Not really. I was just a little mesmerized, that's all." Taylor turned to the gentleman and smiled. "And to answer your question, yes, it is a beautiful way to travel."

"I'm sorry – how rude of me." The man extended his hand in greeting. "I'm Terrance Dubonnet." Taylor stood to come up to some of the height of the silver-haired man in front of her, though she was short by about a foot. Not that she was small, far from it, but he must have been a little over six foot, in her estimation. Their hands connected and she returned a firm handshake.

"Nice to meet you. And I'm Taylor Palmer." Both of them were biting back smiles; they were both looking at sparkling eyes, though different colours.

"Good to meet you, Taylor. May I call you Taylor?"

"Of course, if I can call you Terrance." His face broke into a 'touché' smirk. She had a strong personality; he liked that. He ventured further with conversation, eager to talk to her.

"The new Dreamliner is particularly nice because there are only eight seats in the whole cabin. It's one of the most modern birds in the sky. It's a real treat to fly on one, don't you think?"

Taylor couldn't help the slight blush that crept over her cheeks. Should she say it was her first time in First? But there was no need. The silver-haired gentleman understood immediately.

"Well, if it's your first time on board in First Class, then you really must have the window seat. Then you can add the view to the whole experience. Allow me to swap seats with you. That is, if you would like?"

"Oh, I couldn't ask you to do that! But thank you anyway."

"Nonsense, my dear. I'd be delighted to swap with you. I'll just let the stewardess know. It's my pleasure, as I said." His silver-grey eyes twinkled at her in encouragement. How could she refuse?

"Well, in that case, I'd love to see the view as well. Thank you." Taylor couldn't believe her luck. Could this get any better?

"Splendid. Then you gather your belongings, and I'll let them know we've swapped. Then maybe we can chat again a bit later, during the flight? Perhaps over another glass of champagne?" The man nodded to her flute of bubbles.

"Certainly. It would be my pleasure." Taylor watched as he turned to talk to an attendant, then moved herself across the aisle to the window seat and settled back in. A moment later, she felt his presence rather than heard him, in the seat she had recently vacated, and snuggled back into her own. Closing her eyes to savour the moment, she wondered, and not for the first time, how she had come to be sitting in First Class. Not upgraded to Business Class, even, but full-on First

Class. Some airlines didn't even have a First Class section any longer, and with only eight seats in the cabin, there wasn't room for many to travel in such style. Her smile returned. The gentleman's voice caught her attention again.

"I'm so sorry to bother you again," he said apologetically, "but I thought I'd show you how to turn your seat into a lie-down bed for later. It's a long way back to London. I'm sure you'd appreciate a decent sleep?"

"Oh. Yes. Thank you. That would be great. It's been a long day, actually. I don't think I'll have too much trouble dropping off tonight."

"Well, allow me to make you more comfortable." Taylor removed herself from her private cubicle and watched as he showed her the mechanism. While it was kind of him to take an interest, she was curious why he was doing so. The flight attendant would have helped her anyway. As she watched his body bend to make the changes, she noticed how easy he was for an older man. She guessed he was in his seventies, perhaps; he was very nimble. Her own grandfather barely shuffled around his flat without groaning about being stiff, but not this gentleman. Perhaps he did yoga.

"There you go. It's really very easy." Touching the side of his nose knowingly, he added, "And nobody but us will know you've never travelled First Class." His kind smile filled his face genuinely, his silver eyes and silver hair giving him an air of Santa Claus without the red robe. A man to be trusted. Taylor smiled her appreciation at their secret.

"Now you settle in, and maybe after dinner we can chat more over that drink?"

"I'll look forward to it." Taylor sat back and picked up her book, ready for takeoff. In several hours she'd be back in London, and whilst she was looking forward to seeing her friends and family again, it was going to be tough to get settled in another role. She'd left New York, and everything she loved about it, behind her.

Dinner was served an hour into the flight. Gone were the nasty plastic trays filled with plastic cutlery, tasteless food steamed to death under a tinfoil lid, and the little plastic wine cup. An actual menu had been presented moments before, and she'd decided on herb-crusted lamb with all the trimmings as her main course. But right now, with stainless steel cutlery, Taylor was enjoying fresh lobster with a lemon dressing. Another flute of bubbles was at her side. She thought of what the majority of the passengers behind her in economy would be eating; there was no comparison. And in the back of her mind, still couldn't for the life of her understand how she'd come to be sat there enjoying it all. Perhaps she should buy that lottery ticket when she landed, before her luck ran out.

"More champagne, Madam?" The hostess hovered with a bottle of Laurent-Perrier Grand Siècle in her hand, linen napkin at the ready to catch any drips.

"Thank you – yes, please," Taylor said, and she watched as her glass was refilled for the third time. She caught the eye of her silver-haired gentleman friend as he watched with interest, a slight smile on his lips. She smiled back, and he nodded in satisfaction and went back to his own meal, safe in the knowledge that his plan was taking shape, both on board the aircraft and down on the ground.

The following morning, and an hour before the flight was due to arrive in London, he had his last task to fulfil. He ordered coffee for the both of them and a pot, cups and cream arrived shortly afterwards. He turned towards his new friend.

"I've taken a bit of a liberty, I'm afraid and ordered a pot of coffee. Would you care to share a cup with me?"

"Of course. That would be lovely," she said, closing her book. She watched as he poured aromatic coffee into a second cup and offered it to her.

"Cream and sugar?"

"Just cream, thanks."

"Well, I hope you've enjoyed your trip in First Class. You'll never want to go back to economy now, I expect." He was teasing her; his smile told her so.

"I've no choice, so I'd better get over myself and realize this has been a one-off. Fabulous, but the chance of being upgraded again is fairly remote, I'd say."

"Oh, you never know. Life is full of surprises, my dear. One never knows what will happen to us from one day to the next."

"Quite. I agree." Thinking, she added, "It's been nice meeting you too, and thanks for letting me have the window seat. The whole trip has been a surreal experience for me." She drained the remains of her coffee.

The silver-haired old man could only smile his delight in reply. The last part of his plan was now in place. The rice grain–sized device was now floating around inside Taylor's stomach, and would stay in her system for the next 24 hours, transmitting her location at all times. He sat back in his chair and smiled his appreciation to himself in the privacy of his own cubicle.

Within 24 hours, he'd have another prize to add to his collection. And he couldn't wait to savour it.

Chapter Four

THE MAN PICKED up the new signal almost immediately. He checked the code on the screen to see who had activated it, whom it had been issued to, and smiled as he saw the name of someone who regularly used his services. He never knew his real name, of course; anonymity was crucial all round for their services to work so seamlessly. His records showed the owner of the tracker as 'Quinine,' which meant nothing to him nor anyone else. The tracker device icon pulsed gently on his screen, the dot not far out of London itself, and he flipped to another screen to see where his team were located, who he could pull in for immediate surveillance. He texted the tracker device link to his chosen player, who acted immediately. Watching the movement of the now two different-coloured dots on his screen, he could see the player had moved towards the device's path, closing the gap between the two of them slightly. The easy part was in motion; the harder part would come some time later. In another hour or so by his reckoning, they would have a full visual of the person they were to supply. That was the part that had the potential to be tricky, so it was imperative nothing was overlooked.

The operator hit a series of keys on his keyboard that activated people in the vicinity as well as in an office block not far from where he was. With the aid of intelligence and surveillance techniques, a full profile of the person would be available very shortly so they could find their 'entry point,' the part that would lure the target into their trap. His clients paid handsomely for what they provided, and he took his work very seriously. A small army of people from all walks of life were available at any given time. If they needed a pretty waitress to hover, they had one. If they needed a scruffy tramp to observe, they had one. If they needed an investment banker to talk bullshit, they had one. Every angle was covered for every eventuality.

And that was because each of his clients required something rather particular.

Chapter Five

❧

TERRANCE DUBONNET WATCHED as the woman in his sights made her way through passport control and onwards with the rest of her journey home. She'd acted perfectly, been perfect in every way, actually, and while he lusted after that special something she possessed, he could be patient a while longer. He cut a dashing figure as he moved forward in a casual, relaxed manner, his statuesque body drawing glances from intrigued women of all ages. At seventy, he was in good shape physically, and he wore his expensive clothes like an iconic movie star working the red carpet on Oscar night. He oozed confidence and style. His black patent shoes peeked out from pressed fine wool trousers as his long legs extended gracefully forward. Up ahead, the cognac shade of her glorious hair was only just visible in the distance, and he placated himself with the knowledge that it wouldn't be too long before he saw her again. His phone interrupted his thoughts and buzzed with a message.

Activated. You have 23 of your 24 hours left. Be available. Further details to follow.

His smile stayed on his tanned face for a couple of minutes longer as he walked, cherishing the time to come later. Terrance clicked delete, though there really was no need; the message would have disappeared after he'd read it anyway. But he liked to be doubly sure. The organization he used checked every last detail for his protection, as well as their own. If anyone found his phone, there would be no evidence of their agreement existing, nothing to trace back – to anywhere. Clearing passport control, he headed off to collect his luggage and out to his waiting car and driver. He too loved New York, but it was always good to be home.

"Good morning, sir. Pleasant flight?"

"Good morning, Patrick. And yes – great, thanks. How's the traffic this morning? Same as usual?" His right eyebrow rose in anticipation of good news.

"Yes, sir. More like a car park. Is it ever anything else?" Patrick smiled as Terrance slid inside and made himself comfortable on the back seat. He picked up the morning paper that had been left for him; there was a fresh silver flask of hot coffee in the holder. Patrick had been his driver for more than 10 years and they had an easy, relaxed relationship. Everything about Terrance could be considered relaxed. Stylish, extravagant even, but relaxed overall. Like his car, which was a Bentley. But not the old-man type of Bentley. Terrance had a Flying Spur V8 – silver-grey, of course. And with a top speed of nearly 183 mph, it certainly wasn't an old man's car. Not that he'd ever needed the "zero-to-sixty MPH in 4.9 seconds." It was the luxury, style and comfort of the car that he loved. And he loved beautiful things.

The journey back to his home wouldn't take long. Englefield Green was only a handful of miles from the airport, but congestion often made the trip much longer than it needed to be. If the M25 was crawling, it didn't matter how big your engine was: you crawled along with everyone else.

As Terrance settled in, he looked at his wristwatch and noted the time. He'd started things in motion and had only 22.5 hours remaining, but he knew things were being taken care of on his behalf. He'd be messaged again soon with the next set of details, but until that time, he'd rest. He closed his eyes, laid his head back in his reclining seat, and let the smooth vibration of the car rock him for forty winks.

The sound of the driver's door closing woke him. Shuffling himself upright, he ran his bronzed fingers through his short hair as he readjusted to where he was.

"Sorry, sir. I wasn't sure whether to wake you or not, but I seem to have anyway. We're home."

"Lovely. Thank you, Patrick. I may need you again later today. I'm waiting on a call so I'll buzz you when I'm ready."

"Very good, sir." Patrick helped Terrance out of the car and began to unload the boot. "I believe Mrs. John has baked you a cake – your favourite, coffee and walnut. I expect she'll be glad to have someone to fuss over again now you're home."

Terrance smiled despite himself as he walked towards the front door. The door opened before he had got there himself and a small squeal of delight greeted him. In the doorway stood an older woman, about his own age, he'd often estimated, although he'd never confirmed this. Mrs. John, much like Patrick, had been part of his employ for a good number of years.

"Mrs. John!" he said to her, beaming. "Lovely to be home. I believe you've baked a cake?"

She caught his delighted smile and encouraged him inside before closing the door behind her. "Oh, it was meant to be a surprise! Wait until I see Patrick," she grumbled teasingly. "I have tea ready if you'd like?"

"Thank you, yes, though I'll take it in my room. Even flying First Class makes you feel like you need a proper shower when you get home, and that's precisely what I need to do. Give me ten minutes and I'll be ready."

"Good idea. In that case, you go on ahead and I'll bring it up shortly."

Terrance made his way up the sweeping staircase from the main entrance lobby towards his room. The house was far too big for him now, but it had been in his family for such a long time it didn't seem right to sell it and move on. But what would he use seven bedrooms for, really? The staff had their own cottages on the property, so at night, when everyone had gone home, there was only him. The smooth feel of the wooden banister reminded him of sliding down it as a child, though Nanny had threatened to tell if he did it too often. His parents had been absent during great chunks of his life growing up, so he'd been grateful for a nanny who'd allowed him to have fun while still being in charge. His younger sister Petra had then come along, and most of the focus had shifted onto her as he grew into a young teenager, though Nanny's influence had carried on. Reaching the top of the landing, he passed a door that had once led to Nanny's room when she'd lived in the house. He paused outside it. The room was empty now, and there was that unlived-in feeling about it, like most of the rooms in the house, though Nanny's old bed and some sparse pieces of furniture were still there.

And some of his memories.

His hand rested on the doorknob for a moment as he debated whether to enter or not. No, he'd save it for later.

Chapter Six

A KNOCK at the door caught his attention. From his en suite, he heard the faint clatter of china being laid out on the table in his bedroom and the humming that always accompanied his housekeeper as she busied herself. She never whistled – that would have been too distracting – but she did hum. He found it quite relaxing, almost therapeutic, and he welcomed her presence in the house when he was in residence. The place was too damn quiet otherwise. He slipped into his paisley robe and headed back into his room smelling of fresh deodorant and shampoo.

"Thank you for bringing it up here. I just needed to shower before I did anything else."

"You're welcome. Was it a successful trip?" He watched as she poured tea into his cup and placed a sugar lump into it and then set the little silver tongs back in the bowl. Why did he still have sugar lumps, he wondered? Wasn't it a tad old-fashioned? And did it even matter? Still, he wondered.

"Yes, it was. Though I do think I'm getting a little long in the tooth for so much travelling. I get tired quicker these days, I've noticed. And even First Class can't help with jet lag and time differences." Terrance sat in his favourite old leather chair, picked up his cup and saucer, and took a sip.

"Ah, that tastes good. You always have made a decent pot of tea," he said, satisfied. "The Americans just don't quite know how to get tea just right. Better sticking to coffee." He took another mouthful and sat back. Mrs. John offered him a slice of coffee and walnut on a little plate.

"Freshly baked this morning, if you'd like a piece?"

"Indeed, thank you," he said, and took the plate. Powdered icing sugar stuck to his upper lip as he took a bite, and coffee-coloured crumbs dropped to his plate. Mrs. John hovered as he ate, not sure if he wanted conversation or for her to leave.

"I may not be in for dinner tonight, so don't make anything special. Perhaps leave something in the fridge that I can heat up in case my plans fall through."

"Of course. Going somewhere nice?"

"Not too sure of my plans as yet. I may be going into London; we'll see."

Terrance finished the last of his cake and watched as Mrs. John topped his teacup up. With nothing left for her to do, she carried on. "I'll leave you in peace then, Mr. Dubonnet. You know where I am if you need anything," she said, and headed for the door, a faint hum going with her.

She'd have been a fine-looking young woman in her day, he thought as he watched her walk across the room. Tall and slender for her own years, she'd been a widow for nearly twenty of them, and he'd been tempted at times to state his interest. He never had. Yes, he got lonely rattling around the big house on his own, particularly at night, but she'd never shown any interest in him so he'd left it at that. But then he was her employer, so would she have anyway? And besides, he'd found his own unique and special interest had satisfied him over the years – just another reason he'd never sell the house he'd grown up in.

His thoughts turned to his old Nanny Prue. He thought of her often, like now. She'd been the catalyst for what he desired, he was sure. Where else had it stemmed from? Prue's room was right next door to his own, and without actually moving in there, he was as close as he could be to her memory. The hundreds of nights she'd spent in his room reading him a story, her light perfume lingering once she'd left his side. . . Her face had been so pretty, even to a small boy, her skin so soft. As he'd aged, become a young teenager, he'd received less of her attention as she'd focused on his younger sister, who had been a surprise to the whole family. Petra had needed Nanny full time, since his mother had no interest in looking after her herself, and so he'd seen very little of her. He'd missed her visits back then and somewhat resented Petra for stealing their time together, so he'd taken his interests out on the girls at school when he could. That hadn't been easy and had ultimately gotten him expelled from school for a period of time.

As he'd grown into an adult, his interest had become progressively easier to deal with, though he'd kept it a secret. Now? Well, he'd found the perfect way. If you knew where to look, you could find just about anything you desired, sexual or otherwise. And the service he used was a huge part of his life now, allowing him both freedom and the excitement his prizes afforded him.

A familiar stirring warmed his body as he remembered the red-haired woman on the flight that morning. He'd been able to watch her from the privacy of his seat without too much difficulty while she'd slept, and knowing she was being monitored for his needs right at that moment excited him. Soon, he'd have what he'd paid for, what she owed him in return. He drank back the last of his tea as his phone buzzed with the message he'd been waiting for. His pulse spiked as he read its contents.

The next part of the plan was now finalized.

All he had to do was turn up at the appointed time and location and he'd be in his version of heaven. He pressed delete and the carefully choreographed arrangements disappeared without a trace.

Chapter Seven

"I'D LOVE TO! Can you give me an hour?"

"I'll meet you there then. And Taylor?"

"Yes, Mum?"

"It's good to have you back on this side of the Atlantic for a while."

"Thanks. I'll see you shortly. And I'll tell you all about New York if you want to hear about it."

"Of course I do, darling. See you soon."

Taylor beamed at the now silent phone in her hand. She'd planned on going over to see her mum and dad the following day, but as it turned out they'd had some business in town and wouldn't be that far away. With a small chain of shoe shops on the market, Leonard and Judy Palmer had been meeting with various accountants and lawyers over the last couple of months, one of whom had brought them into Croydon. Close to retirement age, they'd decided to sell up, spend some of their hard-earned cash and travel, then probably buy a small hotel somewhere further down south on the coast. A romantic notion, Taylor thought but never said; many people wanted to retire and run a bed and breakfast.

It made perfect sense for them all to have a late lunch together and catch up. It had been three months since her last visit back home to

Croydon, and it had only been a short one, as she'd been on her way through to Europe; there hadn't been much time to spend with either her parents or her friends. Her passion for art allowed her to travel extensively with work, which she loved; she was sorry that her job in New York had finally come to an end. Now she wasn't sure quite what she might do with the next part of her life, although with the money she'd saved she was in no hurry to decide. Thoughts of travel conjured up the recent memory of being upgraded to First Class. Was that only yesterday? Still clutching the phone in her hand, she smiled broadly. "What will Mum say about that when I tell her?" she said to herself.

With only an hour until she was due to see her parents, she quickly changed into something a bit more feminine than normal, pushed a brush through her hair and then tied it up in a loose knot. She dabbed on some blusher and lipstick and she was all set. Her skin glowed with a light bronzing from the summer sun and weekends spent reading in Central Park, stretched out on the grass. But now at the end of summer, the sun's power was diminishing and cooler mornings and evenings were nudging their way in. The change of seasons excited Taylor – the wrapping up and putting away of one, the unfolding and rejuvenating of another in its place. A bit like changing your wardrobe over and packing away the old season in a box for storage until the following year, she thought. Packed away would be cotton shorts and skirts, and in their place would come light woollens and long-sleeved shirts. It wouldn't be long until the oak trees in the park near her flat would be dropping their fat leaves, the golden and brown Christmas-tree shapes covering the pavements. Pulling on a light cardigan, she closed the door behind her and headed outside to hail a taxi on to the restaurant for lunch. And her parents.

Chapter Eight

"You look lovely, darling! Welcome home."

"Thanks, Mum," Taylor said, hugging her mother tightly. "And how's Dad?" she said, turning and embracing him. She stayed tight in his arms for a moment or two longer as they squeezed each other tenderly. Always a daddy's girl.

"Much better for seeing you," he whispered in her ear with affection. Eventually they both pulled back and her father looked her up and down.

"You look lovely, Taylor, and so happy. And a tan really suits you." He backed up a step to take her in again. "You do look stunning. But then I am biased towards my girl." Anyone looking on would see how proud he was of his beautiful daughter.

"And how are you really, Dad?"

"Ah, well, we're both getting old and tired, but nothing to grumble about. We have our health on our side still, which is the main thing. And hopefully a buyer for the stores. But first let me ask you – any gentleman friends taken your eye yet?"

"Oh, Dad! No!"

"Don't embarrass her, Leonard. She's only just got here. Give her a chance."

Laughing, Taylor answered anyway. "There's plenty of time for all that, Dad. I'm only twenty-six," she said. "And it's a good job I haven't got a man friend now I've come back home. I don't have broken hearts to worry about. I don't think I could deal with being lovesick as well as starting a new career on this side of the world at the same time."

"And quite right too," her mother said, giving her husband a sideways glance in warning. "No rush. Your dad just wants to be a grand-dad, I think."

"It's usually the grandmother who pushes for that, isn't it?" Taylor said, laughing. "Talk about role reversal with you two."

"Well, I'm not pushing, Taylor. You go at your own pace. But let's sit down and you can fill us both in on your adventures as a single woman. And I'm hungry, so let's get a table and order."

The hostess escorted them to their waiting table and they each picked up a menu.

"Let's have a bottle of bubbles," Leonard said, "in celebration of you being home. And hopefully a sale finally." Turning to the waitress, he ordered a bottle of Veuve Clicquot and three champagne flutes. Judy raised her perfectly plucked eyebrows but immediately relented.

"Well, I'm in the mood for a proper celebration. It's so good to see you, Taylor. You do look well on whatever you've been up to, I must say."

A moment later, a bottle with its distinctive orange label appeared and popped warmly as the cork was set free. The pretty waitress filled three flutes and said she'd be back soon to take their lunch orders.

Raising his flute, Leonard said, "Now I'm going to propose a toast. Welcome home, Taylor, and to the smooth sale of the business."

"I'll drink to that!" Judy chimed in.

Taylor saw her opportunity. "This brings back very recent memories, actually – sipping champagne, I mean."

"How so, darling?"

And so, Taylor recounted the story of her First Class upgrade, how she'd travelled in style, and the gentleman she'd chatted to and shared a glass or two of champagne with during the flight.

"Oh, darling, how wonderful. Your father and I have never travelled more than Premium Economy and I can't even begin to imagine what First is like. Any idea why you were upgraded? Just lucky?

"None at all, and I expect it was a random thing, but it was a nice experience while it lasted. Probably never will experience it again." Taylor rolled her bottom lip up over her top, mocking a petulant child.

"And I'm guessing this man you got talking to wasn't your type?" said Leonard.

"Dad! No. He was way older than me. He had to be in his seventies, I think, so no."

"Just enquiring, but I see your point." Judy reached over and pretended to slap her husband on his hand for his comment. "Now let that be the end of it, Leonard. No more talk of men. Do you understand?"

He had the sense to keep quiet and nod his agreement.

"Now let's order." Taylor took charge, putting an end to her parents' jovial spat.

As the three sipped champagne and chatted about their lunch order, the pretty waitress disappeared for the briefest of moments, ducking discreetly into a room off the main serving area.

On the other side of London, her message was received. Taylor Palmer was now under full observation.

Chapter Nine

THE TABLE of three had eaten well, drunk a bottle of champagne between them and were contemplating desert. Half-empty water glasses and crumbs littered their tablecloth.

"Well, I'm stuffed, but the chocolate fondant is calling me so I'm going for that." Taylor placed her order with the pretty waitress, who then moved on to her father.

"And for you?"

"I think I'll go for the same. Thank you." He passed his menu to her as she asked Judy what she'd like.

"Make that three, thank you." She smiled. With all three menus gathered, the waitress moved off and conversation at the table moved on again.

"So darling, what are your plans for the rest of the day? Rest? Jet lag is a funny thing; hits you at all odd hours."

"No, I'm feeling fine, actually. I might just take a look around the shops after lunch, stretch my legs, get some air, then I should sleep properly tonight. Want to join me or are you heading back?"

"We're heading back. Though you are still coming out tomorrow, aren't you?"

"Yes, absolutely. Your roasts are legendary," Taylor said, "though when I've finished off the chocolate fondant, I might never eat again."

"Good. We figured you'd still come even though we've had lunch together." Judy took Taylor's hand in her own. "It really is good to have you back, and you look so happy and healthy. Life in New York obviously agreed with you."

"Thanks, Mum. It's been an amazing couple of years, and it's now time to move on to something else new and wonderful, whatever that might be. And hopefully on this side of the globe." The familiar ringtone of Taylor's phone chirping from somewhere inside her bag stopped the conversation.

"Sorry, I thought I'd switched it to silent before lunch." Taking her phone out to silence it, Taylor frowned as she glanced at the screen. "That's strange. No caller ID." The phone carried on its chirping.

"Hadn't you better answer it? You'll never know who it is otherwise. It could be important." Taylor clicked the green icon to answer it and stood to move away from their table and the other late diners.

"Taylor Palmer," she said.

A man's voice greeted her back. "Hello, Miss Palmer. Please forgive my intrusion but I am calling on behalf of Mr. Terrance Dubonnet, whom I believe you met yesterday."

Taylor thought for a moment, a little confused. "Yes, I did." Wary.

"My name is Patrick. I work for Mr. Dubonnet. He wondered if you might be able to meet him later today. He has a couple of good connections in your professional field that could prove useful to you, and he wondered if you might be free to take afternoon tea with him?"

A little taken aback, Taylor found herself agreeing, intrigued if nothing else. Mr. Dubonnet had been lovely on the flight, and if he did have relevant connections, she'd be a fool to not use them if they were on offer. Someone as wealthy as he was could be extremely valuable in finding her next role, whatever that might be.

"I shall let him know," said Patrick warmly. "He'll be very pleased. A car will pick you up at four pm. What address, please?"

Taylor looked at her watch. Lunch had taken longer than she'd anticipated, and it was already 3.30 pm.

"I'm in Croydon at the moment," she told him. "Will there be enough time? I don't know where you will be coming from."

The man at the other end of the line seemed unfazed by her concern. "That will be fine. If you'll give me the address, I'll be waiting outside at four o'clock precisely."

Taylor relayed the restaurant's address to him, and he repeated it back to her. When the call had finished, she stared at her phone a moment before returning back to her parents, and the chocolate fondant that had been delivered in her absence. A quenelle of whipped cream had started to melt on the desert plate.

"Everything alright?" her mother said, frowning. "You look a little perplexed, if I might say so. Who was that on the phone?"

"It was someone who works for the man I met on the flight yesterday. Said his boss has a couple of contacts for me and asked if I'd care to meet him later today to chat." It sounded astounding to her own ears.

"Well, that's wonderful isn't it?"

"Yes, it is, I suppose. I'm a bit surprised, that's all. A car is picking me up in thirty minutes from outside." She still sounded a little unsure.

"Well, from what you said earlier, he sounds lovely, and good on him for trying to help you. And if he is very well off, as you say he is, of course he'll send a car. Better that than expect you to get on public transport to meet him." She smiled at Taylor encouragingly. "Oh, how exciting!" Judy clasped both of her hands in front of her as if Taylor had just told her she was getting married. But it did the trick and relaxed her a little. A smile crept onto her face.

"Well, I guess there's no harm in going along and seeing what he has to say. It could give me some better options, some more prominent galleries perhaps. And a recommendation from someone like him could be invaluable."

"That's the spirit," Leonard chimed in. "Choices are always good to have."

Judy looked at her watch. "Then we'd better eat up before he gets here. Wouldn't want to keep him waiting."

Forks and spoons clattered as they tucked into their chocolate fondants, and the table fell silent for a few minutes.

At precisely 4 pm, the trio stood outside the restaurant. Taylor kissed both of her parents goodbye with a promise she'd see them the next day and fill them in on the conversation she was about to have, and they wished her luck.

As they disappeared into the distance, she was aware that a sleek black car with heavily tinted windows had pulled up at the curb beside her. She glanced at it, impressed. Even to someone who wasn't a car boffin, the shiny Mercedes was unmistakably a top-end luxury vehicle. A man wearing a smart black suit and driving cap stepped out and held the rear door open for her.

"Miss Palmer."

"Thank you," Taylor said, and climbed into the backseat for another sumptuous First Class travelling experience. Just where she was headed she had absolutely no idea.

Chapter Ten

✿

JUST FIFTEEN MINUTES LATER, the car pulled up outside an older boutique-style hotel. While it was less modern than some in London, it certainly oozed extravagance and luxury, but had she expected anything else? A doorman in a neatly pressed uniform and also wearing a cap was at her door before the driver had a chance to get out. She swung her legs out to the pavement in one elegant, fluid movement. Maybe it was the luxurious car that had encouraged her to act a little more demure than usual when alighting. She never got out of a taxi that way; it was generally more of a scramble. The thought amused her as she carried on with the act of being someone she really wasn't, and found she was enjoying it a little.

"Welcome, Miss," the doorman greeted her, and gave her a friendly smile. He had kind eyes and wore gloves on his hands, she noticed. Not really sure what she should do next, Taylor was relieved when the driver appeared by her side with instructions.

"Please follow me, Miss Palmer," was all he said, and she walked with him towards the lobby. Her shoes made no sound on the thick, rich red carpet. Heavy gilt-framed paintings adorned the walls; the lighting was muted and regal. Patrick led the way through to a small private room. As he opened the door for her, she saw it had been laid out for afternoon tea for two people. Her first thought was not to marvel at how beautiful the elegant room looked or wonder why it needed to be so private; instead, she groaned inwardly at the thought of more food. How was she going to take tea with her new acquaintance and not offend him by not eating? Maybe she shouldn't have had the chocolate fondant, but it was too late now. No, she'd have to manage.

"Please, take a seat. He'll be along very shortly."

Then the driver was gone, leaving Taylor standing alone in the silence as she waited. The faint sound of distant traffic could be heard but not much else. Outside the sun was not much more than a creamy glow, like the light from a candle, as the day wound down. She made herself at home in one of the comfy floral chairs while she waited. No sooner had she sat down than the door opened and a much younger man than she was expecting introduced himself.

"Hello, Miss Palmer. My name is Marcus and I work for Mr. Dubonnet as his assistant."

"Hello. Nice to meet you," she said, standing again and extending her right hand. He really was quite handsome, she observed. Tall and athletic-looking in his suit, he obviously took care of himself. A gold band on a finger of his left hand told her he was spoken for. His sandy-brown hair was styled with just the right amount of ruffle, and a light tan completed the look. The only thing that was missing was a personality, it seemed.

"Mr. Dubonnet has been delayed slightly, so he asked me to ensure you are comfortable while you wait."

At that moment, a woman dressed in a maid's outfit arrived carrying a tray of silver pots, which she placed on the table to complete the set-up, then left as discreetly as she had come.

"I wasn't really sure what type of tea you drank, so I took the liberty of ordering chamomile as well as Earl Grey and Darjeeling. What can I offer you?"

"Darjeeling is lovely, thank you." Taylor watched as Marcus expertly poured the perfect coloured brew into a china teacup. "Sugar? Lemon? Milk, perhaps?"

"Oh, as it is will be fine. Thank you."

Even though she smiled, he didn't. Why was he so austere, she wondered? For a man who looked to be in his early thirties, he was pretty rigid. He passed her the dainty cup and saucer and excused himself, saying Mr. Dubonnet would be along in a moment. Then the handsome but rigid man was gone, the door clicking quietly shut behind him. Sitting back in the comfy chair again to wait, Taylor took sips of her tea and wondered about the last few hours since she'd left New York. So much had happened – the older man she had met, the luxury she had travelled in, and now here she was, sitting in a swanky hotel waiting for him to arrive and give her some gallery contacts.

Taylor glanced at her watch. Since the handsome assistant had poured her tea, ten more minutes had gone by, so she topped her cup up for something to do while she waited. With each minute that went by, she began to feel more and more tired; the jet lag was clearly catching up to her. She sighed and leaned farther back in the chair; the room felt just a little warmer than it had the minute before. Was she imagining it? She didn't think so, but she was powerless to do anything about it. Finally, unable to keep her eyelids open any longer, she allowed them to close, thinking about nothing whatsoever as she fell into a deep sleep.

On a monitor on the other side of town, the operator watched as Taylor drifted into a comfortable, deep sleep and a man dressed in coveralls entered the room. He was pushing an empty laundry trolley. The operator watched as the man lifted Taylor, placed her expertly inside the trolley, and wheeled it back out of the room. A moment later, another man, this time dressed as a waiter, entered the room and removed the afternoon tea party remains. A quick wipe round with a cloth, and any evidence that Taylor Palmer had been sipping tea in the room was now gone. And so was she.

Chapter Eleven

HE AWOKE. Same time every day. The alarm clock on the bedside cabinet bleeped four times and he reached to turn it off. It always bleeped four times, and he was always awake to hear it. His internal alarm clock was in sync with his battery operated one; both alarms were there for each other should one forget. He knew exactly what time it was − it was the same time every morning − and he swung his long legs out of the bed, turning the bedding down over itself, letting air get to the sheets. It takes fifteen minutes for bed lice to dehydrate, for the moisture to leave their bodies, allowing them to die off completely, and this was an important part of his routine.

Don't confuse bed lice with bed bugs: those little suckers are a whole different story and if you've got bed bugs, you have a problem. Everyone has bed lice. But Griffin makes sure his are dead every morning. His routine could be described as normal or mundane, though many would call it OCD. Every day is the same. Nothing deviates. He heads to the bathroom for ablutions, a shave and a shower, and that takes fifteen minutes precisely. Many parts of his life are slotted into fifteen-minute segments. When his morning bathroom routine is complete, he folds the bed linen back in place, smartening his bed for re-entry in the evening. His wardrobe is equally precise: rows of folded clothing, three piles each the same in content, stacked five high.

He dressed in his uniform, a self-imposed uniform of blue jeans, white T-shirt, blue hoody. It hid his secret nicely, a part of him he'd rather other people did not see, and something he hoped would be dealt with soon. But the hoody would have to do the job for now, until he raised the funds and found the appropriate outlet for the task.

He walked through the lounge, which was simple, inexpensive, and immaculate. Ikea had benefited from his wallet. All his flat-packed deliveries had been methodically constructed, neither a gap nor an overlap visible in their build, not a random screw left over. Built to perfection. A couple of neutral-coloured throw cushions on the sofa were the only soft edges in the room; even the rug on the floor was rigid. In the kitchen, he flicked the switch of the kettle that he'd pre-filled the previous night before bed, then poured cereal into a bowl that was already waiting on the work surface, sliced the waiting banana into it, and poured milk from the fridge. The milk was the only thing he had to get from somewhere else. When the kettle had boiled, he poured hot water onto the tea bag that was also waiting in the mug and left it to steep while he ate his breakfast in silence.

Eating finished, he drank his tea and took the little pile of supplements that also awaited him and washed them down in one knobbly mouthful. When he was finished, he placed his used breakfast cutlery and crockery neatly into the dishwasher and turned it on, selecting low wash. Precisely thirty minutes later, he left his flat in Croydon and walked the short distance to catch the train into London, white buds stuck in both ears and the Boo Radleys singing the same 'beautiful morning' song. He loved the beat.

Once he'd boarded the train, along with hundreds of other daily commuters squashed into the metal capsule, then and only then would he allow himself to break out a little before he reached his office. Sometimes it was with Elvis, sometimes it was with Guns 'N' Roses, and sometimes it was with Gershwin. He allowed himself a wide range of music depending on his mood, and the mood of the people in the capsule. Spotify had opened him up to a whole new musical world, and while he'd found it a little overwhelming at first to deviate from his routine playlists, he'd finally embraced the experience and begun to see it as part of his education. He wondered if perhaps the rest of his life would follow suit and he'd break out a little more, one day at a time – break away from the confines that restrained his life, break away from fifteen-minute segments. And perhaps one day he'd find someone to share his life with. But who would want him with his quirky routine? Or his issue? When he allowed someone to get close and they saw what he was hiding, the shock and repulsion on their faces was always obvious. And it hurt. People could be so cruel. And so, it was easier to stay as he was, for now. To stay away from having someone close. But when he finally had the money and had found someone to do the job to his standards and his budget, that would all change. He was sure. Until, then he'd continue working as a sports reporter by day, and searching for the perfect person who'd help him by night.

As the train pulled in at London Victoria, he changed his playlist, the crystal-clear piano notes of Gershwin's 'Rhapsody in Blue' cranked up in his ears. Ironic, really, since the piece itself had first been conceived while George Gershwin himself rode the train into Boston one day. It had since become a classical piece almost everyone would recognize. Griffin worked his way towards the tube entrance onwards to his final destination of Green Park. Thousands of other London commuters had gone before him already that morning to just another day at the office. Griffin himself would be behind his desk shortly – it would take him fifteen minutes precisely.

Chapter Twelve

"Morning, Griffin."

It was Jan, editor in chief at the paper and general pain in the ass. Commonly referred to as 'she who shall be obeyed,' she was an 'in your face' type of boss who frustrated the hell out of most of the team. Including Griffin. He stared at her long red fingernails, chipped at the edges, and then at her folded arms, carefully averting his eyes from her heavily made-up face.

"Morning, Jan." He didn't need or want to say more. So he didn't expand.

"Deadline's eleven am. I trust you'll be on time?"

"It's ready to go," he said, patting the laptop he was unpacking from his satchel.

I've never missed a deadline yet. It's not what I do, remember?

"Glad to hear it. And I've pushed your review session back until next week. Hope you don't mind. I'll send you a calendar date when I've decided on when exactly." Then she was gone as quickly as she'd appeared, the faint odour of stale cigarette smoke overlaid with her vile perfume lingering where she'd stood.

That's not good. Why do you need to change it? What's more important than a person's performance review – my performance review? I like order. Remember?

Griffin stood to make his way to the break room, scraping his chair back noisily on the wooden floor. Anxiety started to boil in his chest. He'd spent time on his performance review and treated it with the importance it deserved, and that would all be wasted now. He'd have to do it all again. And wait for a time that was suitable to her. He stalked towards the small kitchen area and thrust a tea bag into his mug, covering it with boiling water from the heater on the wall. He stood seething as it steeped. It wouldn't last long, this feeling. He'd taught himself how to handle change over recent years. At fourteen years old, he'd found a coping mechanism that worked for him, allowing him to get through his teen years largely unscathed. And that was where his fifteen-minute segments came in. It helped him to get through the anxiety, knowing it would pass soon, within those fifteen minutes. He stirred his tea and waited it out in the calm of the small room. Shortly, all would be well again in Griffin's world. He just had to stand and wait it out.

"There you are." It was Rob, a features writer at the paper and probably the only person on the team who took much notice of him. "Been looking all over."

"Just catching ten before the mayhem starts and Jan starts flapping like a mad woman. I hate deadline day."

"Know what you mean, bro. Me too. You're all ready, though, aren't you, Mr. Organized? I'd be surprised if you weren't. Not like me, eh? Always on the last minute. I'd be late for my mother's funeral I'm sure, never mind my own."

Griffin poured the last tea dregs down the sink and rinsed his mug. "And look at the stress it causes you by being late. You're the same every month. Don't quite know how you manage it, or why. I couldn't cope." Griffin slapped Rob on the shoulder affectionately as he made his way back to his desk, his clean mug in hand. "If you really are stuck, let me know. I might be able to help you. I'm not submitting mine in until eleven am on the dot, just to bug her."

"That's not like you. What gives?"

"She's postponed my review until next week, so if she thinks I'm not important enough, then I feel the same about her lousy paper. Stuff her."

Rob watched with his mouth open as Griffin left the room. His friend was never one for outbursts, though Rob knew he sometimes struggled to contain things inside. And he usually managed to keep them concealed. Rob busied himself making coffee and headed back to his own desk a few moments later. As he passed Griffin, he noted that his colleague's head was already buried in his laptop. Rob tossed a Kit Kat to him, payment for his help that he would undoubtedly need if he was to submit on time. Griffin looked up, startled, as it clattered down by his elbow.

"Thanks, but no thanks, Rob. You eat it. Too much sugar for me. Can't eat it."

"Ah – sorry, mate. Forgot about that," Rob said, and swept in to claim it back. "May as well have it myself then." He ripped into the red wrapper; small flakes of chocolate and biscuit scattered to the floor beside Griffin's desk. "Damn, half of it is broken. Look at that lot – half of it's missing!"

"Well, it's on the floor if you want to get on your hands and knees and clean it up. If you don't, I'll have to."

"Nah, you're all right. Cleaners will get it later," said Rob, his mouth full. And off he went, unaware of just how Griffin was fizzing inside at the new problem around his feet. Try as he might, he knew he couldn't leave it there: the chocolate crumbs would grind under his feet. It would play on his mind too much. Stepping carefully around the mess, he made his way back to the kitchen for a damp paper towel to wipe it up with. Mess just never sat well, and that included around his workspace. It was better than the anxiety-riddled alternative. Jan's voice interrupted him while he was on his hands and knees.

"Listen up, folks. Deadline has changed. Ten am, please. And no buts! So if you're still working on it, get your own butt moving, pronto!"

Rob glanced at Griffin under his desk on the floor and rolled his eyes at Jan's announcement. While it didn't pose a problem for Griffin, he smiled as his friend mouthed 'Butt out' to her retreating back.

Chapter Thirteen

GRIFFIN WALKED from Green Park to Victoria station that night after work. It really wasn't very far, and although normally he took the tube to the station as part of his routine, tonight he felt like the walk. The air was still lukewarm, the remaining sun in the sky weakening as summer moved on to pastures new and autumn moved in in its place. He picked up the pace and headed in the direction of the station like he was on a mission. He was, kind of: to get home.

He'd been a sports reporter for a couple of years, though he'd only been into sports at all for a little over three. He had been diagnosed with type two diabetes at age twenty-two; his doctor had been worried about his general state of health, and ultimately told him that, weighing in at close to twenty-five stone, he had been on a fast track to organ failure. Luckily for Griffin, he'd made the right decision and got himself on the right track. How he'd ever got to twenty-five stone he had no clue. There was no abusive story lurking in his background, no family breakup to blame, no bullying to speak of save for the usual teasing he and others in his class had endured. Yes, his anxiety issues had played a part, but in general, the simple answer to his weight gain had been gaming. He just hadn't moved enough to compensate for the calories he consumed daily. And so his weight had ballooned until his doctor had told him to get moving and change his bad habits. So he had: the doctor had told him to do it, and that's all he'd needed. Direction was his friend. Now, although he was still a little heavy at thirteen stone, he'd lost almost twelve, with just another stone to go. And that's when he'd got his 'issue.' Yes, it bothered him, what he kept secret under the hood of his own engine, but he'd get it rectified just as soon as he had the funds to do so. And found the right person to do the job.

The train was packed like a tin of sardines, and at the end of a hot day, and was just as pungent. But Griffin didn't care. In thirty minutes he'd be back home, changed into his training gear and headed for the park and all the fresh air he needed as he walked ten laps around it to complete his ten thousand daily steps. He had a goal to aim for, and sitting as his desk for most of the day didn't use up enough calories to move the final stone that he still carried. And walking was now a part of his routine. Routine, routine, routine. It kept him sane. Sitting in his seat on the packed train, he closed his eyes and allowed himself to think about having a special someone in his life. One day, he'd have one. What would she look like? How would they meet? What would her friends be like? Would she fancy him? Would she be the one?

He felt the train slow down and pull into a station, so he opened his eyes. He wasn't sure where they were, exactly. That's when he saw her. He briefly caught the eye of a young woman sitting almost opposite him. Briefly, but long enough to note she was pretty, with short, shiny brown hair cut into a smart bob style, thick-rimmed glasses very similar to his own, and a scattering of freckles across her nose. She looked almost like Velma Dinkley from the *Scooby Doo* comic strip, but without the pleated skirt. And she was pretty. After his brief analysis, he chanced a small smile, expecting her to turn away; they usually did. Nothing came back; no smile, no nothing. Just a fixed expression as their eyes caught. Perhaps she was looking past him, not at him at all, or maybe she wondered who the hell was looking at her.

He was just about to turn away himself, before the rejection pricked him in his chest, when her petite mouth lifted slightly at the corners and formed the smallest of smiles. Had he imagined it? Was he daydreaming? He tilted his head slightly as if that would give him a better view, to confirm that she had in fact smiled at him. Or had not.

But to his astonishment, it *was* there, and he chanced another smile back in return. It felt awkward, but the nice thing to do. What would happen now? Would she stop smiling, get off at the next stop and never be seen again? Or would she look away and that would be the end of it?

The train slowed to a complete standstill and people shuffled out, distracting him, making his thoughts scatter inside his head. When the carriage had almost emptied, he chanced a look back to see if she had left with everyone else, but she hadn't. She was still sat there. Not knowing what else to do, he simply nodded in her direction, which she seemed to enjoy, and even though she turned her head away from him, he could see her smile had widened via the reflection in the window. Perhaps she was shy, embarrassed even? There wasn't anything else he felt able to do. He wasn't like other men in the confidence department. No, he'd see where she got off, he decided, and if it was before his stop that would be the end of it. He rested his head back and closed his eyes once more for the remainder of the journey, not daring to look her way again.

As he felt the train finally pull into his station, he gathered his belongings and edged his way to the door, keeping his eyes averted. But there are too many windows on a train not to see a reflection.

That was how he saw her getting off at the same stop as his.

Chapter Fourteen

꧁꧂

TAYLOR FINALLY STOPPED PANICKING and stood rigid in the centre of the room. Stolen her hair? How could that even be? And who would want it? And what did the card mean – 'settled'? So many questions she hadn't answers for fizzed in her head like freshly poured Fanta, though without the zing. Her hands tentatively touched her scalp again for confirmation of what she already knew, hoping she'd been wrong when she'd looked in the mirror. But mirrors never lie, and neither did her hands. The stump that was left was still secured neatly there. The rest of her hair was gone. She wiped away a tear, which was quickly followed by another. Transfixed, she watched them fall through the air and splash onto the thick carpet. Picking the notelet back up, feeling the cool, crisp card in her fingers, she re-read the message again out loud.

Your debt has been settled. I'd advise you to tell no one. It wouldn't be wise.

"My debt?" Those damn questions with no answers.

She glanced at the curled-up sandwiches and the silver pot, which she assumed contained tea, although it was probably cold. While she had no intention of sampling anything, the silver pot reminded her of one thing – her tea appointment who had never shown up. Could he be linked to this, perhaps? Her mind conjured up possibilities that made no sense. Why would he be involved? She hadn't seen him in person, but she had met his assistant. And there was yet another question – had the man indeed been his assistant? And the driver in the fancy Mercedes –had he been real too? What the hell was going on? Deflated, she sat down heavily on the sofa where she had woken up only minutes ago. The simple fact of the matter was that, while her hair had been stolen, she was otherwise unharmed. She picked up the empty cup and took it to the bathroom to fill with water. Her mouth was parched, and if she had been drugged at some point, she wasn't about to risk what might be in the pot. The cold water felt refreshing as it slid down her throat, and she refilled the cup again, sipping it more slowly now that her initial thirst had been quenched, and returned to the sofa.

"Drugged? Me? But why?"

Daring herself, she ran her fingers through the little stump of hair, pulling the hair tie out as they forced their way through the clump that was left. The hair tie pinged off to the side and landed on the carpet. She stared at it. It was black and gold. Her little topknot fanned forward as she bent to look at the tie more closely. She didn't recognize it as one of her own, which raised another question. Had it been bought solely for the purpose of restraining her hair before it had been cut? Had this all been planned, premeditated? Was she part of some sort of vile game, herself the victim? Definitely not the winner if she was.

She pulled the woollen blanket around her shoulders, suddenly feeling chilled, and wondered what to do. The card had said it wouldn't be wise to tell anyone, but she needed to tell. How could she not? If she'd been taken against her will, drugged and robbed, the person or persons involved needed to be caught before they did it to someone else. But what would happen to her if she did tell and go the police? The card had been specific in it being 'unwise.' Was she prepared to find out? Resting her head on the sofa back, she closed her eyes and tried to make sense of what she should do. Stay and call her mother and the police, or go, forget all about it and not risk any possible repercussions? If it had been an elaborate set-up, preplanned, there would be no evidence of any wrongdoing in the room, she was sure. And that would make her look like a madwoman who had lost her hair, the victim of a prank and nothing more. And whoever was responsible clearly had had no intention of harming her physically or restraining her; the blanket and food along with the unlocked door told her so.

On steadier legs, she stood, put her feet in her shoes, grabbed her bag and let herself out of the hotel room.

Chapter Fifteen

THE LIGHT OUTSIDE was almost completely faded and a cool chill clung to her thin cardigan as she stood in the hotel doorway. She shivered involuntarily, not all together sure which direction to turn in. Back inside and report it? Or towards home and forget about it? A male voice at her side made her jump. Turning in the direction of the voice, she relaxed a little when she saw it was the doorman from earlier in the day.

"I'm sorry?"

"I asked if you were alright, Miss. You're shivering." His smile was warm, but not enough to warm her right through. And he was looking at her a little oddly, like he recognized her but something troubled him. She remembered her hair.

Pausing a moment before she spoke, she replied, "Yes, I'm fine. Thank you." Should she ask him a question about earlier? Would he know anything? As she stood in the doorway, still undecided on her direction, she figured if the doorman had been a part of whatever it was she was involved in, he'd have been long gone by now. Maybe he'd remember something. Turning towards the older man again, she asked, "Do you remember me arriving earlier, by any chance?"

"Yes, Miss. I do. I let you out of the car."

Right – that memory returned to her, at least. "Yes, you did. Thank you. Do you know the driver of that car? Have you ever seen it or him before?"

"No, Miss, can't say that I do, but then we have a lot of black Mercedes dropping guests off. Is everything alright?" The corners of his eyes were crinkly with age, the irises a comforting hazel colour. She knew she could trust him.

"You didn't happen to see a tall grey-haired man, probably in his seventies, come in here by chance, did you? Quite a distinguished-looking man, very stylish?"

The doorman thought for a moment and shook his head. "No, Miss, but he may have come while I was on my break. I've been back about an hour. Are you sure you're all right? You seem a little nervous, upset even. Can I get you a taxi somewhere, perhaps?"

Ignoring his question and concern, she asked, "Is there another entrance to the hotel?"

"Not for guests. Only the rear entrance, but that's mainly for staff. You know, for deliveries and the like. He wouldn't have entered that way." The doorman scratched his chin as he thought. "Though he could have if he'd wanted to, I suppose. Highly unusual, though. Why would anyone enter that way?"

Why indeed.

Taylor still had no answers to the fizzing questions, but as exhaustion settled into her bones, she knew what she was going to do next.

"I think I'd like that taxi home, please."

"It will be my pleasure, Miss," the doorman said, and she watched as the kindly man hailed her a cab.

When the taxi had pulled away from the curb, he stood and watched the vehicle disappear off into the distance, the taillights eventually fading to the size of red pinheads. The big question that hung on his heart surfaced again. What had happened to her beautiful hair? It had been the same woman for sure; he wasn't such an old fool to have forgotten it so easily – the colour was glorious. But it was none of his business. Another car pulled up and he greeted its occupants in his usual way.

Back to work, and back to normal.

Chapter Sixteen

STEAM from the bathtub filled her small bathroom and she added a dash of lavender bubble bath; the white bubbles foamed up on contact with the water gushing in. Somehow, she'd given the taxi driver her address and unlocked the door to her flat, though she didn't remember any of it. Maybe her brain was still addled from whatever she'd been given earlier. She climbed into the tub and the warm water got to work on warming and soothing her aching limbs. Stress can do odd things to a person, show itself in odd ways, and Taylor started to shiver uncontrollably as she lowered herself further in. Slipping down so her shoulders were completely submerged, she let out a deep breath and closed her eyes. The lavender smelled good, the warm water felt good, but *she* didn't feel good.

After a few minutes, the warmth began to soothe her, and she let her head slip down into the water. Her roughly cropped hair floated around the back of her head, no longer able to fan out around the front like it used to do. It felt so strange. What the hell was her mother going to say tomorrow when she saw it? Taylor knew she'd be horrified, upset, mad even, but hadn't a clue how to tell her what had really happened.

It wouldn't be wise to tell.

No, she'd have to make her excuses, which in itself didn't sit well. Lying to her parents was something she had never done, even as a teenager growing up. Lies meant you didn't respect that person, and respect was something she had in spades for both of them. Whatever she'd got up to through the years she'd lived at home growing up, she'd told the truth and suffered any consequences that had followed. Even though her close friends had encouraged deceitfulness, she'd never obliged them. Her mother had bored it into her: 'With lies you may go ahead in the world, but you can never go back.'

Yet she couldn't face telling them the whole truth.

Feeling terribly ashamed at having been taken in, she sank her whole head under the bubbles, screwing her face up completely so as not to inhale any water, and there she stayed until she could hold her breath no longer.

"Bwahhh!" she hollered as she broke the surface of the water in a rush. Water sloshed over the sides of the tub and soaked the floor. She gulped air in frantically, trying to refill her lungs with much-needed oxygen. Startling herself, she sat shaking. Involuntarily her face screwed up like a child's, her mouth forced down at the corners, and wracking great sobs erupted from her chest. Tears mixed with lavender water on her face as she let it all out in the sanctuary of her warm bathroom. With no one to hear her cries, she sobbed until she had nothing left to give, and the water had cooled enough to add to her misery. When she was finally depleted, she opened the plug and stepped out of the tub and into her robe. Feeling as tired as she could ever remember, Taylor curled up on her bed. What was left of her hair soaked her pillow, but that was the least of her concerns as she finally drifted into a deep slumber.

Chapter Seventeen

WHEN THE NOTIFICATION had come that his transaction was ready to be finalized, Terrance poured himself a martini and took it downstairs with him. He never referred to the room as a cellar; that sounded dank and fusty. But like a cellar, the room was underneath the main kitchen of the house. Few people knew it existed; certainly, none of the current staff did, and years ago it hadn't held the same things it did now. No, he'd kept his interests away from the house back then – that is, until he'd taken on the place as his own. Then he'd done with it what he liked. And the room had been fitted out. Working after hours, the builder, carpenter, electrician, glazier and others had been paid handsomely to never mention the room to anyone, and as far as Terrance knew, they hadn't.

Leading off the main passageway towards the old coal cellar further along was a door that no passerby would notice; it had been built to match the walls completely. Terrance raised his hand to find the small lever hidden by a beam. The wall slid back and the faint glow behind it spilled out into the corridor. Terrance stood in the doorway a moment to admire his collection from a distance before entering the room fully and appreciating it in its entirety. The door slowly closed behind him as he ventured forward to his wing chair in the centre of the room. It was the only piece of furniture in there save for the purpose-built cabinets that spanned each of the four walls. The chair stood on a circular plinth that rotated 360 degrees, enabling the person seated there to view any wall they chose by pressing a button.

Built of a rich, dark oak, each cabinet was divided up into three separate display cases stood on top of each other; each stacked unit was wide enough to span the entire width of the wall against which it stood. Most of the display cases were filled, leaving only a handful still empty. The brass hinges and knobs of each case gleamed in the light that came from strategically placed wall lights, giving the room an almost golden glow. The temperature of the room was always perfect: never too warm and absolutely never too cold. Placing his martini on the little table that shared the plinth with the chair, he sat down to experience the room in its entirety. He sank back, let out a deep, low sigh and pressed the button, relishing the anticipation. Ever so slowly, the chair turned, giving him a full 360-degree view of all of the items that he had collected over the years, each one with a different story attached to it.

Of course, things had changed, and his collection had increased in recent years thanks to what he'd been able to find on the dark web. It really had been a revelation to find others with similar wants and needs, as well as a way to procure for his own private collection, and all from the comfort of his own home. He barely needed to be involved in anything else but the receiving of his purchases.

The chair continued to rotate and he smiled as the very first piece of his collection came in to view. It was old now, though still just as beautiful as the day he'd taken ownership of it, and it sat displayed in cabinet number 1. There was a small plaque just above the glass, though he didn't need to read it; he knew exactly what it said.

Prudence.

She had been the first, the catalyst for his whim, and she'd been very giving of it.

Eventually.

He took a sip of the martini as the plinth turned slowly. It wouldn't be long now until his new arrival would take one of those reserved places and he could sit and appreciate it from his sanctuary. The thought pleased him; he felt a smile creasing his lips, a familiar stirring in his groin. She had been so delightful, so pretty. But before a cabinet was allocated with the rest of his collection, he'd have the pleasure of her in the privacy of his bed tonight.

He wondered what she'd smell of.

Picking up the remainder of his drink, he stood from the chair and headed back towards the hidden doorway. Before the lights dimmed as he left, he turned and took one last glance into the room to admire his collection so far.

Shining back at him silently, the thirty perfectly displayed glorious ponytails faded slowly as the golden lights dipped. He put a finger to his lips as he bid them good night.

Chapter Eighteen

✦❧✦

IT WAS NEARLY 8 pm when a text alerted him to a delivery arriving within the hour. Always ambiguous, never with a singular meaning, the text disappeared within seconds of him reading it. No one could ever know about the service he sought for his fulfilment, and as always, he was appreciative of the tight security. Since he'd begun using the services of the group, he'd never known the identity of any of the other participants. Each of them had a username that probably made sense to them alone and no one else. Take his own, for example: "Quinine." Nearly 200 years before, Joseph Dubonnet had invented his eponymous drink as a means to make quinine more palatable for soldiers battling malaria in North Africa. Quinine on its own is extremely bitter, though Terrance didn't see himself that way – quite the opposite, in fact – but the link to Dubonnet, however circuitous, was why he'd chosen the name.

Leaving his phone on his bedside cabinet, he headed through to the full-size bathroom adjacent to his room and drew himself a bath. At any other time of the day or night, he used the shower, the raindrop head allowing him the enjoyment of warm running water on his skin without the intrusion of invigorating jets. But on a night such as this, while he awaited his acquisition, he took sanctuary in the palatial room that the queen herself would have enjoyed bathing in. It had been planned out and designed meticulously, and nothing had been forgotten in the effort to make it a room of enjoyment. There was no toilet in this room, for obvious reasons; that was in a room of its own next door. Instead, a chaise longue sat proudly along the rear wall with soft, muted grey throw cushions neatly placed on top; a soft woollen blanket was folded and placed at the foot of it. The bath, with modern claw feet, sat in the centre of the room; cream shag pile carpet surrounded it. Brushed bronze tapware adorned the ceramic fittings, and bronze accessories adorned the room on shelves and small tables, along with a bronze bust of a woman watching over him from the left corner of the room. A picture of the same woman hung on the opposite wall, placed as though to allow the two to look at each other.

Terrance watched as steaming water filled the tub from a bronze horse-head spout, the waterfall cascading therapeutically and mixing with the infused oil he so enjoyed. Lime and basil filled his nostrils. He loved the simple smells rather than more elaborate manufactured perfumes, and that went for fragrances on women, too. He'd much rather catch a vanilla bean on the wind than the cloying odour of something from an expensive bottle; it had more substance. He had fond memories of simple smells from when he was a boy, like Pears shampoo. 'Fruits from the orchard,' she'd told him when he'd admired the smell many years ago.

He stepped into the warm bath and laid his head back on the soft-towelled headrest; it was heated, and the warmth it emitted helped to relax him further. Classic music, the tinkling of piano keys, could just be heard coming from the hidden speakers on each side of his head. The muted lighting, the feel of infused water and oil on his skin and the gentle piano playing in the background was the therapy he needed before he welcomed his new addition.

How long ago it was that he'd first found his fascination. Glancing at the bronze bust looking over him, he smiled at the woman and idly wondered if perhaps she was still alive someplace. He'd never kept in touch after he'd taken what he'd so desired, what she had made him desire. She was the one who had led him to start his collection, to take hers first, to cherish it, to preserve it, to mount it in a cabinet. The first cabinet, the one numbered '1,' with the name *Prudence* on the plaque. He felt himself stir at the thought of her, of how she'd used to sit on the edge of his bed as a young boy and tell him a story. Of how her eyes would twinkle as she spoke, how her soft-looking lips would move with her words and how her hair would shine. But it was when a nightmare came and he called out into the night that she would come from her room next door in her long nightdress, her hair loose around her shoulders. That was what he had found the most fascinating. And soothing. She'd lean in to him and stroke his hair to quiet him down, and he'd catch the smell of her hair. Fruity like an orchard. He could smell it now as clearly as though she were sitting there now, even over the lime and basil; it was there with him, always.

"Your hair always smells nice, Prudence," he'd said one night while she helped him get back to sleep. "And so soft too." His little fingers had reached up and touched it, stroked it and run themselves back down, through it. She'd bent her head into his touch, enjoying the feeling of someone's affection. Young Terrance had fallen asleep filled with calm then, and whenever a nightmare had come after that, she'd used her hair to help him back to sleep. Terrance had had many night-mares growing up, though he could never say what they had been about exactly when she questioned him.

Forty-five minutes later, he emerged from his bathroom feeling relaxed, though anticipation was now subtly taking over. He made his way downstairs to await the text message that would tell him a delivery would be made within the following five minutes. He didn't have long to wait. The lights of a car on his driveway could be seen through the trees now, and he opened the front door and stepped outside. When the black car had come to a standstill, a man in a black suit and driver's cap took a slim, polished wood box out of the rear of the car and approached Terrance with it. It was about two feet long and just a few inches deep. He carried it like he was carrying the crown jewels, treating it with reverence as he walked slowly towards its new owner. Knowing what was inside, Terrance smiled inside and stretched out his arms to take ownership of the latest for his collection. The man handed the box over, then silently turned and climbed back into the black Mercedes to drive back the way he'd just come.

Terrance waited for the lights to completely disappear then closed the door and headed upstairs to his bedroom and the long-anticipated experience with Taylor Palmer's long cognac locks.

As the driver headed away, the tiny chip embedded in the wooden lid confirmed the package had been delivered to the requested address, and a signal pinged on a screen somewhere back in London.

Another transaction had successfully been completed.

Chapter Nineteen

GRIFFIN HADN'T EXPECTED her to get off at the same stop as his; he'd only decided what to do if she got off at a stop *before* his. And that was 'do nothing' anyway, so it wasn't much of a plan. But now she was close by, just behind him somewhere, and he had precisely no idea what to do next. Walking forward down the platform towards the entrance and home, he fiddled with his iPhone and ear buds, his hands all thumbs and no fingers as he fumbled to undo a knot in the wires. He slowed his pace and moved over to the side, out of the way, as other passengers hurried past him.

"Can I help?" The small voice was coming from his left side and he froze. Summoning up his courage, he turned to look at the owner of the voice and was both startled and thrilled all at the same time. 'Velma' was looking at him for an answer.

"I . . . I . . ." he stammered, and then froze again. She smiled. He melted a little. Only a little.

"Here, let me help you," she said. "My fingers are smaller than yours. I'll be twice as quick as you."

She reached for the wires. Griffin found himself handing them over and watching as her nimble fingers did indeed undo the knot in no time at all. She handed his ear buds back, smiling up at him.

"There. Told you it'd be quick." Her petite face took in his, though while hers looked relaxed, Griffin's was tense with anxiety. He still hadn't uttered a full word. 'Velma' waited. It seemed like an age before he finally mumbled his thanks.

"Thanks. It was bugging me." Finally.

"What are you listening to?" They started walking towards the entrance together again. It was less embarrassing than waiting for him to speak.

"Guns N' Roses. Well, I was going to, but I'm talking to you now so I'm not listening to anything." It came out a little more abrupt than he meant it to. 'Velma' felt the sting and glanced up at him. He back-tracked a little.

"Sorry. I meant I *will* be listening to it, but obviously not right at this minute. That would be rude." He chanced a nervous smile, his perfect white teeth peeping out from his lips a little awkwardly.

"I've seen you before. On the train. Where do you work?" Her voice bounced in a sort of singsong as she spoke. And the thought of her noticing him previously sent a tingle somewhere down his spine. He liked it.

"Green Park. I'm a sports reporter. How about you?"

"I work in IT just near Victoria station. I live here in South Croydon. I'm guessing you do too, since you got off here?"

Is she always so chipper and forward? he wondered.

"Yes, I do." They both walked through the exit door and out to the road. "I live over there, just behind the church. I have a flat," he said, pointing to a nearby spire.

"Lucky you. I'm a bit further on down, on Whitgift Avenue. I still live with my parents. Can't afford a place of my own yet. Too damned expensive."

Griffin mumbled a reply along the lines of 'I hear you,' and, still feeling very self-conscious, didn't add anything further. They were nearly at his address when he found his words.

"I'm nearly home now. Thanks for sorting my buds out. Perhaps I'll see you again, on the train?"

"What's your name?"

"Sorry?"

"I said what's your name?"

"Griffin. It's Griffin."

She stuck her hand out and, after several seconds of staring at it, he took it in his. They shook.

"Nice to meet you, Griffin. I'm Vee. That's what everyone calls me. I'm Vera, really, but I don't like it, so stick with Vee."

"Nice to meet you too, Vee."

She was already walking off as he spoke but she turned and gave a little wave. He was sure he heard her say 'I hope so,' or did he imagine it? He hoped he hadn't. She was cute.

Opening his front door, he thought back to Vee on the train when their eyes had caught each other's, and how she did look like Velma Dinkley – glasses, haircut, height, everything about her. And she was called Vee. What a coincidence. And *she'd* spoken to *him* even though it had scared him half to death. That was a good sign, wasn't it? Her speaking to him? Because if it had been left up to Griffin to make the first move in greeting, the world would still be waiting. But then she had been very confident in her approach, something he lacked. When he was at the right place, he'd take a confidence-building course or something, but until then, there wasn't much point. Work, walk, web were the routines of his life, his very existence; his walking counter-acted the time he sat still at work and at home, surfing the web, most evenings. He spent a considerable amount of time online searching each night, trying to find the best option for his situation, and he was still a way off finding the solution. So he kept on looking.

Griffin took his satchel and put it in the cupboard before taking his clothes off and folding them all neatly in a pile on the end of his bed. He replaced them with training shorts and a T-shirt and collected his running shoes from a different cupboard. He downed 250 millilitres of water from the jug in the fridge and set out on his usual route to complete his 10,000 steps, pulling the door shut behind him. His mind ventured back to Vee's petite face. She really was quite pretty. He was almost at the small park when he realized he'd been humming as he'd walked. Griffin never hummed.

But something had made him. Or *someone*, more to the point.

Chapter Twenty

HIS PERFECTLY TIMED repetitive morning routine complete for the day, Griffin left his flat and walked the short distance to the train station. He'd slept well and blamed his slightly lighter feeling on rest as he walked briskly to his usual spot on the platform. Elvis in his ears, he found himself looking around, searching the others who were waiting for the train, but Vee wasn't one of them. Pity. If she was going to catch this one, she'd better be quick, but as the familiar clicking of the tracks sounded, signalling an approaching train, she was nowhere to be seen. The engine pulled up ahead; his usual carriage stopped directly in front of him and he waited for the doors to ping open. One last glance back up the platform before he boarded told him she wasn't going to be on this train.

His train.

Sitting in one of his three usual seats – his choice depended on who else was on board – he resigned himself to the fact his ear buds would be his entertainment for the remainder of the journey in to work.

That evening was a different matter.

At 5.30 pm on the dot, Griffin left the office and headed to Victoria station, buds in his ears, Guns N' Roses playing for his return journey.

He felt her before he saw her. Glancing to his left, he could see that Vee was just about by his side, her petite face with its thick glasses smiling up at him. While she wasn't particularly small, Griffin was nearly a foot taller at six foot four.

"Hey," was all he could muster, though he knew he wanted to say more. But what exactly?

"Hey back. I wondered if I might see you on the way home." Her smile turned out to be infectious. Well, just a little. He smiled down at her through barely open lips, although his smile was nowhere near as blazing as hers.

"Good day at work?" It felt a safe subject, less awkward perhaps. There was always the weather.

"Yes. You?"

"It was okay. Nothing special. Deadline was yesterday so there's always a bit of a breather the following one. Not much goes on." Thinking, he asked, "What is it you do in IT? It's a big subject." They carried on walking towards the station up ahead.

"I'm in cyber security, actually. I work for a private firm. They do a lot of computer forensics for businesses. You know, like when someone leaves a company and tries to take a copy of the database with them. Or trying to defraud the company through dodgy accounting – that sort of thing."

"That sounds interesting. A bit more so than sports reporter." They had almost reached the platform while they talked; Griffin felt a little more relaxed with each step and her easy conversation. And her easy manner.

"It can have its moments. It's mainly dull digging, until you find a clue, that is. Of course, I'm not much higher up than a gopher at the moment, but I'm working on it."

The train was waiting at the platform and Griffin guided them both to 'his' carriage before sitting down. She sat next to him. It felt pleasant.

"I enjoy it," she continued, "though I'd like to get a bit more involved with cases than I am at the moment, but I'm learning. And learning to be patient. And of course, I can do some of my own research in my own time. You know, in the dark web as well as the surface web."

"You spend a bit of time in there, do you? The dark web?" Griffin's interest was piqued a little more. The dark web wasn't something people openly talked about much, though a lot of what a person could find there was perfectly legitimate.

"I do at the moment. Have you ever been inside?"

With her perfectly innocent face looking up at him, he hesitated before replying. Tell the truth or avoid it?

"Just a little." *Each night... There – that wasn't completely a lie.*

"Cool! So if you know about it and have been there, you'll know what I'm talking about."

Oh, yes. I know, indeed.

She went on. "What's the weirdest thing you've ever stumbled across while you've been surfing?"

"I've not stumbled across anything weird, actually. It's a bit hard to 'stumble,' as you put it, but I've checked into some of the drug chat rooms, for article research, you know – doping in sports, that sort of thing. Why? What have you stumbled on?"

The train jolted forward with a clank as they finally set off in the direction of home, the carriage full of tired commuters headed back with them. Vee lowered her voice in the crowded carriage and semi-whispered in his ear. The warmth of her breath on his skin as she spoke felt good. Very good. He hoped he wasn't blushing. He hadn't been so close to a female in a long time.

"Nothing really weird or anything like that. But I have figured out a couple of places I'd like to peek into. I'm a bit scared, though, of what I'll find there, so I haven't bothered." Hurriedly she added, "Nothing freaky – just a bit different. I shall say no more." She gave a sort of half-nod to the surrounding people in the carriage, some with flapping ears no doubt, clearly not wanting to risk being overheard. Having a fair idea of the types of things she might have found access into, he merely nodded to her in reply and said nothing.

And of course, he didn't mention what he had been looking into while he surfed, either. That had to remain private for a good while yet. He hardly knew her; even though he found himself liking her, he had no idea what her reaction would be. No. It was way too soon.

Chapter Twenty-One

TAYLOR AWOKE with sore eyes and turned towards her alarm clock, which sat on the night-table not far from her pillow. After spending a sleepless night filled with questions and tears, she'd finally dozed off. The clock read a little after 8 am; the last time she'd checked, it had read 5 am. Three fretful hours was all she'd managed. And now she felt like shit. Her head pounded like a madman trying to kick his way out of his cell, and she knew without looking in a mirror how red-rimmed her eyes would be. She could almost feel the crimson glow of them as she lay there. There was no rush of yesterday's nightmare returning, because it had never left her in the first place. No rush needed. She felt numb, lifeless even, and certainly not in the mood to celebrate her homecoming at her parents' place, with all their neighbours and friends tagging along. No. Her most immediate problem was how was she going to get out of going today and avoid explaining what had happened. And tidy her hair up in a rush. What was left of it, that is. She reached for her phone and dialled her mother.

"Hello, darling! You're an early bird." Always a happy singsong in her voice; Taylor wished she could match it.

"Morning, Mum. I hope I didn't wake you."

"Not at all. I'm just drinking tea sat up in bed, thinking about your father's and my next trip. I fancy Florence but I don't think your dad's that keen. Says he'd like to go a bit further east and see some of the eastern European countryside for a change. God only knows what for."

"He's always liked the less touristy places, Mum. It's you that dislikes them." Her voice sounded flat and mono in comparison to her mother's bright pitch. Her mother picked up on it in an instant.

"What's wrong, darling? You sound unwell."

Thanks, Mum. That's because I've been violated.

"Well, that's why I'm ringing, actually. I've been up all night and I look and feel terrible. I think I should stay put today. I don't want to wreck your get-together." There really was no lie there; it was God's honest truth.

"Oh, dear. That really is unfortunate. Everyone wants to see you. But if you're unwell ... then I guess you'd better stay where you are. It's probably something from the plane journey home. Your father generally catches something when he travels." That was the truth, too.

"Sorry, Mum. Maybe I'll be a bit better later on; we'll see. And I love your roasts too, so I must be bad if I'm going to miss one." Another truth.

"Well, you stay where you are, dear, and look after yourself. I'll call you later. Try and get back to sleep if you can. The rest will do you good. I'll handle the rest of the family and we'll see you when you're feeling better. Okay?"

"Okay. Thanks, Mum. Love you." Taylor forced a smile as she hung up, imagining her mother sat propped up in bed with pillows, a mug of tea in one hand and the phone in the other. It's what she did on mornings they were both at home together and not rushing off anywhere. Dad made her tea and delivered it every morning. He treated her like royalty.

Taylor pulled the duvet up under her chin, lay perfectly still and closed her sore eyes for a moment. The conversation had been easier than she'd anticipated, but all she'd really done was stall the inevitable. Buying some time wouldn't get rid of the problem, only delay it, but she hoped by the time she had to confront it, she'd be in a stronger state. At the moment, she doubted she had the strength to knock the skin off a rice pudding. With fond thoughts of her father dutifully following her mother around the sights and shops of Florence, sleep crept up on her and carried her on until lunchtime.

For the rest of the day, or what was left of it, Taylor busied herself in her small flat. Being away for so long meant dust had gathered in unseen corners and was a welcome distraction as she vacuumed and scrubbed and generally re-arranged things. By the time 6 pm had come, the place looked like a magazine shoot. A knock on the door startled her. No one knew she was back yet and, remembering the vacuum cleaner's noise, she figured it was probably a neighbour. Without thinking, she opened the door. The look on her mother's face reminded her instantly of the events her spring clean had pushed to one side of her head for a while. Her mother's mouth was wide open in an oval. A small toy train could have driven through the entrance.

Exclaiming and covering her mouth at the same time, she said, "My goodness – your hair! What have you done to it?"

Taylor felt herself go numb. She stared emptily at her mother's horrified expression; vaguely, she felt tears forming of their own free will and trickling down her face. Her mother ventured forward and wrapped her arms around her daughter's shoulders, as a strangled howl burst from her chest. Taylor flung her arms around her mother and pulled her tight, her chin resting on her shoulder as violent sobs wracked her body.

Her mother's shock gave way to concern for her daughter, and she stroked the top of Taylor's head just as Taylor's father appeared in the doorway carrying a wicker basket. Knowing immediately that something was wrong, he silently entered the room, closed the door behind him, and joined in with his arms around them both as best he could.

Finally, Taylor's sobs subsided. She pulled slowly out of her parents' embrace and looked at each of them in turn. Leonard and Judy Palmer stared back at her, dumbfounded. They couldn't even begin to imagine what had actually happened.

Taylor swiped a hand across her eyes. "I'd better tell you both what has happened, then we can decide what to do about it. Though I suspect it might be too late to do anything."

Her parents took Taylor's cue and sat down with her in the small sitting room area. When she'd gathered the energy, she told them both what had happened.

As best she could remember.

Chapter Twenty-Two

It's a common reaction for the mothers of most species: protect their young from harm at all costs. Judy Palmer was like a tiger keeping her cub safe after an intruder had been in the vicinity. She was on edge now, alert, and pacing the room. Leonard had hardly said a word; his wife had done enough talking for the both of them.

Taylor, on the other hand, had calmed right down after she had finished telling her story and almost fallen asleep with sheer exhaustion after too little sleep and too many tears. Through heavy lids, she glanced at her father for encouragement. While she loved her mother dearly, it was her father whom she took after the most in terms of her emotions and mannerisms. They had the same shade of green eyes, though his hair was fair rather than red. And she accentuated the colour at the salon to make it even richer. She absentmindedly reached back now to find a few strands to play with, and then realized there was nothing there. How could you miss your hair so much? Her father brought her back to the present by finally speaking.

"If Taylor doesn't want to report it, then I think we have to honour her wishes, Jude. She's not a child anymore, and if she feels unsure about the threat, as I would, I don't blame her. We don't know quite what she may have been mixed up in." His calming overtones seemed to make the room sag a little and relax from the recent tension.

"And I don't agree at all," his wife shouted from where she was stood looking down at the street below. The sky was autumn grey, and she watched as people below scurried on their way before the threatening rain started in earnest. She turned back into the room.

"Goodness only knows what could have happened in that room – drugged, for heaven's sake! That's serious cause for concern, Leonard."

"I agree, Jude, but apart from her hair, nothing else has been stolen. She hasn't been harmed, thankfully. Maybe we should let it rest and help her get over it. Reporting it will only make her relive it and drag the whole thing out for heaven knows how long. Maybe it's best to start the healing process now rather than in a week or two."

Taylor listened as her parents bantered back and forth like a badminton match. The shuttlecock was now in her mother's court. She picked it up and whacked it hard across the net.

"Trust you to be the one for an easy route, Leonard Palmer. No balls –that's you."

"There's no need for swiping, Mum. Calm down. We can only cope with one person ready to chop heads off, and that's you. Dad is just balancing the situation with calmness like he does when you get so excited."

"I'm not excited, I'm livid!" Judy Palmer screamed at them both and they jumped slightly.

"Mum. Please, try and calm down a bit, will you? It's not getting us anywhere. I've no idea what they meant by 'it wouldn't be wise,' but I sure as hell don't want to find out, either. Let it go, would you?"

Taylor's energy was severely depleted and her nerves were vibrating like banjo strings. Her mother's anger was making matters worse, not better. Taylor moved over to her father and sat on the floor between his legs for comfort. Instinctively he stroked the top of her head, something he'd done all her life when she'd been upset and needed calming. It didn't bother her that, even at 25 years old, she still found it a comfort. Judy relented.

"And what's that about the debt being repaid? What's all that about?"

"I've really no clue, Mum, I've not thought of much else since I got home last night. Nothing makes any sense. You're about as wise to the answers as I am. But I'm not reporting it, Mum. Really, I'm not. And that's the end of it."

"Well, if you've made up your mind, I'll support your decision. I might not agree with it, but there you go." She sounded almost petulant but at least she'd stopped yelling. "I could do with a drink. Leonard, open that bottle we brought in the basket, would you, dear?" Turning to Taylor, she added, "We brought you a plated roast dinner from earlier, in case you felt like it later. Now I understand why you didn't want to come round." Her deep sigh could be heard in each corner of the room, the sound of frustration tinged with disappointment.

"I'll put the plate in the oven to warm through. Then it'll be ready for when you want it," her dad said as he walked to the kitchen for glasses. A moment later, he was pouring three goblets of red, one for each of them.

"Look, I appreciate your concern, really I do, and the roast dinner. But I'm a bit scared of any repercussions and I want to move on and put it behind me. You can understand that, can't you, Mum?" The room stayed silent for a few seconds; not an awkward silence, but the silence of relenting.

"Of course, my darling, of course. But let me do something for you." Finally, she was speaking calmly to her daughter. Normality was resuming.

"What, Mum?"

"Let me see if Jeremy could make a house call and wave his magic wand on the hair you have left. You'd feel better, I'm sure, if you didn't have the constant reminder each time you see your reflection. I'm sure he'd do me a favour and pay a visit. I've been going to his salon for long enough." Taylor knew what her mum was saying was right. She would feel better if her hair was styled nicely rather than the jagged look she currently sported. And if it kept the peace and calmed her mum down, then she could oblige her that.

"I'll call him now and see when he can do it. The sooner the better, I think."

At least now that a semi-unanimous decision had been made not to report the incident, Taylor could get on with the business of forgetting. And having her hair sorted.

Chapter Twenty-Three

❦

"I CAN'T BELIEVE how soon the date has come around, hun. It doesn't feel like five minutes since you told me." Jeremy was trimming Amanda's already short hair as he chatted.

"I know. Time passes so quickly these days. I've no idea where it goes, but I certainly seem to miss it when it passes through. But yes, six whole weeks and we will be bride and bride." The smile on Amanda's face said it all. When Ruth had proposed some months ago, they hadn't seen any reason to wait like many engaged couples did. What was the point? And even now, it was only because the venue they wanted was fully booked that they'd decided to wait. If it had been Amanda's decision only, they'd be doing it in the back garden and having takeaway afterwards, but it wasn't just her decision. And if Ruth wanted a bigger affair, then she'd give it to her. Amanda was just pleased to be making their relationship official in the company of their family and friends.

"I'm so pleased for you, hun. I wish I was the one settling down, to tell you the truth. But alas, still too much of a playboy, I think." He gave Amanda a flirtatious wink. "While I'm still young, that is."

With mock annoyance, she retorted, "Cheeky sod! I'm not old. But I know what you mean."

Jeremy was pumping styling mousse into his hand when he exclaimed, "Oh, I nearly forgot to tell you. I've got gossip." He rubbed mousse into her hair, then wiped his sticky hands on a nearby towel.

"What, you? Jeremy the hairdresser nearly forgetting gossip? Are you feeling unwell, by chance?" Sarcastic. She caught an affectionate slap on her arm for her tone.

"I don't gossip! I've no idea what you're talking about. I've never spoken ill of anyone." Then he added, "But I've thought it," winking at Amanda's reflection in the mirror, and they both burst out laughing. He grabbed the hairdryer.

"But seriously," he went on, "I had to make a house call last weekend, on a Sunday no less. To attend to an urgent matter," he said in a more sinister voice.

"What was so urgent that someone needed a hairdresser on a Sunday?"

"Are you ready for this?" he said, leaning in to her ear so he couldn't be overheard, giving an extra frisson of theatre and intrigue to the coming story. Jeremy had missed his calling; he should have been an actor.

"The daughter of a client had apparently had her hair chopped off. Severed completely. In a prank, apparently. What do you make of that, then?" He stood fully upright behind her, a look of pure incredulity on his face in the mirror as he watched for Amanda's reaction.

She opened her mouth to speak but nothing came out.

"My thoughts exactly," he said in a satisfied tone. "It looked to me like they'd taken her ponytail, from what was left. Tied her hair up high to get the most hair, and then 'chop!'" he added, sweeping his hand down like a guillotine blade. "What kind of friends does this girl have, I asked myself? And she had such gorgeous red hair, too – it would have been spectacular in all its glory. And now it's gone."

"That's meanness on the grandest scale. Who would do such a thing?"

"I know, right? I said she should have reported it to the police." He turned on the hairdryer and it whirred into action. He began to run his fingers running expertly through her hair, tousling it dry. Amanda raised her voice to be heard over its din.

"So why didn't she?"

"Didn't want the fuss, I suppose. And really, what could the police do – slap them on the wrist?"

Amanda had to agree there. An assault charge would be all, and, really, who would bother?

"Well, I hope she'll make some nicer friends and ditch the culprits who did it. Was she bullied, do you know? Is that why these 'friends' did it?"

"Not from what I could see. She was a very beautiful and confident young woman, just home from working in New York. I don't know her myself; only her mother, the one who called me. But who would know?"

He turned the hairdryer off. Amanda's short hair took only moments to dry. They began to speak normally again as Jeremy rubbed hair putty onto his hands. Running his fingers through her hair once more, he teased it into shape, fiddling with the hair around her face. When he was satisfied, he stood back and smiled.

"You look gorgeous. Amanda Lacey, as always. Your hairdresser has done a fine job once again," he said, and beamed at her through the mirror. Amanda rolled her eyes at him and smiled her appreciation.

"Not really sure about the gorgeous part, but you do a great job. Thanks, Jeremy." He pulled her chair back as she stood.

"And only one more visit before the big day," Jeremy said as Amanda paid. He added thoughtfully, "I think I'll open some bubbles at your next appointment to celebrate. What do you say?"

"I say maybe when you've *finished* my hair, not while you're working on it. I don't want to end up pink."

"Now there's an idea! Pink would *so* suit you. You should give it some thought – a nice baby pink." Jeremy was seriously thinking about it now. He struck a pose, his bent forefinger resting between his lips and his hips thrust forward.

"I don't think so. We'll stick to blonde."

He leaned in to peck her cheek. "Well, enjoy your day, and I'll see you in five weeks, hun. Bridal hair, here we come!"

Leaving the salon with his astonishing gossip still ringing in her ears, Amanda's thoughts were with the poor woman who had had her hair hacked off by her so-called friends. What a truly nasty thing to do.

What had the girl done that was bad enough to deserve that?

Chapter Twenty-Four

　　　　　　　　✿

In his secret room, Terrance sat transfixed, perusing his acquisitions in tranquillity and privacy. No one knew he was there; no one could disturb him, and he took his time to appreciate his collection. He marvelled at how large it had become over the years, and yet with each addition, it still excited him to think how many more he could gather to feed his desire. The last cabinet to have been utilized now glowed with the others. Inside it, a long, beautiful piece of red hair was positioned perfectly to catch the light and show itself to him. A smile played on his lips at the recent memory of meeting the young woman who herself had worn it so well. That was why he had been drawn to her. The colour had glowed like a beacon to him, spoken to him out loud, and he had known at once that he had to have it. He hoped the woman hadn't been too distraught when she'd awoken.

There had been nothing in the press; she'd been the sensible type and, as instructed, had left the 'incident' unreported. He silently thanked her for that. Not that it would have come back to his doorstep. Oh, no; the service he paid so handsomely would have seen to that. After all, that's what he paid their steep fee for. Idly, he wondered what was in her past that they had on her to keep her from telling. Yes, he knew just how they operated. He'd seen the evidence, not from his own personal dealings with them, but via others who frequented the very specialized group. And that reminded him he still had a task to complete now he'd had his initial fun.

His smile widened as he thought back to that night – had that only been a few days ago? He'd taken the box and carried it carefully upstairs to his bedroom and placed it on his bed. Then he'd stripped and slid between the sheets, feeling the coolness of fresh cotton on his naked skin. He'd lain down, the box alongside his long lean body, and relished the knowledge that the best was yet to come. How long could he control himself before he stroked it? How long could he bear it so close to him, protected by its casing? His pulse had raced, throbbing in his neck like a second heart, and as his breath had caught in desire, he had known he couldn't stand the wait any longer.

The lid had slipped back silently under his fingers and the fingers of his right hand had dared themselves to touch the contents. As the initial jolt of both satisfaction and desire shocked his body, he'd whimpered. To his touch it had felt like Mulberry silk, the softest silk in the world, and he'd dared himself to place his whole hand into the box and stoke it fully. He'd whimpered again, feeling himself harden, his heart beating hard with anticipation. When he could stand the sensation no longer, he'd pulled the hairpiece from its confines and brought it to his face. Taking a deep breath in, he'd held it. It smelled just as he'd hoped it would, of apples and pears and orchards gone by. With a long, satisfied sigh, he'd let his breath go and drunk its perfume in again, then again, and then again. With his eyes firmly closed, he'd reminisced about his boyhood nanny leaning forward to kiss him good night, her hair falling away from her face and touching his as she did so. It had smelled of orchards. He'd held the piece in one hand, running the fingers of the other through the softest of strands just like he had with Prudence's hair. She'd liked it. And so had he. And it had soon become part of their evening routine together as she sat on the edge of his bed. She'd held her head still for him after each good-night kiss, and he'd taken as much of her hair as he could, slowly, relishing the feel of its softness between his fingers, stroking, enjoying. Her face was as clear in his mind as if she'd been sat there on the bed with him, gazing down at him with her own enjoyment in her eyes. He had smelled the apples and pears of Prudence's shampoo, and, still stroking the cognac locks, had found his release.

Taylor Palmer's glorious hair had been a delight to experience all on his own, to take his time with, but now he had one last task to do to complete the transaction at his end. He pulled his camera out of the secret compartment of the plinth and went towards the cabinet to retrieve the hair. The effect on him was instant as the softness once again touched his skin, sending a frizzle to his groin. He laid the hair down on the table, gently, carefully, as if it were alive, making sure it was well displayed in all its glory. Standing back to admire it again, he snapped several shots of it, allowing the light in the room to show it off from various angles. When he was satisfied he had what he needed, he carefully placed the piece back into the security of its own cabinet and let out the breath caught in his chest. With one last look at the room's contents in their entirety, he slipped the memory card out of the camera and put it in his pocket, then left the room, the lights dimming slowly as he did so. Now all he had to do was log on and share his prize with others who appreciated his collection.

And share in theirs.

Chapter Twenty-Five

✦

"COME ON IN, Jack. You know the way." Amanda held the door open for her partner, or her work husband, as she had been calling him lately. He was more like her work father in reality, though she took care of *him* more than he did her. Amanda watched as he made his way down the hall towards her kitchen at the back, a six-pack of Heineken in one hand, a bottle of red in the other. Looks like he's in the mood for a drink or two, she mused. Placing the booze on the worksurface, he took a can from the pack and pulled the ring open; creamy froth filled the opening. He wasn't quick enough to put his mouth over the hole and froth spilled over.

"Shit," was all she heard, and she smiled at the older man. It wouldn't be long now until he retired, and she often thought about how that would change her work life, having to get used to another person's ways and foibles like she had with Jack. And like Jack had with her, if she was being fair. Still, he had that fatherly thing going on, and since her father was long gone she'd allowed the relationship to swing that way. Even though she was technically his boss, they were more like equals.

As she entered the kitchen and reached for a glass for herself, she asked, "Want a glass or are you drinking from the can today? Which will you make the least mess with?"

"Since I'm at your house, I should have a glass. I don't want to bring the standards down, eh?" His smile was always a comfort to her no matter what her mood, and she reached up for a tall, dimpled glass and handed it to him. He watched as she poured wine into her own before he took a mouthful from his. He clunked his glass with hers and smacked his lips.

"Cheers, Lacey. I've been looking forward to a beer all day. Where's Ruth? She not joining us?"

"She'll be here shortly. She's gone to pick dinner up. I know I said we'd cook, but neither of us has been organized enough, so we ordered take-out."

"Fine by me. I'll eat anything, as you know. As long as it's hot if it's supposed to be hot and cold if it's supposed to be cold, I'm easy." He downed a couple of long mouthfuls, making his glass less than half full.

"You thirsty today, then?" she asked, pointing to his glass. "You'll be on the floor if you're not careful. You know you're a lightweight when it comes to alcohol."

"I must be the only detective in the world that can't hold his drink. Never been any different. Two whiskies, max, and I'm done."

"That's not a bad thing," she said. "I'd rather work with a light-weight than a drunk. At least your head is clear." She sipped her red wine as the front door opened and a woman's voice called 'Hello.'

"Down here," Amanda called back, and couldn't help the smile that broke out on her face. Jack didn't miss its arrival either. He was glad she'd finally found someone to settle down with, just like he had done many years ago with his Janine. But she was gone now, gone from the world forever, but never from his heart. When he was feeling particularly melancholy, he played a particular song from his ELO CD, "Sweet Talkin' Woman." It usually made his eyes well up. He missed his Janine every single day.

Ruth's footsteps on the hardwood floor brought him back to the present, and as she leaned in and pecked him on the cheek in greeting, he realized these two women in his life were a blessing. It's not often a man finds two women to love in his later years; these two were the family he'd never had. Ruth ruffled his salt-and-pepper hair affectionately with her hand, sending wispy bits in all directions.

"Time for a trim, young Jack, isn't it?" Ruth teased him at every opportunity.

"Cheeky sod. When you've not got much up top, you can do with all the hair help you can get. Wait until you get to your fifties – you'll have your own issues to worry about, mark my words. Just different issues to hair on your head." Thinking and grinning he added, "Like hair on your chin." Ruth's hand raised in a mock swipe, pretend outrage on her face. Amanda burst out laughing at them both.

"Would you listen to you two? Anyone would think you're the first people to get old. I'm starved. Can we eat, please?" Ruth handed the plastic bag over; the faint smell of hot Chinese food filled the kitchen. "I got a double of pork balls, purely because Amanda and I will eat so many that there wouldn't have been enough to go round with only one portion."

"I don't know how you keep so slim. Do you not eat anything else?"

"It's called running, Jack. You should try it sometime," she said, and patted his soft midriff as she passed him to get a glass of wine.

Jack one point, Ruth one point.

Amanda changed the conversation to something a little more serious as she removed lids off trays and placed the food in the centre of the table. Sweet-and-sour scented steam rose invitingly.

"Talking of hair, I had an interesting yet a bit disturbing conversation with Jeremy in the hair salon."

"I can see how that would be disturbing," Jack chimed in, and Ruth laughed with him.

"There's nothing wrong with Jeremy. He's just a bit of a drama queen, that's all." She knew she'd said the wrong words as soon as they'd left her mouth, and all three erupted in laughter. Amanda flapped her hands, trying to bring some decorum back to the table.

"No, this is serious. Listen to this." She pushed on. "He was called to a house on Sunday evening, for a woman who was in need of some emergency attention."

"Emergency hair attention?" Jack was confused. So was Ruth.

"Yes. And you'll never guess why."

"So tell us."

"Someone had chopped her ponytail off, taken most of her hair. One of her 'friends,' apparently. Can you imagine that? Why would someone do such a cruel thing? I can't imagine."

"Wow, that's wicked. And it must be distressing, too," said Ruth. "No wonder he had to go over. Every time she looked in the mirror she'd have been horrified, I'm sure."

Jack, ever the detective, had his own thoughts. "It was definitely a so-called friend? Was she bullied, perhaps?"

"I asked that, Jack, but no. A bright, confident young woman recently home from the US. Catching up with friends and her hair gets lopped off in a prank, presumably."

Jack wasn't entirely convinced. "Seems unlikely, though, doesn't it? On the surface, I mean? You haven't seen your mates because you've been overseas, then wham, they move in and, in what amounts to assault, chop your hair off? As a welcome home present? It doesn't fit with me. There's something more to it." He put a pork ball in his mouth and tried to chew the whole thing. Tiny pieces of crispy batter fell from his lips. Ruth couldn't help herself.

"Try cutting it up, Jack. You'll have more joy keeping it all in your mouth." Another point to Ruth. 1–2.

When he'd finally swallowed his mouthful, he said, "Fun fact alert." Both women groaned but listened to what Jack was about to say. "Stolen hair is big business in some countries, actually. Venezuela, for instance. Women have been attacked in shopping malls for some time. One person holds the woman and another chops her hair off. It's over in a matter of seconds and the women are usually too dazed to remember much about their attackers. They sell it on for wigs." Jack was full of fun facts about all manner of things.

He cut another pork ball in half. Sensible.

"You think something is going on here, then, in London?" asked Amanda.

"Could be – why not? Hair is hair, and nothing surprises me anymore. Easy enough to sell on, I expect. You can sell anything these days, and don't forget the dark web. It's a whole shopping mall in itself.

Want something peculiar or particular? There's a place to purchase it from."

"Well, it's going to be a bit difficult to do much. The woman in question didn't report it to the police, so there's nothing to investigate. No case. Not officially, anyway." Amanda topped up her wine glass and Ruth's and opened a fresh can for Jack. "Doesn't stop us keeping our ears open, though, does it?"

Jack understood full well what Amanda's version of 'keeping her ears open' meant.

She'd be digging as soon as dinner was over.

Chapter Twenty-Six

❧❀❧

Ruth, Amanda and Jack had both had more than their fair share of Chinese food, the remains of which still sat congealing in trays on the kitchen counter. Amanda picked a tray up and peered inside, curling her nose up with distaste. Her finger touched the orange skin that had now formed on the food, springy and not too dissimilar to homemade jam.

Ruth watched her. "It's funny how you don't mind eating it when it's hot," she said, "but as soon as it goes cold, it takes on another form. I bet a dog wouldn't be interested in that MSG-laden concoction, and I'm guessing you're not going to save it and reheat it? Or worse, eat it cold later?"

"You're right there. Straight to the bin outside, I think," Amanda said, collecting more trays and putting them all back into the plastic bag they had arrived in. She tied the top in a knot and headed for the back door to dispose of them.

"It was nice, though, as usual. Jack enjoyed it. And the company."

"He gets lonely on his own; I know that. I feel sorry for him sometimes, you know. He's not that old, really. There is still time for him to find another partner to spend his retirement with, but he spends far too much time in his job. And he's not going to find someone at work, is he?"

Ruth watched as Amanda wiped the table down and returned the dishcloth back to the sink so she could finish off. "He'll have to search a bit farther afield than that. I wonder if he'd try Tinder?" Ruth was trying to be helpful. It wasn't working.

"Are you serious?" Amanda said incredulously. "He barely uses email and text, bless him, and he still plays CDs in his car. ELO, for goodness' sake."

Ruth's mouth dropped open at that one. "Eh?"

"Yes – I kid you not. He probably thinks Spotify is some form of acne outbreak. He's a damn good detective, but he's a total luddite."

"Hmm, I see your point. Then we should help him, you know, without him knowing. Not a blind date, but something. Someone in a certain place we all are, you know, and we get chatting."

"He's a detective, Ruth, remember? He'd sniff that out like you sniff bacon cooking next door."

Ruth had to smile at that one. She could never become a vegetarian; bacon was too strong a pull. "Then maybe we should look at our wedding guest list again. There must be a suitable single aunt between us? Sit him with her."

Amanda rolled her eyes in exasperation. What was she getting into?

"No?" Ruth said, still smiling.

"No." Amanda was firm.

"Then I don't know what to suggest. No apps, no blind dates, no single wedding guests. What else is there?"

"Nature. That's what it is, nature. Let it do its thing. Without interference from either of us."

Ruth knew when to press and when not to bother. She left it alone. Some battles you fought, some you didn't. The kitchen once again tidy, Ruth announced she was making hot chocolate.

"Want a mug?"

"Always, thanks. Seriously, leave well enough alone. He may find someone all on his own. Talking of single friends, how is Stephanie doing now she and Aaron have split? Is she dating yet or is it too soon?"

"You can't seriously be thinking Jack and Stephanie, can you? He's as old as her dad, nearly."

"No, of course not. I was just thinking of another of your friends in the same boat. Single. I don't think Jack would be her type, really. Aaron was a good-looking man, but Jack? Well, he's Jack, isn't he? And he needs a haircut."

Back to hair conversations.

"Now that is weird, isn't it? The woman with her hair chopped off. My goodness, what a cruel thing to do." Ruth filled a pan with milk and put it on the stove. "I'm actually meeting Stephanie tomorrow for lunch, so I'll fill you in on any dating gossip there might be."

"Well, say hello from me. It's been a while since I saw her." Amanda said no more as she thought back to the night when Stephanie had got the fright of her life and Aaron had almost lost his. They'd driven up to Grasmere in the Lake District to their cottage, though separately, and things had exploded somewhat, leaving their relationship in shreds. It was beyond repair and would never be stitched properly back together again. Their two young sons were coping well with the new family living arrangements, but it was far from ideal.

"Come on, let's take these up to bed and read for a while," Ruth said, handing Amanda a steaming mug of hot chocolate.

"You go on up. I just need to grab my laptop. There's a couple of things I want to check up on first."

"Jack said as much, didn't he? What are you up to now? I can read you like a book."

"Oh, you just reminded me of something talking about Stephanie again. Someone, actually. In fact, being a techy you might even know the answer."

"Try me."

"Well, if you were up to no good ten or fifteen years or so ago, before the dark web was created, say, how would you get involved in shady stuff, things a little out of the everyday ordinary?"

"You don't need to be a techy to answer that one because there is very little tech involved."

"What do you mean?"

"Well, the gangs and criminals back then relied on their networks mainly; that's how they moved stuff around. The smartphone as we know it wasn't prevalent back then, though there was a small palm-held computer in the nineties, but it wasn't common. I think it was called Simon, actually. But phones and laptops would only have been of use *along* with the dark web, hence the need for physical networks. Crims wouldn't advertise on Google, remember."

"Good to know." Amanda was thinking as Ruth spoke. Why hadn't she thought of that herself? Of course, there wouldn't be much to find on a computer from back then because crims didn't use them. And who kept a computer for more than three or four years anyway? And even if they had, the dark web wasn't operational to the public back then, and again, there'd be nothing to find.

Ruth led the way holding two mugs. "Come on. Let's go and read, then."

Personal networks. Maybe that was how Stevens had operated back then, mused Amanda.

Sebastian Stevens: now there was a name that still sent shivers up and down her spine. Not only had Stephanie encountered him and his strange sexual ways some years back, but he'd turned up dead at his trendy penthouse in Manchester recently after a vigilante who hadn't agreed with his big-game trophy-hunting hobby had sent him back to his maker. Rather gruesomely so, too: graphic photos of his semi-decapitated head had been posted on his personal social channels for the world to see. The perpetrator had made Stevens their very own trophy that night. And although the method had been gruesome, the death of a vile creature like Stevens was not something the world had lost sleep over. Good riddance to him and his kind, thought Amanda.

Chapter Twenty-Seven

RUTH ALWAYS MET her friend Stephanie regularly for lunch. And since the breakup of her marriage, it had been an even more important standing diary date, with a few extra evening wines or morning coffees thrown in when needed.

There had been many such occasions. No one had envisaged their marriage split, least of all Stephanie, but when she'd found out that her husband was a serial adulterer with some rather non-vanilla tastes, well, a leopard never changes its spots. There had been many tears, and still, several months later, a few slipped down her cheeks when she found herself alone and was feeling maudlin. The evenings were the worst. Stephanie looked at the much stronger woman reflecting back from the mirror. She was gradually getting used to being single again and making a life and revised home situation for her two young boys. Stephanie rubbed her freshly painted pink lips together and checked her side view in the glass.

"Not bad for a forty-year-old single woman with two kids."

In fact, she really *did* look good. With long, dark straight hair and an olive skin, she always looked 'not bad,' even first thing in the morning with her hair mussed up. While she didn't think it or feel it herself, she was a stunning woman, a real head-turner no matter what your taste was. Or your sex.

She left her Richmond home and drove to the tube station, destination Green Park and Ruth. And lunch. And a glass of wine. Her mum was picking the boys up from school so there was no need to hurry back. Mum —what would she have done without her? The boys needed continuity and she'd helped provide it for them, and for that Stephanie was eternally grateful.

The train throbbed gently as it sped through the back suburbs of London, and she found the vibration soothing. When it finally pulled into Green Park about half an hour later, her stomach rumbled in anticipation of something good to eat. Breakfast had been a lifetime ago, it seemed. Ruth had suggested Stephanie drop in at the office before they went on to the restaurant in case she was delayed a little, which was a common occurrence. It was better to wait in her office if Ruth's meeting overran than sit at a restaurant table, waiter hovering, looking like she'd been stood up. She entered Ruth's building and smiled at Pete, who was just passing through reception.

"Hi, Stephanie. Ruth is on time for once. She won't be a minute. I'll tell her you're here."

"Thanks, Pete."

He'd been working with Ruth for a couple of years and was almost part of the furniture now. A rough start at home and a stint in juvie had given him 'character,' as he liked to call it, but he'd been on the right road for some time now, with some much-needed support and guidance from Ruth. Not to mention a legitimate job. And one he loved, he'd said. She sat in reception and waited. Ruth's shoes could be heard approaching long before she herself was visible; her steel stiletto tips echoed on the hardwood. As usual, she wore a figure-hugging skirt and blouse, refusing to go the full 'tech uniform' of jeans and hoody, and as usual she looked stunning. Her arms were outstretched as she approached and Stephanie joined her in a full bear hug.

When they finally separated Ruth said, "You look amazing as usual."

"As do you. Love those heels, by the way."

"A girl can't have too many shoes, eh? Now how does a juicy burger sound for lunch, or have you another preference? Vietnamese? Curry? You name it."

"Oh, a burger," she exclaimed, feeling her stomach gurgle like a bathtub emptying. "It's been too long since I last had a proper one, and those skinny things the kids eat don't really count. I'm in."

Ruth hooked Stephanie's arm in hers and the two friends left the building in search of food. As always, conversation between the two of them was easy.

"So, what's new in your world, Steph?"

"Not a lot, I have to say. Just steady. And I think I like it that way." Stephanie beamed at her friend and confidante. Finally, her eyes had started to sparkle again of recent weeks.

"You look great, as usual, but you also look great on a different level too, if that makes sense. I can see you have your sparkle back; you're glowing again, which is lovely to see." Ruth squeezed her arm. "Things are finally settling for you."

"Thanks. I feel much better in myself. Onwards and upwards and all that. I couldn't have done it without your support, though, and I thank you." She squeezed Ruth's arm in return. They walked together in comfortable silence for a few beats, then Stephanie asked, "And what's new in your world, then? How are the wedding plans coming along? We've not really talked about them much." Ruth looked sheepish as she turned to her friend, and Stephanie caught her meaning.

"Ah, I see. Me and my disaster of a marriage. Well, that's all behind me now, so don't worry about mentioning weddings. I'm as excited about your big day as you are, and I want to hear all about your plans. Don't avoid the subject on my account, okay?"

"Okay," Ruth said with relief in her voice. She opened the door to the pub and the smell of beer, old polished wood and freshly cooked fries assailed them.

"Then I will get you up to speed," Ruth went on, "because I'm busting to share them with someone. Amanda agreed for me to organize it all, which is what I wanted to do, so she's no clue what I've got planned."

"Two glasses of white wine, please," Stephanie ordered as a barman caught her eye. Or she his, in reality. Steph never had a problem getting a drink order organized, or any service for that matter. The barman was young, but old enough to be a man. His body shape told her he worked hard at the gym.

"Burger?" Stephanie enquired.

"Burger!" Ruth replied.

"And two house burgers and fries to go with that," she called.

"I'll bring them over. Find yourselves a seat," he called back. His cute smile could have made ice cream melt in an igloo.

Ruth watched with amusement. "Well, he's clocked you for sure. You might be in there. I bet he slips you his number when he brings the food over −mark my words." She winked, making Stephanie laugh out loud.

"I'm old enough to be his mother, so I doubt it."

"I'll bet you a fiver he does."

"Okay, you're on. Prepare to lose a fiver."

Ruth pocketed the fiver with a smile. They sipped their drinks and chatted about wedding plans as they ate, then Ruth exclaimed, "Oh, I know what I meant to tell you. Last night, Amanda was telling Jack and me a story her hairdresser had told her."

And on she went. Stephanie sat back and listened as Ruth went over the story again of the woman whose hair had been chopped off.

"How weird is that?" she said when Ruth had finished. "And how mean." Stephanie felt the colour drain from her face.

"Are you okay? Only you've gone as white as the icing on my wedding cake." Ruth put her hand on Stephanie's arm.

Stephanie took a long mouthful of wine for strength, then enquired, "Was there a card left, by any chance? It's important I know. Do you know if there was?"

"I don't know. Why? Whatever is the matter?"

Stephanie took a deep breath before answering.

"Because remember that night all those years ago when I was drugged by that pig Sebastian Stevens?

"I remember you telling me, yes."

"Well, someone chopped my hair off too. It wasn't him, though; I'm sure of that. But they did leave a card."

"And what did it say?"

"It said, 'Your debt has been settled. I'd advise you to tell no one. It wouldn't be wise.' If this girl had a card left too, then it's still going on."

"What's still going on?"

"I've no idea. Whatever it is, though, they're still doing it."

Chapter Twenty-Eight

✿

RUTH COULDN'T BELIEVE what she'd heard. After all her friend had been through recently, Ruth had managed to drag something up from more than fifteen years ago to add to the poor woman's recent stress. By the end of their lunch date, Stephanie had regained her colour, thanks to a stiff brandy. Ruth had walked her back to the tube station, Stephanie earnestly assuring her she was fine. It had all been a bit of a shock, that was all. As for Ruth, she knew she had to talk to Amanda, and quickly.

"I'm sorry to disturb you at work, but this is important." Ruth hardly ever called Amanda during her shift; she usually resorted to text messages if she had to tell her something. But this couldn't wait any longer.

"What's up? Everything alright?" Amanda was generally cool and in control, but when she'd seen Ruth's name on the call display, she'd thought the worst.

"It's about that woman who had her hair chopped off."

"What's so important about that?"

"I've just had lunch with Stephanie and mentioned it to her because, well, it's an unusual story. And she went as white as snow. I asked her what was up and before she answered, she asked me the strangest thing."

"What?"

"She asked if a card had been left. It turns out that, that night Sebastian Stevens drugged her, someone cut *her* hair off too. And they left a card. Like a calling card, with a message on it."

"What? Shit! What did the card say? And how come she's only just mentioned it today?"

"It said not to tell, that it wouldn't be wise. And I guess it never came up before, with everything else going on."

"I guess not." A couple of beats passed as Amanda thought about the card. "I wonder what it means? It sounds rather threatening. And this puts another slant on things. I'd better pop over and see Jeremy, see if I can chat to the woman involved or at least to her mum; she's the one who told him. If this second girl was given a card too – and we don't know she did as yet – then there is something to investigate further."

"Maybe she had a card with the same message, and that's why she hasn't told anyone. Maybe her own mother isn't aware?"

That made sense. "I see what you mean. But it's a start, so I'll see where I get. And Ruth?"

"Yes?"

"Not a word to anyone, not even Stephanie, about this yet."

"Of course. My work here is done. Over to the detectives." Ruth sniggered lightly.

"Ha, ha, very funny. I'll see you later." Amanda hung up and stared at her phone as if the answer had popped up on the screen. No such luck. Jack was nearby, cajoling the coffee machine to dispense a cup, and his exasperation was showing at its non-delivery. Operator error, Amanda thought, smiling ruefully.

"Give me Nescafe any day. My blood pressure can't stand the disappointment," he grumbled, loud enough for Amanda to hear. She smiled at his agitation and walked over to help. It wasn't the first time, probably not even the tenth time.

"You really do amaze me, Jack. A smart person you are, yet when coffee machines are involved, you're the dumbest of the dumbest. Here, let me," she said, pushing him gently out of the way. Amanda quickly assessed the situation and realized his error. She walked over to the tap and filled the plastic well with water then inserted it back onto the machine, trying hard to contain her amusement. Jack was aware that others in the incident room had stopped working and were watching the performance.

"I find it works better with water myself," Amanda said, slotting the water well back into place. There was no need for her to say anything else. Nor Jack. She pressed the requisite button and the machine sprang into life, thick brown aromatic liquid filling his mug with a satisfied 'chug, chug.' There was almost a round of applause, but no one wanted to be the one to start it, so the air took on a sort of silent applause in its place, one that could be felt rather than heard. Grinning faces returned to their duties. Rather than hang around while Jack's mug filled, Amanda left him to wait for his brew and calm himself back down.

A couple of minutes later, when he was back at his desk sipping contentedly, she approached him with the news. "Listen, Jack. We might have something going on with the hair chopping case I told you about. Seems there might be more to it."

"Oh? I didn't know there was a case." A milky moustache covered his top lip and Amanda motioned with her fingers to her own top lip. He got the hint and wiped it away. The foam was now on the back of his hand. He stared at it.

"We didn't, but I've just heard about another woman from some years ago who had her hair taken. And get this: whoever did it left a card saying not to tell, that it wouldn't be wise. I'm off to see Jeremy, see if I can speak to the more recent woman or her mother and find out if they also had a card. You coming?"

Jack raised his coffee mug as if to say 'I've just got this' and said, "No. I'll stay here and get some paperwork done. I'm drowning in it. You go. Let me know what she says."

Amanda watched as he wiped the froth from his hand with his handkerchief. Finally. She grabbed her jacket off the back of her chair and headed out to the hairdresser's for the second time in a week.

This time, it wasn't for tea and gossip.

Chapter Twenty-Nine

⟡

"LET ME GUESS. My roots are that bad you thought you'd better come back and do them before much longer." Judy Palmer smiled as she kidded him. He'd only ever been to their house once before. Jeremy's face told her he wasn't feeling quite so jovial today.

"Hello, Judy. May I talk to you for a moment, please?"

She opened the door wide and stood back, beckoning him through. "Can I get you some tea? Though you look like you might want something stronger. Are you alright, Jeremy?"

"Tea, thank you. That would be nice." He climbed up on the bar stool that stood by the breakfast bar, his body half twisted towards Judy as he watched her make the tea.

"What's on your mind to bring you back out here?"

"I've got a confession to make. And I'm hoping you're not going to be angry. But you might be." He said the words slowly, with trepidation.

"Oh? Go on."

"I might have mentioned to a woman in the salon that I'd been called out to help a woman because a prankster had chopped her pony-tail off. And that is was spiteful, nasty." Judy stood quietly, but he could see by the tightness of her lips she wasn't happy. He carried on. "I was just chatting – nothing malicious, just expressing my incredulousness at how someone could do that to a so-called friend." He stopped at that and waited for her reaction.

"So, Taylor is the subject of your idle chit-chat, is she? But looking at your face, I'd say there was more to it than that. What else?"

He could feel her anger almost palpably bouncing off the tiled wall of the kitchen.

"She's a detective." He winced as the words crept out of his mouth.

"You told a detective? How dare you! How dare you first of all talk about our private business, and second, you must have known she was a detective? Why on God's earth did you feel the need to share it?"

Jeremy could feel himself cowering as her voice got louder, loud enough that Taylor herself came through from the next room where she'd been reading her book.

"Mum? What's going on?" Jeremy had the sense to stay quiet while Judy explained to her daughter. Taylor went as white as the tiled walls, her lower lip quivering as she took in what she was being told. When her silence had gone on long enough, Jeremy dared to add the last piece of why he'd actually gone to the house.

"Look, I'm really sorry that I mentioned it to anyone, but it seems that Taylor may not have been the only one that this has happened to." He watched as both women looked at each other silently. Taylor's lip had begun to tremble. He pushed on. "The detective would like to talk to you and find out a little more, so I said I'd call over and forewarn you both. I hoped I was being helpful. After my mistake."

"It's a pity you didn't try and be 'helpful' before you told half the salon! What were you thinking, you stupid man?"

Jeremy bowed his head. Taylor's voice broke the silence.

"I didn't want the police involved, but now you've ruined that. What am I supposed to do now?"

He watched as her lower lip trembled harder before her face crumpled fully and she fled from the room in tears. He could hear the first deep sob and he felt wretched for instigating it. Judy glared her displeasure at him.

"You'd better go. The damage is done."

Silently, Jeremy slid off the stool where he'd been perched, uttering a final abject apology to Judy's deaf ears. Letting himself back out the front door, he exhaled the trapped air in his lungs and replaced it with fresh, trying to make himself feel better. It took several attempts as he walked out to the road and his parked car, but he wasn't interested in his own car. Parked further up the road was Amanda, and he slipped inside into the passenger seat.

From the way his head thudded onto the headrest, Amanda didn't have to ask how it had gone.

"I feel bloody awful now. Taylor is sobbing, Judy is angry and I'm depleted. Why couldn't I have kept my big mouth shut? Other people's misery is off the table of conversation forevermore," he said emphatically, his arms crossed over his face in anguish. Perhaps if he couldn't see, it hadn't happened.

"Well, I'll go and see how receptive they are in a few minutes. If there are others, and there may only be the two I know about, they could help stop whoever is doing this. And of course, the fact that both women had had the same thing happen to them could also be a simple coincidence." She was silent a moment, pondering. "But as a detective, I kind of don't believe in coincidences."

Jeremy grunted, more from embarrassment than as a proper reply to her comment.

Ten minutes later, Jeremy stayed put in the front seat and watched Amanda's blonde head disappear around the front gate and up the driveway, headed for the Palmer residence. He slunk down in his seat to wait it out.

Chapter Thirty

AMANDA HAD LEFT THE PALMERS' place with what she'd wanted – almost. While Taylor had obviously been scared to talk about what had happened, Amanda had persisted gently with her, and now felt she had the start of something to investigate. Given Stephanie's snippet of information, some fifteen years belated though it was, she didn't believe the relationship between the two incidents was a coincidence. Not at all. When she'd mentioned the card and its message to Taylor, the look of pure horror on her face had sung to her like a Welsh male voice choir. Not even a rookie would have missed it. But the thing that had puzzled both victims, as she now referred to them, was the part about 'the debt being settled.' Neither woman could throw any light on what it could possibly have meant. Now back at the station and headed to fill Jack in, she wondered what they could be dealing with. And just how long whatever it was had been going on. At least fifteen years; maybe longer.

"Crickey, that's weird," Jack said. "And from so long ago too? Did someone resurface, I wonder, or has it been going on all these years and we just haven't heard about it?' Jack was twiddling his moustache between two fingers, a habit that amused Amanda, and something he did usually while deep in thought.

"No clue. But I'm going to get that laptop out of the evidence locker if it's still there, the one that belonged to Sebastian Stevens that we found after his death. If he was with Stephanie that night, it may have been him who took her hair, though Stephanie felt sure it wasn't him. Or it might still be a coincidence. Worth a look, though: fresh eyes, now we know a little more."

"First, Lacey," Jack put one finger up, "you don't believe in coincidences, and second," he put a second finger up beside it, "that computer will only be a handful of years old, so I doubt there's much of use on it."

"I know that, Jack, but he may have been active with others more recently so it's worth a look, isn't it?" Jack conceded the idea and picked his phone up to make the call. "Let's hope we still have it, then. We'll soon find out."

Amanda watched her partner as he asked the question and waited for the reply.

"We're in luck," Jack said after he'd hung up. "They're pulling it out for us. Are you giving it to computer forensics, then?"

"Not much good me looking at it, so yes. But this time, we know a little more about what we're looking at. Sort of."

Jack raised his brows in a doubtful manner but didn't say anything. Sometimes, he let Amanda have her own way without much discussion, and over the years they'd been working together, she'd been more often right than not. She sat back in her chair and started to tap her teeth with a fingernail. It wasn't lost on Jack that she was playing with her own virtual moustache.

At length, she spoke up again. "You know, if you were up to no good these days, there are plenty of ways to hide your activity. If this is something dodgy, chances are it's not found on the regular web but in the dark web. Why would you risk it otherwise? And anyone can get access to the dark web now; it's not hard."

"And if that is the case, it'll be almost impossible to find. Whatever it is. That's the whole point of it – that much this luddite does know." He pointed to his chest with his thumb.

While he was useless with gadgets, particularly coffee machine gadgets, Jack did keep abreast of what was out there security- and crime-wise. He just couldn't make it work for himself. Amanda conceded that he was right. They needed to find out what they could the old-fashioned way and then enlist the help of the cyber team with their more specialist knowledge. And tactics.

And she could chat to Ruth if she needed to. She knew everything about everything tech.

Later that evening over dinner with Ruth, Amanda broached the subject of the dark web.

"Can someone simply stumble across something strange, say a hit man for hire?"

"No, not really. You still have to search for what you want. Why? Thinking of knocking me off once we get married? For my millions?" Ruth grinned at her.

"No, just curious. The dark web is not somewhere I hang out, so I don't know how it works, really. I leave that to the cyber guys."

"And girls."

"Eh? Oh yes, and girls. Sorry, Miss Tech-head."

"Apology accepted. What is it you *really* want to know about?" Not much got past Ruth's bullshit antennae.

"Look, I can't tell you details, but it's to do with Steph's revelation about her hair being chopped off and the more recent woman. Since we've no clue what we are looking at, I thought it may be something deeper. And darker, perhaps. Like on the dark web."

"Well, aren't your cyber team helping?"

"Not yet, no. Nothing to go on to get them involved. Just my mind working scenarios. Or scenario, actually, I haven't got another."

"Well, the answer is still the same. You need to search for it and there's the clue – *search*. The dark web is just a list of un-indexed pages, and they're not all peddling weird stuff. You'll find legitimate sites too. Anyone can look, but users make themselves anonymous by using a TOR browser, which encrypts and pings around a whole bunch of servers around the world so their IP address can't be traced back to them. Simple to do but it also makes it hard to find those who peddle stuff they really shouldn't be. Like child pornography, drugs, and, yes, hit men. And hit women."

Amanda smiled at that one.

"Look," said Ruth, "I'll give you a demo when we've finished, open your eyes a little."

Amanda wasn't sure if she liked that idea or not. You can't un-see something, she knew, and who knew what she might find.

"Don't look so scared. We won't be going to *those* types of pages – what do you take me for? And until you start clicking on dodgy images or videos, or interacting in something illegal, you'll be as safe as on the regular web, maybe even safer. Now eat up and I'll show you."

Amanda was about to have a lesson on what others do for kicks in their spare time.

Chapter Thirty-One

GRIFFIN AND VEE had started seeing a little more of each other, though there was nothing *official* about it. Since Vee had caught up with him a few evenings ago and solved the puzzle of his knotted ear buds, they'd caught the train together to and from work on several occasions. And even though it interfered with his practiced routine, his morning one in particular, Griffin had found himself able to relax about it a little. To his surprise, he hadn't stressed about it as much as he once would have. And that was because he was enjoying her company, her lively but not overbearing chatter, her forwardness and the warm breeze she brought into his otherwise still and functional world. He'd found himself thinking of her at all times of the day – while he waited for sleep to come, while he waited for the kettle to boil and while he finished his steps off for the day. Not in a sexual way; more of a 'not-really-sure-why-I'm-thinking-about-you-all-the-time-but-I-am' kind of way. Did that even make sense? He enjoyed her company, fair and simple. The thought occurred to him that maybe there might be other parts of his routine he could break out of if it brought him the kind of enjoyment that Vee had shown him. And he'd quite like to take her out to the pub, but did he have the courage to ask her? And then what? If they got on well and they carried on seeing one another, there would eventually come a time that she'd want more, expect it, even.

'More' included her seeing him naked, and that he wouldn't do at all. Not yet.

He placed his breakfast crockery in the dishwasher, switched it on for a low wash and headed for the train. He was fifteen minutes later than he had been with his routine of recent, but it meant they could ride together. He picked up his pace as the station came into view. And the rear of Vee. Smiling to himself, he wondered what she was listening to as she walked; her ear bud wires just visible, resting on her shoulder. If he called out to her, she'd never hear him, and Griffin didn't have the confidence to do that anyway. So, he watched her from the comfort of twenty paces away, knowing she'd be stood on the same platform as he would be in a few moments. And that comforted him somewhere deep inside.

She spotted him as soon as she turned into the entranceway.

"Morning, Griffin." Her smile was as bright as a daisy drinking in the summer sun, and just as pretty.

"Morning, Vee." While he smiled in greeting, he couldn't compete with her confident way, and looked more like a cheap chrysanthemum that had been far too long in its cellophane flute on a garage forecourt. He did his best anyhow.

"I fancy a coffee. Want one?" She looked up at him expectantly. "I'm buying."

He hesitated.

"No?"

"I usually drink tea."

But not until I get to the office.

"Can I get you a tea, then?" The daisy-like smile glowed again. How could he not? He checked his watch for the impending train. Some habits were harder to break.

"Great, thanks. I'll come over with you," he said, and they both made their way to the coffee cart along the platform. A couple of minutes later, they had their drinks. When the faint throb of the approaching train could be felt, they stood where Griffin usually stood in the hope of getting a couple of seats together, though the later train time had proved a bit more difficult to manage. Still, they each had their music for the short journey, and they were together at least. As the train pulled up in front of them, they could both see they were out of luck. Vee looked up at Griffin and screwed her face up in disappointment as the people ahead of them crowded into the carriage, taking the last remaining single seats. Standing for the journey wasn't really a problem, but conversation was almost impossible with other people's faces only a few inches from their own. It meant those close by heard every word, and that made it embarrassing to have a conversation for just about everyone. Travelling on a morning commuter train was not too dissimilar to travelling in a stock truck, though rather than being nose to tail, morning travellers were nose to nose. It was only marginally more pleasurable. Some people really needed to attend the dental hygienist a little more regularly.

With their ear buds firmly in place, they stuck it out until they reached London Victoria, Griffin with Gershwin, Vee with Sia, each in their own world thinking their own thoughts. Vee glanced at Griffin but he didn't notice, lost in the sound of piano keys as Gershwin reached a crescendo. When the track changed he looked up from watching the floor and caught her eye. She took her buds out and he followed suit, aware she was going to speak. What was she going to say in a place where she could be overheard?

"Fancy a drink straight from work?"

Griffin couldn't believe his ears. How could she be so brazen, so confident and so forward? And in such close confines, too? He stood there, stunned, like a mackerel ready for the pan. He hadn't been prepared for such a direct question and at first wasn't sure what to say. He knew what he *wanted* to say, but here? With all these people listening? He flicked from her face to the stranger's face a few inches away and back to Vee. As he stood with his mouth open slightly, hoping the appropriate words would somehow fall out, she prodded him.

"Well? Yes or no to a lager?" At least she was smiling – in amusement? The stranger caught his eye and nodded ever so slightly, he too prodding him to answer Vee's question. Griffin fumbled and mumbled, but eventually released a coherent answer.

"Yes. I'd like that." He breathed a heavy sigh as he relaxed, his anguish passing over and leaving his chest as it drifted off down the carriage and out of an open window. The stranger gave him a half smile, a 'well done,' like a teacher dishing out a red star to a good student.

"Great! Do you know The Baskerville? It's not far from my road. Why don't we meet there at, say, seven pm? Will that give you enough time to do whatever you need to do beforehand?"

His steps. He did a quick calculation in his head; he'd have to walk faster if he was going to make it. There was no way he could do less.

"Can we make it seven fifteen? That would be better. So I'm not late."

"Seven fifteen pm it is."

Griffin couldn't believe what he'd just agreed to, and so publicly. What would the strangers be thinking of him? Were they thinking anything? They all knew where he'd be tonight at 7.15 pm and who with. Did that matter? Thoughts bumped around inside his head as the carriage doors opened and strangers flooded out onto the platform and forward, each on their own way to work. As Griffin was swept along with them, he felt a small hand find his and slot itself in. It was Vee's. And it felt comfortable. He glanced down but she didn't glance up, and didn't take her hand away either. And neither did Griffin.

Chapter Thirty-Two

GRIFFIN COULDN'T HELP the bats fighting in his stomach. At 6.30 pm, he stood in the shower letting the warm water cascade over him as he contemplated the evening ahead. A bat thumped him with its wing from the inside as he opened the shower gel to wash away the day's grime. Pine forests filled the cubicle as his thoughts darted back to the evening ahead. Normally, he'd shower and surf after dinner, the end of his normal day of work, walk and web. That's how it was, always had been for as long as he could remember, but then Vee had come along and things had started to move, to change. First his morning commute, now an evening out. What would be next? Soap bubbles slid down his naked body as he washed half-heartedly, not really concentrating on what he was doing, until his thoughts jolted back to his problem.

Soon.

He'd learned to keep it in perspective, to tell himself that it would be dealt with soon enough.

Just as soon as he'd found the right person at the right price.

He grabbed the loofah and scrubbed his body all over, the rough surface sending a tingling over all that it touched. By the time he was completely washed, his skin glowed like light sunburn and felt cleansed. The rest of his routine was much the same as every day, though tonight he dressed in clean jeans and another hoody instead of his normal pyjamas. A splash of aftershave and he was ready to go.

'It is just drinks, for heaven's sake. Get a grip,' he told himself repeatedly on the walk over. "Nothing to be worried about." But he didn't feel relaxed; he felt exactly the opposite.

Vee was already inside chatting to the barman when he opened the front door of The Baskerville, and he took the opportunity to stand in the doorway and take another deep breath to steady himself. From his vantage point, and knowing she hadn't seen him arrive yet, he appraised her from top to bottom. Deep red Doc Martens on her feet, an obviously vintage floral dress that totally suited her and an aura about her that spoke volumes about her relaxed and rather lovely disposition. He dragged some courage up from his own boots and stepped forward to greet her. He opened with a well-planned-out 'Hi,' and hoped he'd figure the rest out from there.

"Hey! Hi yourself. You smell nice. Sort of like a forest." Her smile was as bright as it had been earlier that morning, and he found himself relaxing as she beamed up at him. Deep red lips and dancing eyes caught his attention. She looked even more striking than she had that morning. "What can I get you to drink?"

Finding his voice, he said, "I'll get these. You bought tea this morning. It's my turn. What would *you* like?"

"In that case, I'll have a Snakebite, please."

Griffin looked at the barman, who raised his eyebrows and nodded that he'd heard the lady. "Make that two, then," he added. He was not a big drinker; he'd see if he liked the taste and go back to his normal slimline tonic if not. He didn't want to appear a party pooper on their first outing. He wasn't calling it a date; it was just drinks. That was how he was reconciling it in his head to keep the fighting bats quiet.

"I'll bring them over. Pints or halves?" asked the barman. In unison they both said the opposite to each other.

"Pints," said Vee.

"Halves," said Griffin. It broke the ice and they both burst out laughing at themselves, and at the complete reversal of the norm.

Men drank pints, didn't they? No, not this one.

The barman understood and busied himself with their order as Vee led the way to a table on the far side of the pub, away from the rest of the customers dotted about, some nursing a pint solemnly, some giggling over wine.

"So," she started, "why don't you tell me a bit more about yourself. All I know is that you're a sports reporter and where you live. Then I'll tell you about me if you like."

Griffin wondered if she was always so forward or if it was just with him because he was reserved in his ways. And where the hell should he start? He looked aghast at the prospect but relented; they had to start somewhere. Or sit in near silence. Taking a deep breath, he began, the words tumbling out like the passengers on their commuter train did at Victoria.

"Griffin Stokes. Twenty-five. Lived around here all my life. Single, a self-confessed nerd. Used to be into gaming but no more, and I walk daily. I like a wide range of music, eat healthily but never used to and have lost about twelve stone; still another one stone to go. Oh, and I'm an only child. I think that's about it. Your turn." Phew.

Vee smiled her usual bright smile and Griffin wondered what was going through her mind at that precise moment – good or bad? He hoped it was good.

"Vera Dobbs, but my friends call me Vee. Twenty-five, same as you, about a foot shorter than you at five-foot-four, can be a bit of a geek at times, spend too much time on Facebook, wondered about going vegan but like my bacon too much, two sisters and love the movies. Oh, and I quite like gardening, not that we have much of a garden at home, which, yes, I still share with my parents." She'd mentioned before that she still lived at home and he raised his eyebrows inadvertently. Vee raised her own in reply.

"What?" she asked. "Plenty of people still live at home at twenty-five. I can't afford to move out yet; not around here, anyway." The arrival of their drinks halted the conversation, giving Griffin time to make amends for his slip-up.

"Sorry, I didn't mean to embarrass you."

"You didn't. And I'm not embarrassed. I'm saving hard to get my own flat, but until then, home it is. It won't be for much longer, anyway. I've nearly got a deposit together." She took a long gulp of her Snakebite and looked at Griffin expectantly for his response.

"That's great. It's hard saving up a big chunk of cash; I've done it myself. And I'm doing it again." Griffin realized his error as soon as the words had left his mouth and quickly added a question. hoping to deflect attention away from his comment. "Where will you buy? Something local or further out?" It was an opportune time to taste his Snakebite, leaving her to answer the last question. He hoped.

"Ideally. It's handy for work and I'll still be local to my family, so yes. Just got to find the right place at the right price. What's the Snakebite like? To your taste?"

His tactic had worked. She'd missed his slip. Or hadn't mentioned it, at any rate. "Not bad. It'll grow on me."

Grinning, she said, "Maybe if you've nothing better to do this weekend, you could help me find a place? There's a couple I want to look at." Vee was looking at him across the top of her pint glass, a sly smile on her deep red lips. He watched, somewhat mesmerized, as her top lip vanished into the glass to meet the amber liquid.

"I'd love to."

Chapter Thirty-Three

JOSHUA AND JASPER were upstairs in their room, tucked up in bed reading with their flashlights. Stephanie had turned a blind eye to their refusal to go straight to sleep, knowing full well they were tired out and it wouldn't be long before they were asleep anyway. And reading a book was a useful hobby to have, far better than playing with a screen just before sleep. Feeling like an early night herself, she watched bubbles gather on the surface of the milk she was warming in a pan for a mug of Horlicks to soothe her nerves. She hoped the malty drink would help; in the absence of wine, it would have to do. Since she'd told Ruth about losing her hair that day, she'd not thought about much else.

Losing her mind, more like.

Why had she said anything, raked it all back up again? It had been years ago, long before she'd married and had a family, and since she'd been out having a good time that had then ended up with her in bed with a man, there had been no point in reporting it. They'd both partied hard, she'd gone to his room and the rest had, well, happened. What she hadn't expected the next morning when she had awakened, though, were the tiny nicks on the backs of her thighs, the kind made by a knife, and her beloved long dark hair gone, leaving nothing more than a short basin cut.

While her missing hair and the mysterious nicks had been a shock, it was how those things had happened at all that had alarmed her. Yes, she had partied hard and downed shots as well as copious amounts of wine, but she never touched substances, not even the odd joint. The only way what had happened to her could have happened was if she'd been drugged.

By someone else.

She grabbed a chocolate biscuit from the jar and took the steaming mug with her to her room where she slid between the sheets and sat thoughtfully with her drink. Crumbs dropped on the bed as she bit into the biscuit, and she absentmindedly brushed them to the floor, not particularly caring. She was due to vacuum tomorrow anyway. Her phone chirped a message and she reached over to the side table to see who it was. Did she want to talk? Probably not. Ruth's name filled the green text box.

"Just saying hi. Hope you're okay. Sorry to have dug up the past. If you need me, you know where I am. xxx"

Smiling at her friend's thoughtfulness, she tapped a text in reply.

"Just sat in bed, with Horlicks and a biscuit. How sad is that? Seriously, I'm fine though. Thanks for checking in."

Since Amanda had been to the Palmers' home and found out Taylor, too, had received the same card, the idea of its being a coincidence was seeming less and less likely. If whoever had assaulted her all those years ago had surfaced again only recently, something or someone had activated them, to her way of thinking. Unless of course they had never completely gone away.

"When are you going in to the station to fill out a report?"

"I'm going in tomorrow. There is no real urgency, just getting it on paper really. It may help someone else."

"Yes, that's the spirit. Well, good luck. And good night. Xxx"

"Night. xxx"

Stephanie stared at the screen and re-read the message. While it was probably too late to get justice in her own case, she hoped her experience and any evidence she might be able to give would help catch the perpetrator and prevent it happening to anyone else. Had

Sebastian Stevens still been alive to tell his side of the story from that night, that might be a different matter.

Opening her Kindle, she turned her attention to her book and finished her Horlicks as Jack Reacher chased a badass through a crowded market. If nothing else, it took her mind off her own life's issues, and she allowed the fiction to cover her like a soft blanket. Half an hour later, she was sound asleep, her bedside lamp still blazing, the boys in the other room still reading. It was a little after 1 am that she woke with a start and went to check on them. Both were by then fast asleep. She turned off their lights, tucked their blankets around them and crept back into her own room, now lit only by the moon streaming in through the window. She lay listening to the night – a couple chatting quietly as they walked on the pavement below, their voices carrying upward on the still air; the distant sound of a dog barking a couple of times before settling again; and a car cruising to a standstill nearby. A car door slammed shut and she heard the sounds of two people saying goodbye. Then silence returned.

She turned over in bed, wide awake again. Tomorrow, she would report what she could remember. Which wasn't much. There had only been herself and one other person in the room that night. They'd had a good time, pushed some boundaries, and afterwards she'd fallen asleep. Or so she had thought. A vague recollection came back to her as she lay there and delved a little deeper. She reared up in bed with the sudden realization of something.

"Oh shit!" she said quietly, her heart rate picking up speed as she remembered back. There had been an argument, the sound of another male voice in the room for a brief time. But she'd been half out of it and fallen back into oblivion. What had all that been about? She lay back down to think through the events that had followed.

Sebastian Stevens had still been lying next to her the following morning, and he'd been the first one to point out her hair was gone. He'd sat bolt upright in the bed, pale as a ghost, and said "What the hell happened to your hair?"

She'd rushed into the bathroom to look in the mirror and stood there open-mouthed in shock. It couldn't have been him; otherwise, why hang around until morning and act the way he had? In a panic, she'd gathered her belongings, dressed and fled back home. It was when she'd got in her own shower that she'd noticed the little blobs of dried blood and felt the stinging on the backs of her thighs as the water washed over her. *That* was what had really concerned her. The card she'd found later on, just inside her handbag, and reflecting back now, she realized it had been placed where only she would have seen it. Yes, she'd wanted to report it, but the message on the card had been clear. As was the voicemail Sebastian had left on her phone after she'd fled.

"No one will pay you any attention after what you agreed to last night."

She had known that was true. What they'd done – the sex, anyway – had been consensual. But what about the nicks? And why had her hair been so cruelly taken? And by whom, for what? She had never asked him, had wanted to simply put the whole eerie incident behind her and forget it, and him. Over the following weeks, she'd willed herself to put the whole thing out of her mind, learn from it and move on. Resolutely, she'd vowed never again to pick up a man who seemed too good to be true, and to run for the hills when the coke came out.

Tomorrow's report-taking would drag it all back up in detail, she knew, details she'd rather forget. But if someone else had been involved that fateful night and the police managed to track them down, her day in court would come.

Snuggling further down into the bedclothes, she willed sleep to return.

Chapter Thirty-Four

INTERVIEW ROOMS in police stations were set up not for victims but for criminals, Stephanie thought. Uncomfortable plastic chairs and functional cheap tables made anyone who sat at them feel uneasy in their surroundings, and the discomfort only added to Stephanie's anxiety. At least she knew the friendly faces on the other side of the table, which eased her mind a little. But she'd been drained before she'd begun: thinking back to an event that she'd rather have blocked from her mind, one that had happened fifteen years ago, wasn't an easy task, especially coupled with a fitful sleep the night before. She'd never smoked a cigarette but was desperate for one now.

Jack was the one asking the questions. "Let's start right at the very beginning, then, before you met Mr. Stevens. What were you doing that night, and who with? Then fill us in from there. Don't leave anything out: the smallest detail could be of use and I'll prompt you along the way if I need clarification on anything. Okay?" He smiled encouragingly at her.

Though she was still feeling wound up, Stephanie took a deep breath in, exhaled and started on her account of that night's events. Jack scribbled as she talked.

"I'd met a man, who turned out to be Sebastian Stevens, in a bar one night. I'd had quite a bit to drink. My friends had split up a little, and I found myself propping the bar up. That's when he said hello. He seemed nice enough and I allowed him to buy me a drink." She sipped water from a plastic cup. "He had started out with some other friends, I assumed, and a bit like me, he'd split off from them. We chatted, we drank, we flirted and later that night, he escorted me out to his car. He said he had a driver, which I believed because when we got outside, there was a man in the driver's seat of a flash black car. And he, I mean Sebastian, was as drunk as I was, so I was glad he wasn't driving.

"I got in, and we went back to his place. It was only a mile or two away, but too far to walk in my heels, and like I said, we'd drunk quite a bit." She took another deep breath and carried on, knowing that the next part could be embarrassing. "We went inside his flat, which was more of a penthouse, so I knew he was really well off, what with the driver as well. He poured us drinks, and one thing led to another. I'm sure I don't need to spell the next part out to you."

"Do you remember, and I'm sorry to have to ask you this, but were you still coherent at that stage or not?" Jack was embarrassed too but needed the answer.

"Yes, I was alert. Pissed out of my head but alert. We got into bed, and I remember having sex but I must have passed out shortly after that. The next thing I remember was a vague conversation sometime in the night. Not Sebastian, but another voice, like there was someone else in the room. But I drifted back to sleep again. When I awoke in the morning, Sebastian was still there in bed and it was him that noticed my hair had been cut off. And not just cut off but stolen. Then I panicked. Sebastian was as shocked almost as I was, I think, and swore it hadn't been him. And I believed him, because why would he? And he was still there with me. If he'd done it, I figured he'd have been long gone, but then we were in his place. A hotel room would have more suitable, had that been his plan, not his home.

"My hair wasn't in the room. I looked. It had definitely gone. So I left as fast as I could and got a taxi home. That's when I discovered the tiny nicks on my thighs. That, I believe, was him."

"What made you think that?"

"Because he wasn't the usual vanilla in bed. He was," she paused for a moment, "more adventurous. He wanted me to do things I hadn't done before. He encouraged me to try stuff, and he liked to dominate. He wanted me to be submissive, stay on the floor on my knees, that sort of thing."

"Did you confront him after that night, about the tiny cuts?" Amanda said gently, aware that this was extremely personal territory.

"I didn't. Because he sent me a text telling me nobody would listen to me so not to bother telling anyone. I'd gone to his room for sex, and that was that. My own stupid fault." Stephanie's bottom lip started to tremble and she fought to keep control of her emotions. "I didn't consent to that though – my hair being severed," she wailed, tears spilling down her cheeks.

Amanda passed her a tissue and looked at Jack sympathetically. "Take a moment," she said. "There's no rush. Then can we go back to when you thought you heard another voice in the room."

Stephanie nodded and blew her nose. When she'd regained her poise, she rewound back to where Jack wanted her to be.

"I don't know what time it would have been. We didn't get to his place until around one am and I left at around seven am. I remember the sunlight streaming in – that's what woke me in the morning, I think. It was so bright. He hadn't closed the curtains. Anyway, all I can remember from earlier was I was in bed. It was dark, but there was a muffled sound, conversation, two deep voices. I assumed one was Sebastian and one was another man, though I've no idea who. Like I said, I was pretty out of it."

"Was Sebastian out of it too, do you remember? Had he taken anything, and had you?" Stephanie looked a little sheepish and the answer was obvious.

"He took some coke – I think it was coke. But I never touched it. I've never done drugs. He wanted me to have some, but I said I didn't need it. He took some, like they do in the movies – you know, up his nose. He said it relaxed him." Turning to Amanda quickly, she asked, "Do you think that's what he drugged me with – cocaine?" Her voice rose in panic.

"Probably not, though we'll never know. If you had been drugged to knock you out, it would more likely have been Rohypnol – 'roofy' is the street term for it, and it's also known as the 'date rape' drug."

Stephanie sat speechless for a moment. At least she hadn't been raped; her experience had been consensual, although only marginally so.

Jack broke the silence. "Can you tell us anything, anything at all about the other voice? Accent maybe, old- or young-sounding, foreign possibly? Anything?"

"No. It was just a blurry voice, like I was hearing it under water. I wish I could tell you more."

"It may throw some light on what happened. As Mr. Stevens was murdered, we can't ask him about that night. And you seem pretty sure he didn't have anything to do with your hair being cut. So let's get to the part about the card, the note you found. Go on from there."

"When I got home, I showered, got dressed and sat on the sofa, trying to sort my thoughts out, really. And figure out what had happened, what I was going to do next. I grabbed my bag, looking for something, though I can't remember what. And then I saw an envelope sticking out. It had my name on the front. It just said 'Stephanie,' so I opened it. The single piece of card inside said 'Tell no one. It wouldn't be wise.' And that the debt was settled. Or words to that effect. It spooked me, and I assumed it was to do with my hair being taken. I'd already had the text from Sebastian about being game, so it didn't make sense for it to be from him. I do remember it looked very elegant though, a swirly handwritten script, not from a computer."

"What did you do then? Did you tell anyone about the card?"

"No, I didn't tell. I was too spooked all round. I threw the card in the rubbish and that was that. My hair would grow back, and I figured I'd had a bloody lucky or unlucky night, depending on how you looked at it. It taught me a lesson, I can tell you."

"Is there anything else?" Jack sensed she had finished, had told all she knew and was ready to wrap it up.

"No. I'll let you know if I think of anything. Can you tell me why this is so important now, after all this time and Sebastian being dead?"

Good question. Jack took it.

"There may be another case that's recently come to our attention.

Quite by accident. She had a similar card left and thought she'd been drugged."

Stephanie's hand flew to cover her mouth.

"And her hair?"

"Sadly, gone."

A groan of disbelief and anguish escaped her mouth. Fifteen years later it was happening again. Had it ever stopped?

"My god. It's been happening all this time and nobody knew." It was a fact, not a question.

"Well, we do now."

Chapter Thirty-Five

⚜

IT HAD BEEN a harrowing hour or so at the police station, regurgitating events from so long ago, events that she'd worked hard to forget. Now they were back swimming around the inside of her head like sharks circling in shallow water. A nuisance, and frightening. While she probably hadn't been much help – she hadn't seen anything of use – if it helped to catch whoever was responsible for the latest victim and prevent more women from going through this, then it would have been worth the pain.

As she walked, a thought nagged at the back of her mind now – the reference on the card to a debt being settled. At the time she'd wracked her brains, wondering what it had meant, but nothing had come of and it had been forgotten with the rest of the nightmare. But now, having told Jack and Amanda about it, she began uneasily to ponder it again. *Your debt has been settled*. But what debt, and to whom?

Right now, she needed a drink. There was a place up ahead that would do.

Stephanie opened the door to the wine bar and found a vacant stool at the bar. She didn't want to be totally on her own, but she didn't totally want conversation either. She hoped a glass in the vicinity of others would soothe her nerves. A young man dressed in a denim apron with "Matt" embroidered on his nametag approached her, smiling pleasantly.

"A glass of white wine, please," she said. "A large one."

"Coming right up." She watched him pour from a bottle in the fridge, salivating at the thought of the crisp, cold liquid she was about to consume, then silently reprimanded herself.

You sound like a desperate alcoholic.

"Thanks," she said, and greedily took three large mouthfuls.

Matt raised his eyebrows at her. "Are you okay?" he asked. "Only you'll be falling off that stool in a minute if you're not careful." His concerned look told her he wasn't being a comedian or an asshole.

"Rough day, that's all." She put her glass back down. It was now only a third full. "And I know it's still early, but really, it's been a crappy day already."

Matt took the hint and busied himself further down the bar to give her some space, and she nursed the rest of her glass at a more leisurely pace. She'd been sat there thinking for about twenty minutes when the door opened again and three women walked in, chatting earnestly together, and headed to the bar to order. All three women would have been in their thirties, and from the way they were dressed, probably office workers of some kind, and well paid, judging by the shoes they were wearing. Stephanie loved nice shoes. One of the women was telling a story, the other two listening intently as Matt approached, and Stephanie's ears perked up, not out of nosiness but because the woman was obviously wound up – probably the reason they were in the bar in the first place, much like Stephanie. One of her colleagues took the liberty of ordering them gin and tonics, and Matt began to mix them, shooting a quick glance at Stephanie.

"Honestly," the first woman exclaimed. "It's like Hollywood in that place now, probably worse. What's his last indiscretion going to do to the company's reputation now, eh? I'm getting pretty sick of fighting his fires because he can't keep it in his pants, or his hands to himself. He's a bloody nightmare to have around. I'm seriously thinking of talking to the board. It's not good for business." The woman steadied herself with a deep breath before taking a large mouthful of her drink. Her hand shook slightly, and the ice cubes rattled. The other two women sipped slowly; so far, they'd only offered the occasional 'oh' and 'ah' to confirm they were indeed listening.

The speaker set her drink on the counter and began talking again, her voice vibrating with anger as she spoke. "It's Lisa I feel sorry for now. Having put up with his advances all this time, it won't be him that moves on, but Lisa, and she's a damn good team member. Not like Mr. Shitty Sleazeman."

One of the other women nearly choked on a mouthful of gin, coughing and smiling at the same time. "Sorry, that's actually quite funny," she apologized, wiping her mouth. "Cheeseman, Sleazeman. Who made that up?" She giggled and took another sip of gin.

"I think he earned that name himself don't you?" said the first woman. If the cap fits and all that."

The three women stood in silence for a moment, contemplating what was obviously an embarrassing and awkward situation back at the office. The ringleader carried on. "We've got to find a way to stop him. Otherwise, we won't have a team – or a business, at this rate. Sexual harassment is not to be taken lightly; it's a serious offence, for both parties. If Lisa leaves because of it, she'll be marked a trouble-maker, and if she presses action and wins, she'll be labelled a trouble-maker too. Meanwhile, Sleazeman gets to have a giggle about the whole thing and life moves on for him. Until the next one. And the next one. And I'm sick of trying to sort it out. Perhaps *I* should leave and leave him to it." The other women watched as she slammed her empty glass down on the bar with a thud, catching the attention of Matt.

The first woman said, "Let's order some food and another round, and sit down and make a plan. You're right: the problem won't go away on its own. We have to do something." The third woman nodded her agreement and gathered three menus. As the others moved to a table, she called to Matt for three more drinks.

Stephanie had always believed in chance, in fate, in being offered an opportunity at the oddest of times and places. Listening to the women's heated conversation had jogged something loose, something from the past that now swam in front of her eyes like it was only yesterday. That shark again, or something else as deadly. Open-mouthed, she ran through what she'd only moments ago realized, a piece of the puzzle from her past now making perfect sense.

Her debt had been paid.

She'd been the one being harassed by a director back then. *He'd* been the one to make her life hell to the point that she'd begun taking anti-depressant pills. And then, just when she'd thought she couldn't stand it anymore, it had stopped. Like someone had severed his hold on her, cut the cord with a knife. Nothing further had happened – no more quick touches as they passed in the corridor, no more lewd looks and sexual innuendos. No more chance meetings in the tearoom when everyone else had left for the evening. She shuddered at the memory, and what she'd done to him that night. He'd left rather suddenly and never said a word about it. At the time, she'd wondered why. And now she knew. Someone or something had intervened. While she'd been thankful it had ended, there was a question to be answered.

Could she have ended up in someone's debt?

Chapter Thirty-Six

HOW COULD she have forgotten that important snippet? She slapped her forehead with the palm of her hand. He'd left suddenly, with no warning and no explanation, and she had felt relief like never before. It had all come to a head. All the flirty remarks and comments, and suggestions of dinner after working late – all the classic 'want you in my clutches' letch talk that she and probably others before her had endured – had finally flicked a switch in her mind.

Late one night, she'd been finishing off a project. Most of the team had left for the evening and she'd been rinsing her mug in the kitchen. Quietly, he'd entered the room while she had her back to him and had locked the door. When she'd turned and seen him standing there, the look of 'got you' written on his face and his lecherous smile, her stomach had nearly emptied itself into the sink. It had been obvious what was to happen next. She remembered how he'd leered at her, taking in her long legs, licking his lips as he'd walked towards her, savouring his prize like she was an ice cream he was about to devour.

But not tonight. Never again.

She'd waited patiently for the right moment, for him to get close enough. Kicking him in the nuts wasn't an option: he was already too close, and there was not enough room to swing her foot up. No, she'd had a better plan, one that could get her the sack, or even worse, a record for assault charges. But that didn't bother her. *He* bothered her, and he had to be taught his advances weren't welcome, ever.

She'd fixed a 'come and get me' smile on her lips and stuck it out. He'd probably been surprised at her smile, and pleased that she was going to submit without a fight, that she had realized she couldn't stop the inevitable. That bit had pleased her, because he was almost correct on that score. Except it was *he* that couldn't stop the inevitable.

As she'd leaned back into the kitchen counter and he'd made contact, pressing his body into hers, she'd stayed focused on what was to happen next. She'd turned to her right slightly and let him kiss her neck, all the time fighting the repulsion of his damp, hot breath on her skin. She'd tried her best to relax, to let him know he'd won and she was enjoying his touch. How far from the truth that was. Her right hand had clenched stealthily around her weapon of choice and with one strong movement, she'd thrust the fork prongs into his shoulder as hard as she could.

It took him a fraction of a second to realize what she'd done and release her, but she was well ahead of his thought process. Like a firework, she propelled herself at the door and unlocked it, flying out into the main office and into the midst of the cleaning staff who were working there. Pausing just for a moment to grab her bag, she watched as he stared at her from the doorway, his face crimson with pain and fury. And a fork sticking out of his shoulder. That part had amused her, and she'd smiled mirthlessly as she fled the building, leaving him to it.

At least she'd won on this occasion, though it wouldn't be the end of it, she knew. Tomorrow, she'd be lucky if she still had her job, not to mention the police at her door.

She'd hit 3 on her speed dial as she legged it towards her car. Chris had picked up quickly, his voice chipper, pleased to hear from her as always. They'd once had a serious thing but were now on and off regularly. She knew Chris wanted them to be permanently on.

"I've fucked up," she blasted out in a rush. "I think I may have gone too far."

"Slow down. And tell me what's happened."

"Meet me somewhere?"

"Anytime – you know that. Where are you now?"

"Just left work. Headed home."

"Then jump in a taxi instead and come straight round. I have wine." Chris always had wine; they'd drunk a fair bit of it together in the past.

"On my way. See you in ten."

He was waiting at his front door and walked down to the pavement as she pulled up. In the back of the taxi she'd had time to calm herself down a little and wasn't so frazzled. Chris paid the driver as she got out and he turned to her. His arm slipped across her shoulders in comfort like close friends do. Once inside, she'd told him the whole sordid story. Of how her boss, William Botham, had tried valiantly over the previous months to make her his prize. Of his disgusting habits and ways of speaking. Of how she knew she wasn't the only one going through this, though no one had dared make a formal complaint. And of how, tonight, she'd finally had enough and decided to beat him at his own game. He'd set her up in the kitchen by locking the door, and she'd set him up by having the fork ready at her fingertips. The only reason she'd chosen a fork over a knife was because a knife really could have been termed a weapon. A fork? More opportunistic, less premeditated. Though it had probably hurt just as much. She'd certainly hoped so, and his yelp, like a wounded dog's, had confirmed it.

Chris had sat quietly taking it all in but couldn't help himself smiling proudly as she described the scene just before she'd fled. The wine was helping her relax.

"I felt like Sarah Connor stabbing the Terminator – strong, in control and damn hard," she'd said, and they'd both laughed. Her tension was easing.

"Did you wear jeans and a vest covered in sweat? And big boots?"

She knew when he was taking the piss, but it felt good to laugh at the whole scenario before the inevitable shit set in. He'd held her close as their laughter had died down and they both thought of the possible consequences. It was assault, after all, and she'd no proof of his wrong-doing – and Botham was in a better position to persuade the authorities if he chose. Getting her fired wouldn't have been a problem in the slightest.

"Look, stay here tonight," Chris had said. "I'll sleep on the sofa and you have my bed. In the morning you'll feel better and be ready for whatever the day brings."

Stephanie had agreed.

He'd hugged her tight, and she had felt glad of his friendship.

Chapter Thirty-Seven

✦❦✦

Fifteen years before

Chris Meeks had never been much of a sleeper. He'd regularly operate on four or five hours per night and often wished he could sleep for longer. His body just didn't need it, and the many physicians he'd consulted as he was growing up had all come to the same conclusion – he was just wired differently. They'd advised him to just let it be, and as a result he read huge amounts at night or listened to audio books as he lay in bed 'resting' his body, with his mind whirling round digesting the words. Late-night radio bored him senseless but podcasts on various topics filled the gap; he'd found they were a good alternative to fiction.

It was during all this spare time, when others slumbered and snored all around him, tucked up warm in their beds with loved ones, that he had taught himself how to code and to set up a business. But his business was a little different from the conventional ones a client might find listed on Google. His business lived in a secret place, a dark place, one accessible only by invitation to select and affluent clientele. When he'd first had the idea and begun to put the bones of it together, he'd been surprised at the custom that had come his way – not so much the volume as the customers who had seen the opportunity for him to expand his offering to so much more and had been willing to put money into the venture.

Of course, he'd started small, and had done the majority of the work himself with the help of actors looking to pay bills of their own. He paid much better than waiting tables. Some of those early actors were still with him today, though times had changed with the advances in technology. Still, Chris's business wouldn't work without the humans involved; not everything could be left to technology. No, humans were the very essence of his group. And they had their needs.

Back in 2004, there had been only a handful of sites like his, and he'd had to use the common web to get things going. That and dank basements where others involved in illegal activity did their trading. It had reminded him of prohibition and illegal underground bars: secret locations, secret access and secret clientele that could be trusted.

Trust.

Trust was essential for a business like his to operate outside the norm, and he'd come up with a foolproof way to ensure nobody blabbed.

Self-incrimination.

In order to gain entry, a member had to supply proof of their desires and proof of themselves satisfying those desires. That way, if anyone felt like snitching, there was evidence of their own full involvement – and who would be crazy enough to drop themselves in it and report him to the authorities? So that's what kept his service running smoothly, without aggravation from law enforcement. Even if an undercover officer managed to gain entry with an invitation, they were never going to supply their own proof of incrimination, and Chris would sniff them out immediately.

The other built-in security measure he'd added was the constant merry-go-round of site addresses. He used these like squatters use derelict homes, moving from one location to another at regular intervals. A short time before the group went live for the evening, a link would be sent out to his client base with the address where the gathering would be held encrypted in the message. Illegal dog-fighting rings did the same, except they met in the woods in person, while Chris's group met in the cloud under pseudonyms.

Sat at his desk as Stephanie slept in his bed, Chris entered the group under his usual admin login and sent a message to the rest of his 'management team,' those who co-owned it. He had an opportunity lying fast asleep in his bed next door, and he knew there would be the perfect match-up for her somewhere. He just needed to find out who. He stepped back into his bedroom and took a picture of her lying fast asleep, her beautiful hair on show and her sweet face in blissful repose, looking like she didn't have a care in the world. He knew otherwise. He typed a short message and attached the image, then hit 'send' and waited while it pinged across various servers around the world. It wasn't long before the first response came back.

Hair for a hijack, read one.

A beating for two pints of red, read another.

Feet for finances drained, read the third.

Chris smiled at the devilish delights his clients were willing to give in order to get what they wanted. While he himself would have liked to put a hit out on the man who had upset Stephanie, the rules of the group were clear: no one got physically hurt. No one would die, no feet severed, no eyeballs collected. Nothing to cause physical pain was ever to happen. That was not the business he was into. His role was arranging pleasure and fulfilling sexual fetishes for one group in return for something the providers would appreciate or enjoy themselves, and ensuring that neither party realized the two parts of the transaction were connected.

As he put it, he offered a dark service.

Since he himself was the client in this particular scenario, the 'hair for a hijack' offer stood out to him now. Stephanie could cope with losing her hair, he decided. It would grow back, and setting up the perfect hijack would be fun: William Botham would be scared out of his sleazy mind when the time came to throw a sack over his head and manhandle him out of his home.

He sat back in his chair, fingers steepled together in thought as he quickly worked out the logistics. He wanted it done tonight. He glanced at the clock on his computer: it was just coming up to midnight, which gave him around five hours tops, and since he knew nothing about the target as yet, he'd have to work quickly to get the pieces in place. While he felt sorry for Stephanie, since she'd undoubtedly be upset for a few days, he knew she wouldn't be harmed in any way. Using a hijacker who demanded only money for the service was not how these exchanges worked: Stephanie needed to frighten Botham into silence, so there needed to be a forfeit in return. So there was no way around it: Stephanie would have to give up her beautiful long locks.

He got to work with his plan. First was a background search: his client's location, activities and finances, both company and personal. It made him smile as he dug into what the man had been up to; his credit card statement read like a porn library and it seemed he had more than one property listed to his name.

"Which one are you sleeping in, Mr. Botham?" he said to the screen as he typed. He sat back and looked at the current power consumption of each of them. "Ah, I guess one is a bolthole for 'special occasions.' I wonder if your wife knows about it. Shame you're not there in that flat. It would make the job a little easier later on." He searched on and was pleased to discover Botham had a regular gym session with a personal instructor at 6 am each workday.

Well, he wouldn't be going tomorrow.

He walked into his bedroom and bent at the side of the bed, kissing Stephanie lightly on the cheek. She really was a beautiful woman, and her long brown hair fanned out gloriously over the pillow.

"It will grow back, my love," he whispered, "and your problem will be solved." He slipped into bed beside her and stroked the very hair that would soon be appreciated by someone else.

Chapter Thirty-Eight

HIS SHOULDER THROBBED. Was there any wonder? William looked at the red and now quite swollen skin in disbelief. Four little dark bloodied holes seemed to glare back at him, and he did his best to ignore them.

"Bitch," he said to the reflection in the mirror, then peered more closely at his wound. His pyjama top had kept it concealed from his wife in bed; otherwise she'd have been asking awkward questions, questions he didn't want to answer. How exactly do you explain that you were stabbed by a woman at work whom you were teasing? What was she on, anyway? Couldn't she take a joke?

"Bitch needs an orgasm to release her pent-up frustrations," he grumbled. "Probably not had one for years. Stuck-up cow – who does she think she is, attacking me?" He roughly lathered his face in foam and began to shave quickly, all the time cursing inwardly at the woman who'd taken him aback the previous night. He'd have to deal with *that* little problem later today: nobody got one over on him. In frustration, he swept his blade over his chin far too quickly and nicked himself. Claret mixed with creamy white, like strawberry coulis on vanilla ice cream.

"Shit!" he cursed out loud as he watched the red drop travel south.

"Bitch," he added again, and kicked the wall to vent his annoyance at something that wasn't going to fight back.

Twenty minutes later he was on his way down to the underground car park and an hour punching a bag with his instructor at the gym before work. Still seething, he unlocked his car as he approached. It beeped in response and he flung his kitbag on to the back seat. As he got into the driver's side, a figure slipped into the passenger side next to him, startling him. Even in the dim light of the garage he could see the person was wearing a black balaclava. Adrenalin poured into his bloodstream.

"What the fuck? What is this?" He turned to the figure and his face met the muzzle of a gun.

"Shut the hell up and drive. Head for the gym – as usual."

It wasn't lost on William that the 'as usual' meant whoever this was knew his movements. "What do you want? I don't have any cash if that's it. But I can get it later. Just leave me alone," he said, his voice quivering.

Chris smiled inside the balaclava. This one was going to be too easy. It always amused him, when he undertook this role, how people reacted, how they'd start spilling their guts, what they started offering. And sometimes *who* they offered. He shook his head and tutted softly; this guy would probably sell out easily. He was tempted to ramp things up a notch. But he wasn't there to harm the man, just scare him shitless. He spoke with a practiced fake Irish accent that even to his own ears sounded menacing.

"Shut the fuck up and drive. Don't make me have to tell you again." He pressed the gun into Botham's thigh.

Botham took the hint and started the engine, pulling out of the dark garage and out into the weak morning light. He tried to look down at the gun, but the man pressed the muzzle in harder.

"Watch the road. You know what this is so don't make me use it." He felt Botham quiver slightly and hoped he wouldn't wet his pants. Some of his victims had, and he hated the smell, but this was only going to be a short journey. He got down to the business he was there for.

"You weren't very friendly last night. Now you'll pay for it."

"What? What do you mean?"

"Are you really that stupid? Perhaps you are. They said you weren't particularly bright. And I'm inclined to agree. Think back, dumbshit."

A moment passed before Botham spoke. "Really? It's about the bitch from the office?"

A punch to the side of his head sent the car careering into the other lane for a moment until Botham managed to correct it back to his side of the road.

"There you go again, disrespecting a woman. Not bright."

"Oh, now I get it. This is my warning to stop, is that it? Who the hell are you, her boyfriend?"

Another blow caught him hard and he winced, closing his eyes for a second as the pain sliced through his skull.

"Do I sound like her boyfriend? I doubt she'd date someone with my particular skills." He chuckled snidely and noted with satisfaction that Botham swallowed hard. The gym was just visible in the distance now.

"Pull into the car park and park over in the far-right corner, behind the shed."

Botham obliged and steered the car into the space he'd indicated. "Turn the engine off and stay facing forward. Keep your hands on the steering wheel. If you move, it could get messy. And I don't like mess."

William sat po-faced like a naughty child doing as he was told. He felt movement at his side but dared not to look. Then suddenly everything went black as something – a sack? – was placed over his head. He gasped in panic as the smell of damp earth from the sack filled his nostrils. When nothing else happened, he tried to relax a little and keep his wits and bearings. He heard the strike of a match, and the stench of cigarette smoke filled the car. He waited for the man to speak, to find out what was coming next. The smell of smoke became stronger as the man exhaled, and William tried not to cough.

"Here's what's going to happen," the man said at length. "Go about your day as usual. Do not under any circumstances speak to, look at, touch, or do anything with Stephanie today or any other day. If we hear of any contact with her whatsoever, your wife will be notified about the little love nest you keep for your extracurricular activities and the women who frequent the place with you. That should lead to quite a nice divorce settlement for her, I should think." The man took another long drag on his cigarette, and William could just see the red glow of the ember through the woven sacking.

"Okay, I hear you. Can I go now?"

"Not quite. As a little reminder for you, in case you get tempted to digress, I want you to remember our conversation with this."

The man gave no warning as the cigarette seared the skin on the back of William's hand; he yelled in pain as the man increased the pressure, stubbing the cigarette out fully on his skin. He clutched his hand, gritting his teeth in pain.

"Now remember what I said or there will be more where that came from, much more. Look at the mark every time you see her, as a reminder of our conversation."

William heard the car door open, and the man slipped out without another word and shut it quietly behind him.

William sat aghast. What the hell was going on here? First his shoulder, then his shaving, topped off with two blows to the head, a sack over the head and a burn on his hand. He was beginning to feel like Michael Palin in *A Fish Called Wanda*. All he needed now was a bloody nose.

He sat still, listening, for several more minutes. Finally, hearing nothing, he dared to turn his head. Had his assailant gone? He chanced lifting the sack away from his face and, squinting in the early morning light, looked cautiously around the vehicle. No, he was alone. He climbed gingerly out of the vehicle, cradling his burned hand, headed to the back door of the gym and went inside. While he wasn't going to work out, he relished the sanctuary the building offered, and he felt his thumping heart begin to slow down. The bright receptionist, his current plaything, smiled coyly at him, but he was in no mood for flirting today. Maybe never again.

"Done?"

"Done. And what a pathetic excuse of a man he turned out to be. Bullies often are. He won't be any bother now."

The driver started his engine. "Excellent. Fancy a Sausage McMuffin?"

Taking his balaclava off, Chris replied in a very English accent, "Love one."

Chapter Thirty-Nine

✿❀✿

SHE'D AWOKEN in a strange bed. Chris was lying fast asleep next to her and she palmed her forehead in dismay. Has she really stayed over at Chris's? And what had happened to him sleeping on the coach? Her head hurt from downing too much wine too quickly, and she jolted back to the events of the evening before.

At work. And what she'd done.

Grimacing, she gently folded the bed linen back and crept out of the room in search of the bathroom. Locking the door behind her for privacy, she examined her face in the mirror and took in the swollen eyes and blotchy skin. She looked like she'd had a good cry, that's for sure, and she didn't have any make-up with her. She flopped down on the toilet and took a pee, head in her hands. A light knock at the door pulled her out of her thoughts.

"Are you okay in there?" Gentle as ever; he'd always been the perfect gentleman.

"Be out in a minute," she called back. "I need to get home and changed. I look like hell."

"Never, but yes, I'll drop you home. Time for a cuppa first?"

She had no idea what time it was, but if she was late, she didn't really care anyway. She'd be lucky if she still had a job to go to, but she wasn't going to stay away completely.

"Please."

The smell of toast wafted up the stairs and met her on the landing. Her stomach grumbled in appreciation. When Stephanie eventually entered the kitchen, Chris had laid the table with juice and cereal packets.

"You may as well eat here," he said, busying himself buttering toast. She took a slice. Butter ran close to the crust edges and she licked at it greedily. Chris couldn't help but notice.

"Thanks for letting me stay last night. What happened to the sofa, though?" Chris smiled. "Relax, we didn't do anything. You weren't that out of it."

Relief relaxed her shoulders a little and she smiled back. "I didn't think so. I guess we can be two adult friends and sleep in the same bed, can't we? Others manage it."

"Well, while I don't know of any, we managed just fine." Changing the subject, he asked, "How do you feel about going in to work? Are you alright?"

"I'll be fine. I might not have a job later this morning, but I'm not staying away. Or I could be answering questions down at the police station, of course." She chuckled to let him know she wasn't stressing too much about it. The beating of her heart was another matter, but what was done, was done.

By the time she'd finally got to work, every fibre of her body felt as tight as a stretch band. She stood in the lift taking deep breaths to steady herself for what was probably going to be an unpleasant experience. She'd dressed in a navy-blue pantsuit, the one piece in her wardrobe that she felt invincible in, like Wonder Woman without the cleavage but equally as strong. Last night she'd barely thought about her actions and her brute strength had surprised her, but today she needed all the help she could get, and from wherever. If power dressing was a crutch, then she'd lean on it for all it was worth.

The doors slid open and her booted feet stepped out into the reception area as she tried her best to ooze confidence and strength. While she looked great on the outside, on the inside she oozed about as much strength as an empty tube of toothpaste. As she made her way to her desk, she chanced a glance to either side of her, expecting either security guards approaching ready to remove her, or at the very least William's P.A. hot on her heels. But there was no rush from either side – no men in uniform, no demanding P.A. She was surprised, but shrugged it off and carried on to her desk, quickening her pace only slightly.

Mid-morning came and went. Nothing.

Lunch came and went. Still nothing.

Surely mid-afternoon? No, nothing.

End of the day? Ditto.

At precisely 6 pm, Stephanie gathered her things to head out for the evening, still expecting a tap on the shoulder, a summons to his office after hours even, but when his P.A. shouted "Good night!" as she too left for the evening, she finally let herself breathe a little easier. Maybe her attack had done the trick and he'd been too embarrassed to mention it. Maybe he was avoiding her for fear of being stabbed again. Or maybe he just had better things to worry about. Hopefully that would be the end of it.

"Oh well. Whatever," she mumbled happily as she slipped inside her car and drove home.

The man in the dark corner of the car park sent a message back to the operator. It read "No contact all day. She's headed home."

The reply came back. "Perfect. We'll activate the next part."

The man pulled out of his hiding spot and stayed within a safe distance of her car. She'd be going out later, though at this point she didn't know it yet. He knew where she lived, so cars pushing in in front of him as they drove didn't worry him, and actually made his tail even more natural. He observed as she approached her flat but he carried on past, opting to park further up the road. She wouldn't be going for at least another hour, so he settled himself in and opened his flask of hot coffee to wait for further instructions.

From his own computer in his own flat, Chris watched as the various points came together on his screen. She was home. He hoped she'd had a rather more pleasant day without the sleaze ball hounding her around every corner. He pressed send on his phone and it connected almost immediately.

"I'm guessing it was all okay today. I didn't hear from you." Chris sounded like the caring friend he was.

"It was the weirdest thing," she replied. "I kept expecting something, a tap on my shoulder, but no, nothing. I'm half wondering if he wasn't that bothered. Or better yet, maybe I've warned him off properly. Maybe that's it now. I hope so."

Chris smiled at her optimism. "Well, that's great I'm pleased for you. I've been thinking about it all day but didn't dare to ring or text. Look, I'll buy dinner, something casual, then what do you say to a couple of drinks? Nothing heavy, but a bit of a celebration, eh?"

The air went quiet between them as Stephanie was obviously considering his offer. Chris was quick to interject before she could find an excuse. "In fact, let's go all out and eat at that new champagne bar in town, then drink champagne there! We could dress up nice and be toffs for the night. Sound like fun? I'm buying."

Her giggles rang in his ear; he'd hit the right spot. "Great! Get your best dress on, then, girl and I'll meet you in sixty minutes. Is that long enough?"

"Yes. Sounds great. You're on. I'll see you in an hour. I'd better get a move on."

He smiled. She sounded lighter and ready for some fun after her ordeal yesterday, and he was pleased with how things were turning out. He really hoped what was about to happen didn't upset her too much, but it had to be done. The debt had to be repaid.

Even for the rather lovely Stephanie Michaels.

Chapter Forty

"YOU LOOK GORGEOUS AS USUAL, Ms. Michaels. Care to take my arm?"

Chris stood in the doorway smiling broadly at Stephanie, arm proffered for her to take, gentleman style. She linked hers in his, and they set off towards his car, which was parked at the curb. He opened the passenger door and she slid in, careful not to expose too much thigh in his direction. She didn't want him getting ideas about anything other than friendship. She gave a mock royal wave with her right hand as though she was riding in the golden horse-drawn carriage. In actual fact, she had been poured into his Mini. Top-end model, but still a Mini. She examined her surroundings, taking in the flight deck of clocks and the various knobs and buttons. The leather interior invited her to stroke it.

"What a beautiful interior. Small, but beautiful."

Chris got in beside her and started the engine. He revved it a couple of times for her benefit. "Listen to that purr. She's like a big cat." He gently revved a couple more times, listening himself to the power tucked inside the bijou casing. "Ready?"

"Let's go!"

And off they drove to the champagne bar that would become their venue for the majority of the evening. There was no need for the tail. Chris knew exactly where she would be tonight: right by his side.

For the time being.

Chapter Forty-One

IT WAS a couple of hours later that he made his approach. Chris had gone to the bathroom, leaving Stephanie alone for a short time at their table, which was his signal to take over. A suave blond-haired male approached the table, a Margarita in each hand. "May I?"

Stephanie looked up from her thoughts, straight into the deepest blue eyes she'd ever seen. For a moment, she didn't quite know what to say; she felt almost hypnotized as he gazed back, but his smile broke the spell.

"I – I'm with someone tonight, actually," she stammered.

"I know. He's just gone to the gents so I thought I'd bring you a drink. I didn't think you were actually an item together, which is why I'm here."

She smiled at that. "Oh? What makes you think that?"

"Your body language together. I've been watching. You're just good friends, am I right?" His eyes danced as he teased her and she found herself staring at them again. And blushing. He sat down next to her. "Here," he said passing her a cocktail glass. "I took a chance on a Margarita. You look like a woman with taste."

"Are all your chat-up lines so cheesy?"

"I'm afraid they are, and they rarely work, but I live in hope they will tonight." They both laughed. He put his hand out to introduce himself. "I'm Sebastian, and you are. . .?"

"Stephanie." She took his hand and they shook gently.

"Well, that has a cheesy ring to it already, doesn't it? Stephanie and Sebastian. Heavens, it sounds like a posh kids' store. We're doomed before our drinks are over!"

Stephanie laughed again and raised her glass. "May as well finish your drink first. No point in wasting it." Over Sebastian's shoulder she could see Chris approaching the table, when another woman grabbed his attention. Stephanie watched as the two of them embraced like old friends, hugging and laughing together. Chris pulled free to look her up and down. She suspected he was saying something along the lines of 'You look great! You've not changed one bit.' She caught his eye and gave a little wave to tell him to carry on; she was fine with the cheesy guy for a while. Chris immediately got the message and acknowledged it with a slight wave back. They were there as friends for the evening after all, not on a date. With Chris busy with his old friend, she turned back to her guest.

"So, Sebastian, tell me. What brings a man like you to a place like this?" She tried her hardest not to giggle but failed miserably, and they threw their heads back in unison.

"I guess two can play cheesy, eh?"

"Oh yes. But seriously, tell me about the man who takes random drinks to random women when they were sitting with another man. What kind of guy does that?"

Over the following couple of hours, Sebastian and Stephanie drank several more Margaritas and several more glasses of champagne while Sebastian filled her in on his life and asked her questions about her own, and they generally got on like peanut butter and jelly on sliced bread.

Chris had stayed with his old friend, giving Stephanie the occasional wave to make sure she was still okay, but he knew she was. It was all part of the plan.

"Let's go back to mine," Sebastian said to Stephanie as the witching hour approached.

Stephanie paused to think for a moment, looking across to Chris who was still enjoying himself with the other woman. *What the hell – why not?*

"Sounds good," she said, flirting back somewhat drunkenly, and got to her feet.

Once back at his apartment, Sebastian had poured them both a nightcap, then pulled out a little box where he kept his cocaine and cut a little on the dining room table. He turned to Stephanie, passing a glass to her.

"Would you like some, to relax with?" he said, indicating the coke.

Stephanie had never tried the hard stuff in her life and wasn't about to start now. Taking her wrap off, she made herself comfortable on the sofa, sipping her drink. "Not for me, thanks, but don't let me stop you." She kicked her shoes off and lolled her head back. Seconds later, Sebastian was next to her, planting kisses on her neck. She let him, stretching her neck to him for more, enjoying the feeling it gave her. They both knew what was going to happen next.

"Come," he said, as he pulled her up and guided her to his bedroom. There was no resistance from Stephanie. Even though she had drunk far too much champagne and too many Margaritas, she was still in the mood for Sebastian.

It was sometime after that that things had gone blurry. Had Stephanie not drunk her spiked brandy, she would have been awake when the visitor had knocked an hour later and Sebastian had passed another keycard through the door. She would have felt Sebastian on top of her, and she would have felt the blade nicking the backs of her thighs as he straddled her, watching tiny beads of blood rise to the surface on her glorious legs. She might have even been aware that another man had crept into the room some hours later and severed her hair, leaving it rough and clumpy.

But she had drunk it. And Sebastian had swapped that keycard for a single baggy of cocaine – the value of her hair.

Chapter Forty-Two

Stephanie sat staring into space, lost in her own world of distant memories, jarred loose by the women's discussion of "Mr. Sleazeman." As their chatter quieted and they tucked into their food, she realized with a start that Matt the barman was hovering nearby. It was obvious he had spoken to her, though she had no recollection what he'd said. She shook her head gently as if shaking out the cotton wool in her head.

"Sorry, I was miles away."

"It's okay. I was merely seeing if you wanted a top-up. Or something to eat. Can I get you anything?" He had an easy, welcoming smile and gentle, soothing eyes. Or was that the glass of wine on an empty stomach? She checked her watch. Did she have to be someplace?

"Thanks. I'll have one more, and how about a chicken salad sandwich with fries? That should soak the wine up and put my day back together."

"Coming right up."

Stephanie took the opportunity to make a phone call; she wanted to talk to Ruth. She pressed her speed dial number and Ruth answered on the third ring.

Breathlessly, Stephanie blurted out what she'd remembered.

"Whoa, whoa, whoa!" said Ruth. "Slow down – you're not making any sense. Now start again, slowly."

"I overheard a conversation about sexual harassment in this woman's workplace and her having to clear his mistakes up again and how much damage it's doing to the company's reputation. She was really heated up about it, and it jogged my memory about something that happened not long before my hair went missing." She paused to catch her breath.

"Go on," Ruth prompted. "Tell me what happened. From the top."

And so Stephanie relayed the story of how her boss had become too familiar with her, and cornered her in the kitchen one night, and how she'd basically stabbed him. And how, the following day, the problem had vanished. He'd never mentioned it, she had certainly never mentioned it, and the whole thing appeared to have gone away.

"I can't believe you stabbed him, Steph!" Ruth said incredulously. "That was a big risk. Mind you," she went on, "I'd have probably done the same if it had been me. And he never said anything about it again?"

"That's right. If someone had stabbed you with a fork, you'd have said something, wouldn't you? And being the boss too?"

Ruth thought for a moment. "I wonder why not."

"Well, that's just it, Ruth. I told my friend Chris that night, nobody else, and I wonder if the whole thing is linked with something else that happened?"

"Oh?" Ruth's voice perked up. "What?"

"Well, the following night after work, Chris and I went out for drinks and, well, that was the night I ended up with Sebastian Stevens, back at his place. I think."

"Go on," Ruth prodded again, her voice serious now.

"Well, Chris was with me for most of the night. And then he went to the loo, and that's when Sebastian came over and sat down. After a while, Chris started back to our table, but he bumped into an old girlfriend. I gave him the signal I was okay with Sebastian, which I was, and Chris stayed with his old friend. I never saw him again that night after we left the bar. Sebastian and I went back to his place, and then I was drugged, and you know the rest."

Ruth was quiet on the other end of the phone for a moment. "So," she said at length, "you're saying you wonder if your friend Chris set you up somehow because he'd done something to stop your over-amorous boss?"

"I think so. Yes."

"Wow. That's a big jump. Are you still in touch with this Chris guy? Does he have a surname?"

"Chris Meeks, and no, he moved away soon after that night. I've not heard of him since. I can't help thinking there are too many coincidences, though – that I was set up, that a debt I didn't know I had was paid back. In full."

"Shit. Have you told Amanda yet? You're going to have to, you know."

"I know. I wanted to run it past you first."

"Well, even if it is something to do with this Chris guy, she'll need more than hearsay and gut feeling. I'd start thinking about how you might find him again. And I'd write out what you've remembered. It might help jog more memories loose when you read it back again. She's going to need some help, and the name 'Chris' and not much else is a bit thin, I reckon."

Stephanie knew she was right: she had to come up with more. The arrival of her sandwich and fries distracted her, and her stomach growled in anticipation.

"I'll write it all out, then I'll call her later," she said. "May as well get it all out of the way. And if he was involved then, and another woman has lost her hair now, there will probably be others."

"Keep me posted, Steph, and you know where I am if you need me."

Stephanie blew her friend a kiss down the phone and hung up. She picked up a couple of the hot fries and chewed on them, thinking. The salty grease tasted damn good. If she had put the right pieces together and figured it out, then someone needed to track Chris down. Rather than waiting, she picked her phone up again and called Amanda while it was all summer-fresh in her mind. She'd know how to find Chris.

If Chris Meeks was his real name.

Chapter Forty-Three

GRIFFIN LAY IN HIS BED; the alarm was due to go off in a few more minutes. It wasn't unusual for him to wake before his alarm, but it was unusual for him to lie in bed. Eventually it was his bladder that made him get up. He tapped the alarm button as he passed his clock, just as it was about to bleep, and dragged the bedclothes back so the sheets and mattress could air. As always, he gave a moment's thought to the bed lice, and then almost forcibly switched the thoughts off again. Bed lice were invisible to the human eye, he told himself again, so technically what the eye couldn't see shouldn't worry him. And he wasn't about to get a magnifier to feed his curiosity.

As usual, his routine was precise, and fifteen minutes later he was in his tiny kitchen pouring milk onto his waiting cereal. Weekends were much the same for Griffin, though without the need to head into town, but he still kept to a regular timetable of sorts, just a little more relaxed. He took tea at home rather than at the office.

The morning sun streamed through the kitchen window, giving a yellowy glow to the room as he ate his Special K. Milk spilled from his spoon onto the table as he completely missed his mouth.

His mind was elsewhere and he knew just where.

Today, he'd agreed to meet up with Vee again and look at a couple of the flats she had lined up to view. The thought of spending the day with her thrilled him; he was finally beginning to relax in her company a little, although it was tough going. Yes, he'd had a girlfriend before, but that had been some years ago, before he'd grown in size like a blow-up paddling pool. Now, he'd shrunk back to a healthier and near normal size for his height. Vee seemed to like him. And if last night was anything to go by, they were getting on nicely. He'd walked her home and they'd stood on the back step, but with her parents inside, he hadn't dared to lean in and give her a quick kiss. And that had been the excuse he'd stuck to. Draining his bowl of the last of the milk, he wondered how he'd avoid the situation again should it arise. Which it would. His lack of confidence could be a pain sometimes.

On Saturdays he had a slice of toast after his cereal, and he put a slice of bread in the toaster while he waited for the kettle to boil again. His thoughts drifted back to the previous night: drinking Snakebite in the pub, her beating him at darts, and their stroll home under the amber glow of streetlamps. The toast pinged up and gathered his attention, so he spread peanut butter on it for his morning protein. He was finishing the last mouthful when his phone chirped like a bird. A text had landed.

"Are you up yet? I guess you are now!"

He smiled at her cheekiness. *"Of course I am. You?"*

"Awake, but still in bed. You still up for today?"

"Of course. Where and when?"

"Coffee first?"

"Excellent idea."

"Come round here and we'll go. 10 am suit?"

"Perfect. See you then."

Griffin waited for a moment in case his phone pinged again, one last emoji perhaps, but it didn't. He found himself slightly disappointed. He gathered his crockery and placed it in the dishwasher as usual and went through to the living area to retrieve his laptop. With a couple of hours until he was due to leave, he put the time to good use and carried on with his research. Depending on how far they walked today, he could get the remainder of his 10,000 steps in at the end of the day. He opened the lid and the screen sprang into life, the login prompt flashing at him like a pedestrian crossing light. Entering his details, he brought up the TOR browser and continued his search. And there he sat until it was almost time to leave.

He could see her in the distance, stood on the front step of her house chatting to someone. A parent, maybe? From what he could make out, the person looked about the right age, a male, but as he closed the gap, he could tell by their body language that Vee wasn't the man's daughter. In fact, moments later the man turned and walked back down the path towards a car that was parked at the curb. As Vee turned to go back inside, she saw Griffin and waved at him. He could see her bright smile easily and he found himself smiling back. She really was pretty in that special way of hers, and he was beginning to enjoy her company more and more each day. He'd even found himself thinking about her while at home on his own, and he couldn't remember when he'd last done that. Or with whom.

He waved back. She began walking back down the path to meet him.

"Good morning," he said when they were a few feet apart.

"Good morning to you too, Mr. Formal." She was teasing him already.

"How am I supposed to greet you – with a 'Yo'?"

"Good morning is just fine. I'm teasing you, silly." She threaded her arm through his and they walked up towards the front door. It dawned on him that he was about to meet her parents. No sooner had the thought entered his head when an older male and female filled the doorway. The woman looked like an older version of Vee: same small nose and fine face structure, though her hair had lost its colour some time ago. Her father, on the other hand, had a thick head of dark brown hair, with just a few wisps of grey at his temples and around his ears. There was no mistaking these folks were her makers.

Here goes.

"Good morning. I'm Griffin," he said, extending his hand. He caught the woman's eye as he shook with her first. She had the same vivid hazel eyes as Vee.

They shone back at him as she replied, "Lovely to meet you. I'm Vera and this is my husband Bruce." She nodded to her husband. He too reached out to shake hands with Griffin.

"Nice to meet you both."

It was Vee who broke the moment's silence that followed. "Yes, I'm named after Mum. 'Little Vee,' as I've been known since I was born. But I've grown up to simply be Vee now. Perhaps when I get as old as Mum, I'll blossom into a fully-grown Vera," she said, winking and smiling at her mother. There was obviously a deep bond between the three of them, Griffin thought as he watched their gestures and expressions. Love was written all over her parents' faces.

"We'd better get a move on," Vee said. "I don't want to be late for the first one."

"Right. Okay." He turned to follow Vee, who was already making her way back down the path, and nodded at her two waving parents. "Good bye, then."

When they were down the road a little way, Vee turned to Griffin and said, "I hope that wasn't too embarrassing. I should have warned you they'd be nosey and want to meet you, but they mean well."

"You look so much like your mum, but with your dad's colouring. Who do you take after most?"

"Oh. Probably a big chunk of each. I look more like Mum, but I think I take after Dad with my mannerisms and laid-back approach to things. But if something bugs me and I get a bee in my bonnet, then I'm more like Mum. She can be a feisty so-and-so when she gets riled up. My sisters and I used to get her in a fizz sometimes. How about you? Who do you take after the most?"

Griffin had to think about that one. He wasn't particularly close to his parents and hadn't seen either of them for at least twelve months, probably longer.

"I'm not really sure, to be fair. I've never really seen eye to eye with Dad. He just thinks I'm odd. And Mum is a bit of a social butterfly, so I didn't really fit in with her 'perfect son' goal, either. So we speak occasionally but hardly ever get together. It's too hard, all the pretence of being something they want me to be rather than who I really am."

They both fell silent as they walked towards the train station, both thinking about what Griffin had just said. As they approached the entrance, Griffin tried to lighten the mood. "Well, that kind of killed the conversation, didn't it?" He was smiling as he turned to her and spoke the words without malice. Vee hooked her arm through Griffin's a wee bit tighter and squeezed some affection up his arm.

"I'll look after you."

Chapter Forty-Four

❧❧❧

THEY WERE on their third property viewing, and almost the instant they set foot on the cracked path up to the house Vee knew she might as well go no further. From the outside, the place looked reasonable, though rundown, and she was prepared to keep an open mind, but waiting outside she'd become more and more dismayed at the place. The only vibe she'd picked up so far on the small estate was a dodgy one. Small groups of youths milled around looking for something to do, and she guessed that would probably include petty crime. Had she asked them, they would have confirmed her suspicions – that is, if they'd dropped their attitude and been civil in conversation.

The estate agent arrived and let them in, then led them straight upstairs. But Vee knew this was never going to be the place.

"And a view out over the local area," the agent gushed, pointing out of the smeary window like she was pointing to the Atlantic Ocean. In Croydon, the only water feature would be the pond in the back garden, if you were lucky enough to have a back garden. To appease the woman, Vee looked out at what she thought was so impressive. Or maybe the so-called view was the only good bit of the pokey property the agent could find to comment on, more like. Vee wrinkled up her nose.

"Not for me, thanks. A definite no-go, in fact. Thanks for showing us, though," she said, and walked towards the door. Griffin followed dutifully, leaving the woman to lock up. She didn't look too pleased at having her time wasted. As they made their way back down the weed-ridden path to the road, Vee let out a disappointed sigh.

"Don't be despondent yet," said Griffin. "We have one more to look at, and the first one we saw was quite good. Needs some work, but at least it was a decent-sized space in a nice part of town." He looked at his watch. They had plenty of time until they were due at the next and last viewing.

"Let's take a break and grab a drink before the next one, eh? We've walked for miles and I know my feet could do with a rest."

"Alright. Mine too, actually. And a cold one would be nice right now. Café or bar? What do you fancy?"

"Let's get out of this dump first, then see what comes along. How about that for a plan?"

"Perfect. Let's go."

Twenty minutes later they came across the first place that looked half decent. A pub it was to be, then. He opened the door for her and she stepped inside. The interior was dark and cooling after their walk in the warm sunshine.

"Snakebite? Or too early?" Griffin had his wallet out ready.

"Too early for me. I'll have a Coke, please. But I need to pee, more importantly. I'll be back in a minute." He watched her disappear around the corner and he approached the bar.

He ordered two Cokes —one diet, no ice in either.

He waited. When she reappeared, he steered her to a vacant table in the corner and motioned for her to sit on the bench side. Covered in a deep burgundy-coloured velvety fabric, it looked more comfortable than the wooden chair opposite. Placing her Coke in front of her, he said, "I assumed you meant regular Coke, not diet? Not that you need diet, I should add. And I didn't get ice. Wasn't again sure if you took ice. But I can easily get you some if you wish?" He was babbling a little and he knew it. She smiled at his efforts.

"Full-fat Coke is fine. No ice is also fine, thanks." Then she added, "For future reference though, I drink Diet Coke and don't care either way about the ice."

For future reference. He liked that.

He watched her gulp down almost half the glass in one go, mesmerized by the dark liquid disappearing down her throat. When she'd come back up for air, she asked, "What have you been up to this morning then, before we met up?"

"Catching up on some research. I'm writing an article on doping within amateur sports. It's becoming quite an issue and quite commonplace. It's not just the big names anymore, but the weekend warriors, the serious amateurs. And it's rampant."

"Really? You mean in cycling?"

"I mean many different sports now, even golf. There's quite a market, evidently. Look at the people who compete in Masters, or age-grade competitions in any sport. They are still serious, even though they're not professional, and they all want the edge over their competitors. Cycling is probably one of the more common sports you'd think of, but as I say even golfers are doping now. And from what I can gather, it's prescription drugs mainly that are available and being misused for something else." He took a breath and paused for a moment, letting what he'd said sink in. He took a long mouthful of Coke.

"I can understand something like cycling, but how does doping work in golf, for example?"

"You've heard of beta blockers and what they do?"

"Yes, my dad is on them. Helps keep his blood pressure under control."

"That's right. And they'll probably be in the bathroom cabinet and you could get to them. If you wanted, you could take a handful here, a handful there maybe. And sell them."

"But I don't understand what a golfer would need them for. What am I missing?"

"Drugs will steady them – steady their movements, lower their blood pressure a bit. And as I said, the prescription forms are all perfectly legal to take, but they can give athletes an edge over someone who isn't taking them. How unfair is that? It's a form of doping, and doping is cheating."

"So where do they buy them from? Not exactly off eBay, I'm sure. The dark web?"

Griffin wasn't surprised to hear her mention the dark web; she worked in cyber security all day long, not that they'd talked about it much. He made a mental note to bring it up in conversation another time.

"Yes, or a dirty doctor somewhere. That might be harder to find, though, unless you have the contacts. With some team sports at a higher amateur level, the coach may be the one organizing things. And no one wants to let the side down, do they?"

Vee was silent, pondering what he was saying. She'd probably never thought of it before, but then why would she have? "And what have you found out so far, for your article? Have you uncovered something big?"

"Oh, this is big, alright. And the more I dig the worse it appears to be. There's so much available – prescription drugs galore as well as other things."

"Other things?"

"Like how to cheat by using substances that occur naturally in the body anyhow, so things like EPO, which is where they take blood from their own body to make the body replenish itself, then reinject the blood back in on top at a later date, getting the benefit of all those extra red blood cells. This is usually done by endurance athletes, like long-distance runners, and it's hard to detect, which is why they do it. But then you are starting to get into quite a dangerous area, messing with your blood cells. Get it wrong and you could be dicing with death, literally. I actually heard of a cyclist that used dog blood, which is a definite no-no. But to answer your question, it's all there for sale. And on the dark web. I've spent a bit of time there recently, actually. I'm beginning to know my way around quite well."

"Wow. Good on you for doing it, bringing it out into the open. What will you do with the article? Sell it?"

"That depends. Officially, I work for the paper, but I'm tempted to try this freelance, see what I can get for it. Trouble is, it could cost me my job in the process."

They both fell quiet and sipped on their drinks, deep in thought. Finally, Vee spoke.

"We should get going. But for what it's worth, I think if you can sell it for a decent fee, and if you've got the evidence in your research that this could be big, you should go for it. You'll get another job easily enough. You have the talent. Or you might choose to go freelance. Could be your real destination."

Griffin downed the last of his drink and followed her towards the door. He'd told her what he was working on: she was the only person who knew. Had that been the right thing to do? He hardly knew her, really, knew anything of her background. Hell, her dad could be a dirty doctor for all he knew. He caught her up as she held the door open for him. While he'd told her of his doping research, he hadn't dared tell her of the other reason he spent so much time on the dark web.

Maybe he never would.

Chapter Forty-Five

BY THE END OF SATURDAY, they'd both had enough, and Vee was feeling despondent with what they'd seen. Or not seen, to be more precise. She took her heavy Doc Martens off and flung them across the lawn with a groan. Griffin sat on a lawn chair and watched her toes wiggle free as her socks followed her boots up the grass.

"Oh. That's. So. Much. Better," she groaned, lying back under the late afternoon sunshine. With her eyes closed, she couldn't see him watching her with amusement. Somehow, though, she sensed it.

"What?"

"Maybe some lighter footwear in the summer would be a good idea? Your feet must boil."

"Technically, it's autumn, but I know what you mean. All in aid of fashion, though." She waved her arms above her head dramatically. "What can I say? I'm a slave to it," she called out, then immediately rolled on to her stomach. She looked at Griffin, who had joined her and was also now lying in the grass. A lawnmower hummed in the distance and someone's sausages were burning on a BBQ nearby. They still smelled delicious.

"Did you think any of them had potential? Could you see the future in them?"

"Personally, if it was me, I'd look at the two bigger ones again. But next time, go with the idea of what they *could* be, not what they are now. Your first home will never tick all the boxes unless you have a rich daddy to buy it for you, and I don't believe that to be the case here. You'll be surprised what a wall shifted or a clever colour scheme can do to a place."

She nodded in silent agreement.

"How many have you looked at so far?" he asked her.

"Too many. Probably at least twenty." As she said it, she realized how silly the number sounded. "Perhaps I am being too picky, want too much. What was your first place like?"

"Quite nasty to start with, but I had space. And it was my space to make my own. Then when I could afford it, I moved up the ladder another rung and my current place is much nicer. You should come over soon, see what you think."

"I'd like that, thanks." She thought for a moment then added, "Maybe I am wanting too much. Mum and Dad have both said the same, but I've written their advice off because, well, they are parents, aren't they? They say sensible stuff like that. Perhaps they *are* right."

"Look, here's what I think." Griffin looked at his watch and pointed to the clock. "It's gone five pm now. Why don't you come round to mine later? I'll order pizza and get some cider and lager for you to mix, and you can see what can be done with a larger small space." As an afterthought, he added, "You'll be quite safe – just food and Snakebite and flat talk."

She grinned at him and accepted his invitation with her smile. "On one condition."

"Name it."

"I pay for the pizza."

Griffin nodded. "Deal. Seven pm work for you?"

"I'd better grab a shower, then, and yes."

Griffin gave her his address and they said their see-you-laters. On the way home, Griffin stopped and picked up Snakebite ingredients and a tub of chocolate ice cream for dessert. He figured he'd be safe with chocolate; everyone ate chocolate ice cream, didn't they? Then it was his turn to hit the shower and wait for his guest.

Chapter Forty-Six

SHE WAS PUNCTUAL, 7 pm on the dot. He liked that. The pizza guy didn't make the same grade but conversation filled the gap until he did arrive. When they'd finally got a slice and a drink each, they settled back into an easy silence, one that didn't need filling continually. Finally, Vee wiped her chin with a napkin and broached the subject of her hobby, or one of them.

"Earlier, we were talking about the dark web, and your research." She took another bite and chewed before carrying on, tomato sauce gathering at the corner of her mouth. Griffin let her continue, intrigued as to what she was going to ask him. "Well, I know quite a bit about it, with my work as you can imagine. But I also use it myself. For personal interest."

So she wasn't going to ask him a question.

"Yeah? What sort of personal interest, as you put it?"

"I'm an admin of one of the chat rooms. One rather close to my heart, actually. Online revenge, to be precise. My main clientele are those who have been targeted with revenge porn – you know, nude photos of themselves being posted all over without their permission or knowledge."

He let her pause and go on again before he said anything, noticing the change in her demeanour as she'd raised the subject. The words 'close to my heart' hadn't gone un-noticed. He nodded in encouragement.

"Well, I may as well tell you the whole story then, now that you've probably guessed it happened to me." She took a deep breath, put her pizza back in the cardboard box and wiped her fingers. "My last partner and I enjoyed our private life together, you know, in the bedroom. We did some stuff that, well, others might think a bit kinky, but we were both consenting adults. You don't need to know the details. And he filmed it sometimes. On his phone usually. Then we broke up, and I started seeing his friend, long after we'd finished, so there was no affair, no overlap. But my ex was pissed at me and decided to post one of our videos to get back at me."

Griffin could see she was struggling a little and didn't want to pressure her either to go on or to stop. He let her have some space and sat silently.

Finally, Vee resumed her story. "He posted it in a chat room, and thirty thousand views later I got wind of it by a tip-off. I'm guessing it was someone at work but I can't be sure." She raised her voice and added, "As if the video being out there isn't enough, a work colleague had to see it too." She took another breath and returned to normal volume. "Anyway, by the time I was aware of it, it was on several more revenge sites with god only knows how many views. Long story short, it hurt, and I mean it *really* hurt, and there's not much I can do about it. That's why it's on the dark web, not the surface web. At least I could ask Google to take it down if it was on the regular web. These guys don't play by the same rules, though, so I assume it's still out there. And you just have to read the news to know that there are many more victims like me." Turning to Griffin and reaching for her pizza again, she went on with an invigorated spark of energy. "So now I play a role in helping others who have had the misfortune to have dated a fuckwit."

So matter-of-fact.

Griffin wasn't really sure what to say or do. Should he refresh her drink? Give her a hug, perhaps? Commiserate, even? Or change the subject? He leaned into her a little and took her hand in his, squeezing it affectionately. At this point in their relationship, and given his uncertainty about what to do, he called it a hug.

It would do for Vee too.

Chapter Forty-Seven

HE NEVER LAY IN BED, but since he'd met Vee, things had started to change. Spending a few extra moments in bed in the privacy of his mind as well as the empty room, he let images of her drift in and out. Everyone had a past, but thinking about her with someone else – the issue of the revenge porn aside – he knew it was jealousy he was feeling. She was cute, no doubt about it, and they got on. And she was smart, and different and knowledgeable and .... And what?

And he was jealous.

He threw the bed covers back and headed to his morning routine to shake the notion from his head. It was all in the past, nothing to think about now. So why was he? And who was the prick who had posted the videos of her for all to see? Upsetting Vee had been the goal, but why? So many questions and no answers. He lathered his face in white cream and wondered if he could track down the guy without her knowing about it. At the very least the prick would inform Vee of his involvement, relishing in the glory of her latest boyfriend getting jealous. If the prick had been capable of revenge porn posting, he'd lap up interference from her latest boyfriend. And she'd be pissed, that much he did know about her. For a small packet, he reckoned she'd throw a hard punch, physically and metaphorically. No, while he admired her, he wouldn't want to cross her. She'd already mentioned her mother's temper; Vee would likely be just the same. The thought actually made him smile and his razor nicked his chin. He winced as crimson mixed with the white foam. Again.

They'd had a good time, though, the previous night. They'd chatted a little more about her role in the support group, and he hadn't pried into her experience for any more details than she'd already given. There was nothing to gain from it. He knew her story now, and that was all he needed to know about it. He knew the real value of privacy and appreciated it himself. They'd ended up watching TV, relaxed in each other's company, while she'd finished off the Snakebite and most of the tub of ice cream before calling it a night, and Griffin had walked her back home. They'd chatted about nothing and she'd kissed his cheek before eventually heading inside and leaving him to wander back to his flat alone. She'd waited after she'd kissed him, but he had felt too awkward to turn a peck on the cheek into something else, something a bit longer. A bit more precise. Like a kiss on her lips. So he'd kicked himself on the walk back, annoyed that the moment had fizzled like a wet firework and swearing he wouldn't let it happen again. No, next time he'd be ready, take the lead even, and kiss her properly.

That alone scared him.

While it was only a kiss, it was a kiss he wanted, though he was acutely aware of what it could lead to; that frightened him. Had that been his reservation, his avoidance – that a kiss would lead to something more?

Get real, Griffin.

What were they going to do, get hot and amorous on her parents' doorstep? Would he accost her and ravish her in her room while her parents listened on below? No, of course not. He shook his head to dislodge his wild, accusing thoughts and strode home quickly.

He made himself a mug of tea, then opened his laptop and resumed his research, research for his *other* interest. The one that had nothing to do with amateur sports doping.

But that had been after he'd fired a quick message off to a friend, a friend with particular tech skills who was no stranger to the online space and might be able to help track down the videos and the culprit himself, legally or otherwise, through backdoors he knew she had keys to. She was clever and covered her tracks well, though that wasn't her day job. More of a side angle, a Robin Hood of the web or a grey hat, if you wanted to use the techy term – someone who obeys morals but not necessarily the law. As a legitimate developer of things techy, she ran an above-board business building apps and websites and did very well for herself. So her 'side hustle' was something that stayed there – at the side. It had to. She was about to get married to her sweetheart.

And her sweetheart was DS Amanda Lacey.

Chapter Forty-Eight

❦

Downstairs in the kitchen, Ruth opened her laptop. Above her head she could hear taps running and muted singing as Amanda filled in the bits of the song in her ear buds she did know and missed out the bits she didn't. Blank chunks filled the air interspersed with semi-shouting. In reality, there wasn't much of the Shania Twain song that was recognizable. She smiled as Amanda pumped out another 'That don't impress-er me much, oh, oh, oh, oh.' Sadly, there's where the song ended each time, for another few seconds at least until the chorus came back round and she ruined it again. Thank goodness they weren't having karaoke at their wedding, Ruth mused.

When Amanda had had her soak and finished playing Moby Dick in the bubbles, she'd grab a shower of her own, but now they were spending more time in the same house together, she let Amanda have her bathroom time. Alone. Not that her eardrums could stand the noise.

Messenger pinged.

"Hello, stranger. It's been a while," Ruth said to the screen. "How you been?"

"Hey Ruth. Can I ask a question and more likely a favour?"

She tapped back a reply. *"Sure. What's up, stranger?"*

"A friend of mine has been the victim of revenge porn. Any way to find the files on the dark web? And where he posted them from? I'd like to cut him off."

"So would I if that's what he's been up to, but I'm really not sure if I'm clever enough to do that. Anonymous IP addresses and all. How serious?"

"Serious enough to piss me off, though it happened a while back. She never got to the bottom of it so assumes they are still out there being viewed. Video."

"Shit. Privacy isn't your own anymore. Do you know the sites, perhaps? What am I looking for?"

"Good question. I'll find out more and get back to you. Wanted to see if you could perhaps help. Hate to ask her for more details. Anything you can do without me having to ask?"

"Maybe. I could probably do with a picture of her face. Might be able to find it with facial confirmation software perhaps, though it's a long shot. It's different from facial recognition software but could do the job. If the video is really low quality and grainy, it won't work. Can you get me a picture, preferably from around the time it happened?"

"Will see what I can do. Thanks, Ruth. I appreciate it. See you soon."

Ruth sat back in thought. The singing from upstairs had finally stopped, though she could hear Amanda moving about in the tub. It sounded like she was farting but she knew the deep sounds were her backside or heels rubbing on the bottom of the cast iron as she washed. Still, it sounded funny in the quiet. Knowing Amanda's routine, it wouldn't be long before gurgling water would be heard as it emptied through the pipes and then ran down the outside of the building and into the drains of Croydon. Approximately five minutes after that, a rather pink and shiny-looking Amanda would emerge wrapped in her bathrobe, hair tied in a towel. How she stood such hot water Ruth could never understand.

Who was Griffin seeing, she wondered? Not that it mattered. It was good that he was seeing someone; he wasn't the easiest person to be around sometimes. *Shy* and *eccentric* were words that came to mind. She'd wondered in the past if he was somewhere on the spectrum; it wouldn't have surprised her. He was hideously smart; everything had to be just so and on time, and since he'd lost a great deal of weight, he was looking great. Closing her laptop for the evening, not even sure what she had opened it for in the first place, she made a note in her grey matter to arrange to meet Griffin for coffee soon. His office wasn't far from hers and it would be great to see how he was doing before the wedding. And now he had a friend in tow, she wanted to find out more, purely from a nosey point of view. She liked Griffin and his particular ways.

A shuffling near the doorway diverted her attention to Amanda, dressed exactly as expected, with the addition of sheepskin slippers on her feet. She glowed like a pink candle, and Ruth smiled her affection across the room, landing slap-bang in the middle of Amanda's chest. They hadn't been together that long, a couple of years at most, but they'd both felt the connection when they'd first met during a case Amanda had been working on. Ruth had been involved because she ran the local community online page, which had discovered dog-nappers working in the area. Several dogs had been held for ransom money but then things had turned even uglier and Amanda had stepped in in her role with the police. Eventually the two of them had met, and the rest had slotted into place like the last two pieces of a jigsaw. And in a few short weeks, they'll be getting married.

"What are you smiling about? You look like you've been up to something the way you're holding that laptop," Amanda said mock-accusingly.

"I was just chatting to Griffin, actually. And you'll never guess. He's got himself a girlfriend. Well, he didn't quite call her that, but a woman knows these things," she said, tapping the side of her nose as if to say 'I know.'

"Well, that's great news. We'll get to meet her as his plus-one at the wedding, I expect." She took her towel off her head and her blond hair stood up at all angles.

"I want to meet her, or find out more about her at least, long before the wedding, purely out of interest. I daresay we'll be a bit occupied on the day and I don't want to miss out."

"Such a Nosey Parker, Miss McGregor," Amanda said, approaching her, "which brings me onto a very important subject."

"Oh? What's that?"

"Have you thought about our names, our surnames when we get married? Will we keep our existing ones or take each other's?"

"Hmm. I hadn't given it much thought, to tell you the truth. What are your thoughts?" Ruth stood and the chair scraped noisily on the floor.

"We could hyphenate, maybe. That way we get to keep them both. McGregor-Lacey. Lacey-McGregor." Amanda tried them both on for size.

Ruth said, "They both sound nice to me, though Lacey-McGregor sounds like Lacey is my middle name, don't you think?"

"Hmm, maybe. Let's think about it. And the other options are to stay as we are now, which means no paperwork and our work names stay as they are, or we decide on something completely new."

"Now, I hadn't thought about that. Something completely new, eh? Like "Monaco" or "Postlethwaite," perhaps." Ruth was enjoying teasing Amanda and knew exactly which way the naming was going to go. Amanda stood laughing inside the doorway.

"Don't laugh – Postlethwaite worked out well enough for Pete Postlethwaite, did it not?"

"I think I'd rather go with Monaco if those are the two options. It worked out fine for Princess Grace!"

"Well, that's debatable. She died, remember? Car somersaulted over a cliff in the early eighties."

"Then let's forget either of those two options and mull it over in our heads. We'll have to figure it out before the big day. We can't have him asking us as we put rings on each other's fingers. It will be funny enough when he declares us 'wife and wife.' There's bound to be someone in the congregation who still finds the concept amusing, even though they know us."

"I know, but I don't suppose too many people have been to a same-sex wedding before, so we'll forgive their ignorance." Ruth fell thoughtful for a moment and Amanda knew exactly what she was thinking about. She strode over and wrapped her arm around Ruth's shoulders and pecked her with a kiss on the cheek.

"Your mum will be watching her gorgeous daughter from way up high. She'll have the best seat in the house, and I know she'll be smiling down on you."

"I know. But it would be nice to see her again, in person. There's so much I want to say to her that I missed by being such a pig, and now it's too late."

"I know you do." The two women hugged tight, until Amanda was sure Ruth was okay. It was Ruth who pulled away first.

"I'm fine. Thanks, love." Looking up at Amanda, she added, "Oh, and my new name? It will be Ruth McGregor-Lacey. But you can call me Ruth Lacey."

Amanda smiled her delight and said, "I'll let the registrar know."

Chapter Forty-Nine

AMANDA AND JACK were parked up not far from Stephanie's place, sipping coffee. They had spoken to her at length about the night with Sebastian Stevens, and she had surprised them both with her idea of how it all connected. It did sound plausible, but where was the evidence? And where was 'Chris Meeks'?

"You ever had a really close friend who simply up and disappeared, Lacey? One that you didn't try too hard to track down, see if they were alright?" Jack was asking the questions and couldn't quite get his head around the fact that Stephanie and this Chris fellow had lost touch so abruptly after having had such a close friendship. Did people do that?

"I guess she and everyone else thought he'd gone off and found someone special and settled down. Nothing sinister to wonder about in a regular guy's life. Why would there be?" She wrinkled her nose. "Did you get sugar in this coffee? It tastes sweet."

"Well, I didn't ask for any. I'm trying to give it up. Want to swap?"

"No thanks. Your lips have been all over it."

"Then swap the lid over. I thought you were a detective, full of sharp ideas."

"My repertoire doesn't include my own practicalities," she said peeling the lid off her paper cup. Jack followed suit. When their cups had been swapped and lids reattached, Jack took a sip and winced.

"See?" said Amanda. "Definitely sugar in there, and a lot. Detectives know this shit." Sipping her own, she added, "That's better," and smiled at Jack, knowing just what he was thinking. He never said a word about the coffee and steered the conversation back to grounds he could win on: the case.

"So we have a name, which may or may not be his real one. A date that goes back fifteen years and one recent victim. There could be others, but we have no idea one way or another at this point and diddly-squat else to go on. How are we meant to solve this one? Any ideas?"

Amanda could hear the exasperation in his voice. In truth, she had no clue either. "Well, a couple of other officers have begun looking into what little we do have. There are about twenty Chris Meekses that fit his age range, and they're narrowing it down for location and job etcetera, so I'm hoping there will be a shortlist of them to talk to very soon. Hopefully he didn't move too far afield. We have his picture from back then, so even if he's changed his appearance, grown his hair out or whatever, we should be able to match his old picture with one of them. I'm hoping, anyway."

Her phone rang and she rummaged in her bag to retrieve it. Looking at the screen she added, "This could be news now." She answered, "DS Lacey. You've some news, I'm hoping." The car was quiet as Amanda listened to what the caller back at the station was saying, and Jack waited patiently.

"Thanks. That gives us something," she said at last, and hung up. Turning to Jack she said, "Seems our boy is a clever so-and-so, a bit of a geek. And the 'Chris Meeks' we know him as has been in trouble before, though not under that exact name. We have his charge sheet as Chris Smeeks, subtly different but him just the same. A clever bugger online; got done for hacking some years ago. Never did any time, but guess what he hacked into?"

"A ham sandwich? Come on, Lacey. I've no idea, have I? Spit it out."

"He hacked into a model agency's database. But this particular model agency deals in . . ." She paused for effect. There was almost a drumroll in the air. ". . . body parts. Feet, hands, hair, teeth – you name it, they have a perfectly photogenic body part for your every need."

"Holy shit."

"Exactly. So they're definitely linked now. That's too much of a coincidence, and since we don't believe in coincidences..." Amanda paused again. "And apparently, after the breach, a chap was cautioned for becoming too much of a nuisance outside their offices – waiting for girls to come out, wanting to talk to them, offering them money and all manner of weird stuff. Spooked the girls, and he was cautioned."

"Was that our man too?"

"No, someone else entirely, though I have a feeling we'll be chatting to him very soon. Again, it's odd that at the time of the breach, someone else interested in particular body parts turns up. I wonder what his interest was. Or is. If he had an interest then, does he still?"

"After Mr. Smeeks' caution, things quieted down for the agency and everything went back to normal. I say we start there, see what low-hanging fruit might still be left hanging that wasn't picked last time around." Amanda handed her coffee to Jack and started the engine. She read out the address to Jack. "See what Google Maps says is the best way to get there. I'm not entirely sure where it is."

She watched Jack out of the corner of her eye trying to type the address she'd given him into the maps app. He was no fingers and all thumbs. As he finally pressed 'go' and the mechanical voice announced the directions, she noticed something else: Jack was grimacing slightly.

"Are you okay, Jack?"

"Eh?"

"Are you okay? You looked in pain there for a second."

"It's nothing. I keep getting a twinge down my right side, that's all. Nothing more than gut-ache."

"How long has that been bothering you?"

"Only a day or two. It'll be gone soon. It's nothing, really. Old age. Or that corned beef sandwich. The pickle on them always gives me gripe. I don't know why I eat them." He turned to her and smiled his 'don't worry' smile. "You just drive and I'll worry about the corned beef and pickle doing its thing."

Navigating the late afternoon traffic, Amanda drove them out to an industrial estate on the edge of town. They parked outside and she craned her neck to look up at the building from the safety of the driver's seat. An ugly two-story clad building, it could have been the office for any number of things, but a small sign on the entrance door announced the occupants.

"This is it," said Amanda. "'Body-licious.' It kind of sounds more like a kink place, doesn't it? Somewhere you might go to indulge in a particular fetish, like for vampires. Go and lick something for pleasure. No wonder odd men sit outside waiting, with a name like that."

Jack nodded. "Let's go and find out," he said, and was half way out of the car before Amanda had unfastened her seatbelt to follow him. Jack strode up to the door, pulled it open without knocking, and set off up the steep concrete stairs on the other side. He was puffing and panting hard, clutching his side, when Amanda caught him up. He caught her stare.

"And now I've got a stitch on top of the pickle," he grumbled. "Relax. I'm fine."

Amanda gave him a look that said 'I don't believe you,' and they entered the small reception area, which was empty of people. Framed pictures on the walls confirmed they were indeed in the business of body part modelling: there were photos of stunningly immaculate feet peeping out of high-heeled sandals, perfect hands that had never done dishes advertising washing-up liquid, and pristine pearly-white teeth smiling unnaturally from between perfectly plump red lips.

A young woman entered the room and gave them a grin to match the teeth and lips in the picture. Maybe they belonged to her.

Jack took the lead.

"Hello. I'm Detective Jack Rutherford and this is DS Amanda Lacey. Are you the owner, by chance?"

The woman smiled again. "I'm afraid not. That would be Jules. I'll go and get her. May I ask what it's regarding?"

"We'd like to ask a few questions about an old case, a menace who was cautioned for approaching the girls."

"I thought that had been solved."

"It has, but we would like to chat to Jules again, if you could go fetch her. Thank you."

The young woman's smile faded fast as she left the room in search of Jules. Amanda stood back and let Jack handle things. In a few moments, stilettos could be heard approaching from the distance. They were fast and loud and sounded unhappy. The door opened and an austere-looking, well-dressed middle-aged woman with short-cropped dark hair and gold-rimmed glasses looked Amanda quickly up and down.

She had a wide streak of white hair by her right temple that reminded Jack of Thomas Mallen, the nineteenth-century Northumberland squire who had had the same feature. A TV program had been made about him and his family, called – unsurprisingly – *The Mallens*, and his mother had used to watch it. As a teenager it hadn't been his thing, but that distinctive white streak of hair had been a talking point for the many years the show had run.

The woman glared at the two detectives now, though Jack had no idea why. Amanda picked up on her perfume – Chanel No. 5. Her red-soled shoes meant only one brand: expensive.

"I'm Jules Monroe," she said. "What can I do for you both?" Her attitude screamed *busy* and *in a rush*. They both felt like intruders, which was, of course, the whole point.

"Sorry to bother you," Jack said, "but we're hoping you can help us with an old case. You may recall a man was cautioned for harassing the models."

"How could I not remember? It was creepy. But that was tidied up, was it not?"

"It was, yes. You are correct. But there may be a link from your case to something that happened only recently. You also had another case where you were hacked, if I am correct? Your database was broken into?"

"Yes, it was, but you know all this. Nothing seemed to have been taken – case closed. I'm not sure how can I help you. . .?" She checked her gold wristwatch as if to hurry him along. It glistened, matching the gold rims of her spectacles. Amanda assumed they were more than gold-coloured.

"We think the person may be connected to your break-in and may also be responsible for another crime," Jack went on. "Or crimes. Did you ever find out why he hacked in? Did he ever have any further contact with you? Messaged you, perhaps?"

Jack wasn't getting to the point quickly enough and it was obvious he was grasping at straws. Amanda stepped in before the woman got seriously annoyed and stormed back to her office.

"Ms. Monroe – Jules," she began. "Recently, a number of women have been the targets of an extremely upsetting type of personal assault, probably the work of the same person. To be perfectly honest, though, we have very little to go on. We think the hacker who targeted your business may be the link between these crimes, so we would appreciate anything you can remember about that incident: a text, any reason they may have given for the hacking, a message, a threat down the phone – anything you can remember at all could be helpful in tracing this person so we can talk further. If it turns out they have nothing to do with these current cases, we can move on, of course, but if they are involved, then they need to be stopped."

Jules's shoulders visibly drooped as she stood thinking, a finger against her lips. At length, she sighed and began to speak.

Chapter Fifty

✦❦✦

"IT's good to see you haven't lost your touch, Lacey."

They were heading back to Croydon to the station. Out of the corner of her eye, Amanda could see Jack was touching his side occasionally.

"Sometimes you need a little 'woman-to-woman' to get the desired result, and she wasn't responding to you."

Jack grinned. "Is that what you call it now, eh? 'Woman-to-woman'?"

She grinned back. "Just because I'm marrying a woman doesn't mean I fancy *all* women, pea-brain. Just like you don't fancy *all* women either. I'm no different, you know."

He knew. "Well, it worked, so that's all that mattered. I wonder why she didn't come out and say anything before, though?"

"Quite. I guess they were more concerned with the stalker than a seemingly random hacking attack where nothing was taken. A guy waiting outside your office is much more 'in your face,' and more of a direct threat to their employees. So I suppose that's what they focused on in the end."

"So what was the real reason for the hacking, I'm wondering?" said Amanda, almost to herself. "Why would someone want access to that company and then not use it maliciously? That we know of, at least. Ms. Monroe said herself she'd have known if her competitors had accessed her files, and they clearly hadn't. It's amazing they even knew they'd been hacked, come to think of it – it's not like these people leave a trail of breadcrumbs. There has to be something else we're missing. Another reason."

They fell quiet as she drove, then Jack piped up again.

"Unless it was to see if they could do it? You know, like some folks climb mountains, just to see if they can? Though if that was the case, it doesn't really help with our victims." Jack fell quiet again.

"You know, crime has changed over the years." Amanda, too, was thinking. "It may be worth a chat with National Cyber Crime to get their take. For example, credit card fraud is old hat, and maybe something more lucrative has taken its place. Otherwise, why would someone hack a database and not sell the contents to a competitor? No one else would want it, would they?"

"I can't see an obvious reason, no. Ask your Ruth; she'll probably know more than the cyber guys, and she'd be a damn sight quicker to get an answer from, too."

"I'll do both. Though she's pretty full-on with her own things and the wedding at the moment."

"And how's it going, the planning?"

"Fine, I think. She's taken it over. I just need to show up on the day at the required time. And get a dress made."

"And I'm hoping at this late stage you have that in hand? You can't turn up in your work suit and boots to this one, Lacey."

"All in hand. Matching fabric, different dresses. I hope I don't let the side down."

"How so?"

"I don't want to look like Little and Large as we walk down the aisle together. She's somewhat more feminine than me, with a much nicer figure."

"You'll look great together, I'm sure," he said, smiling at her side. She caught it from the corner of her eye. He said the sweetest things sometimes.

With the end of that particular topic, Jack reached up and pushed play on the CD player. He'd always found music a tool to help him think and, as they were a bit stuck, he figured he'd give it a try. Pink rang from the speakers.

"Don't you have anything else? Something a bit more . . . male?" he groaned?

"I don't keep CDs in the car. I'm not even sure what that one's still doing in there," she said, pointing to the CD slot.

"What do you listen to, then?"

"I stream, like most folks in 2017. Don't you?"

The only stream Jack knew about ran near the bottom of his road and dried up in summer. She caught his frown. Rummaging in her pocket as she steered, she passed him her smartphone.

"What am I supposed to do with this? Phone someone?"

"You're such a luddite, Jack. Look for the Spotify icon and open it." Glancing over, she smiled as he searched. "It's green and black. That should narrow it down." She watched his chubby finger finally press the correct icon. He needed to trim his fingernails.

"Tap in the search box what you want to listen to, and then choose it," she instructed. They were nearly back at the station by this stage, but she didn't say anything. He hated being thought of as a luddite, but he made no attempt to be anything else. As she turned into the station yard, the distinctive first guitar strings of Rainbow's "Since You've Been Gone" filled the car, and Jack threw his head back in delight as he realized he'd actually done it. For a detective, he didn't explore much in his own life – only in other people's. She pulled into a parking space and turned to him.

"Well, it's a bit too late to listen to it now, but you'll know how to do it for later," she quipped, and smiled along with him. Jack was a huge ELO fan so it was no surprise he'd picked something similar from around the same era. And she also knew what he'd *actually* been thinking about in the car a few minutes earlier as they'd talked about weddings. *Since you've been gone...* Amanda knew how he'd struggled when his wife, Janine, had died, and that he thought of her often. He'd almost gone out of his head, she knew, but he'd muddled through with the help of those around him. Janine had been his teenage sweetheart, and Amanda had arrived at Croydon not long after she'd died. A close bond, almost father–daughter, had developed between them, and they'd been very close friends ever since.

"I think I'll sit here a bit and think things through," he said now. "I'll be in in a moment. You go on."

She was about to admonish him about brooding but thought better of it. Sometimes he just needed his alone time. "I'll make us some coffee, then. Come when you're ready."

Chapter Fifty-One

✦

JACK SAT BACK in the passenger seat of Amanda's car and closed his eyes. The lyrics were still dancing in his head, and he thought back to Janine. What would she think of him now? Would she tease him as a luddite? Would she have reprimanded him over his slight shabbiness, his hair that always needed a trim, or his fingernails? She'd had a thing for neatness and he'd always pleased her, but now as he looked at his tie, he knew he might have let things slip. His tie was clean, but in what century had it been purchased? Not a recent one. He opened the door slowly and put one foot on the ground, ready to push himself up and out.

But nature had other plans.

The pain tore through his right side and then stabbed him hard in the groin. He cried out, then gasped and breathed deeply through the spasm. It only lasted for a few seconds, but his brow was damp with sweat and he took out his handkerchief and wiped it. Taking a few more deep breaths, he waited until he was sure the pain had completely gone before stepping towards the rear entrance of the building. The car door clicked shut behind him and he made his way into the coolness of the corridor. While he wouldn't admit it to anyone, the jolt of pain had frightened him, and he did his best to rearrange the mayhem that was written across his face before Amanda asked him what had happened. Keeping his head bowed as he entered their office, he took the proffered mug of coffee and made for his desk chair to sit down. No one was any the wiser.

But it didn't stop Jack worrying.

Chapter Fifty-Two

AMANDA DROVE the short distance home. The rest of Rainbow's "Since You've Been Gone" was playing, having been picked up when she'd turned the engine on. Ah, the magic of Bluetooth, she thought, connecting itself automatically. While she typically enjoyed music from after the eighties, these lyrics still made her smile. She'd never met Jack's wife Janine but knew all about her from Jack; sometimes she even felt Janine was in the car on a case with them, hanging on for dear life in the backseat, watching and wondering.

As the music ended she absentmindedly turned the stereo off and listened to the relative quiet of rush hour traffic travelling along with her on Purley Way. Could it ever be truly quiet in Croydon? She pressed her favourite speed dial, and Ruth's voice connected through the speakers. She sounded like she was outside somewhere.

"Hey, Amanda, you sound like you're driving."

"Hi, hun. That's because I am. Headed home for a shower – how about you? You sound like you're outside somewhere." A horn, probably from a truck or a bus, sounded somewhere in the distance through the loudspeaker. Maybe Ruth was still in town.

"Just heading to the tube and home, so shouldn't be too long myself. Are you coming over, or shall I head to yours?"

Even though they were engaged, they still each had their separate houses and lived separate lives. For now. And that was something they'd both have to adjust to when they did get wed – living together full time. They both secretly hoped it wouldn't be too much of an adjustment.

"Thought I'd ask you a question now before you put your work brain to bed. I didn't want to talk shop at home."

"Sure, fire away. What is it?"

"Why would someone hack into a company's database other than to steal the contents? Like a competitor, for instance? What else would they want it for?"

The hands-free loudspeaker throbbed with the sound of traffic as it chugged past Ruth walking somewhere on the other side of London. Amanda could almost smell the exhaust fumes that would be mixing with the occasional greasy roadside food vendor and it made her gag. That aspect of London never appealed to her.

"Good question. And one that deserves a good answer." Amanda could almost feel Ruth smiling down the phone.

"Care to share?" Amanda smiled back.

"Well, the most obvious reason after database theft is to sell access to it for some other reason, something more sinister maybe. Probably through the dark web or another connection already in place. Stolen 'access to order,' perhaps. If it's not a competitor, I'd say it's someone up to no good."

That was an angle Amanda hadn't considered. What would a model agency specializing in body parts have that someone who wasn't a customer would need access to?

"What's the scenario?" Ruth asked. "Hypothetically, of course. Maybe I can be of more help." This was her way of helping Amanda talk about a case without disclosing information she shouldn't be discussing with a civilian.

"Of course. If you don't mind?"

"Fire away, until I lose you in the underground, that is."

So Amanda fired away. What Ruth then told her made perfect sense.

"So a certain someone wanted a way in so they could see the *models'* data, not the business's data."

Now it fit perfectly: the guy who had been cautioned for approaching the models, the theft of Stephanie's hair fifteen years ago, and the theft of the more recent victim's hair. An agency that specialized in people with perfect body parts and two cases of perfect hair being stolen could point to a fetish service of some kind. Was someone supplying hair, and God knows what else, to order, perhaps? Fulfilling clients' desires at the expense of others?

Amanda furrowed her brow, thinking. "If you had access to the system in question, hypothetically again, could you see how they got in or who they were? Could you trace their steps back? Does it work like that?" She was hoping it really was that simple.

"I'd very much doubt it. If they were clever enough to hack in, they would have covered their steps. And it was also a while ago. Still worth a look, though. Does your cyber team have any hackers on board? Ideally, a kid who's been done for hacking and given the option of working with a security team as their penance after a crime."

"I'll ask," Amanda said. "But I doubt this case will be a priority for them. Unless there's been a heinous crime like a murder, a bit of hair fetishism will go to the bottom of their pile in a flash. It could be months before the case sees the light of day again. Hence you."

"Before you ask, Ms. Lacey, no. And you know it wouldn't be admissible in court even if I found something. I'm not a detective, remember? I'm just the fiancée of one."

Amanda knew she was right, and her heart missed a beat at the word 'fiancée.' Hell, she loved this woman. She started to reply, but her voice was cut off as the phone coverage dropped out. Ruth must have entered the tube station. With a heavy sigh, she stared at the blank phone, half expecting it to jump into life again. It didn't. But at least she had some partial answers, a clue as to the direction the case might be heading, even if she had no idea how to find whoever was responsible.

The name Chris Smeeks would be the place to start.

Chapter Fifty-Three

❦

THE FOLLOWING DAY, Amanda arrived at the station earlier than usual. Having stopped at McDonald's and grabbed an Egg McMuffin and fresh coffee, she'd sat in the small car park as early rush hour commuters sped past on their own way into work – if you could call two lanes of traffic on Purley Way heading north into London 'speeding.' At just gone seven in the morning, rush hour was in full flow and had been since about 6 am when the early shift headed in for the day. Amanda hadn't slept too well. Jack had sent her a file on the man who'd been cautioned after harassing the modelling agency, and it had been disturbing. She had been fully awake by 4.30 and had seen no point in trying to doze off for another couple of hours, so she'd slipped out of bed and made coffee downstairs. The morning sun had been slow to rise, typical for the start of autumn, but as she sat in her car eating the greasy egg sandwich, it streamed through her windscreen, warming her. She smiled at the word 'streaming' as she thought it.

Jack was a good man but behind the times in so many things. His delight had been amusing as Rainbow had filled the car and she'd explained what streaming was. She wiped grease from her mouth with the napkin and scrunched the paper packaging up while she chewed the last mouthful thoughtfully. They needed to speak to the man who had been cautioned for harassing the modelling agency girls. Yes, she'd read the sheet about the incident and his warning, but it would be useful to meet him herself, see if anything came up that they could use. When he'd been interviewed at the time, there had been no reason to connect him to anything larger. Like fetishism on a grander scale.

The hot, dark coffee tasted good and strong, and was a welcome hit of caffeine on top of her first one earlier in the morning. Her stomach gurgled in satisfaction. She'd regret it later, she knew. The gurgling made her think of Jack again and the obvious discomfort he'd been in, though he'd tried to shrug it off. She knew that, living on his own, he didn't eat as healthily as he should, and often she and Ruth would have him round for dinner and company. He needed someone to help take care of him, if only a decent housekeeper who cooked. A thought occurred to her that she put to one side to percolate and chat about with Ruth later. Her phone rang. It was Jack.

"Morning, handsome," she said, bright and breezy. The second coffee had hit her bloodstream.

"What have you been smoking so early, Lacey?" She could hear him chuckling.

"Must have been the magic mushrooms in my omelette. Too early for smokes." She loved their banter and so did he.

"Very funny. On to more serious stuff, I've fixed to go and see the kinky guy who was cautioned. You coming too?"

"Of course. But you can't go calling him 'kinky guy.' What's his name again, his real name?"

"Hadley Spinks. Who the hell would name their kid Hadley Spinks, for heaven's sake? He'd be better off with 'kinky guy.' Did you read his file I sent you last night?"

"Yes, I did. That's why I've been awake half the night. I look like shit." She glanced into her rear-view mirror while she spoke and prodded at the bags under her swollen eyes. They looked more like overstuffed hold-alls after a bank raid. She could have done with a bit of Ruth's make-up this morning.

"Well, any dude with a ponytail is dodgy if you ask me, and any dude with both a ponytail *and* a thing about feet is double dodgy. Nonetheless, he's agreed to speak to us at four pm at his workshop.

He's at a trade show most of the day but will be back later. And as you know, he's a footwear designer – how apt."

Amanda thought for a moment, sending a 'hmm' back to Jack to let him know she was still there but thinking. "Well, I'm not a psychologist or whatever the correct 'ologist' is," she said finally, "but I'd say that for someone with a fetish, which by the way usually means something sexual in its devotion and an abnormal degree of sexual gratification, working with feet all day would be absolute hell."

"Eh? How do you work that out? He'd be in heaven, wouldn't he?" asked Jack.

"Well, no, I don't think he would. Imagine being surrounded all day every day by the very thing that arouses you the most. It would be quite stressful trying to hide your excitement, like an alcoholic working in a wine shop. Not to mention exhausting." She let that sink in with Jack, then carried on after a moment of silence. "I'm wondering if he avoids beautiful feet completely to minimize his stress. Maybe he works as a shoe designer, for example, so he doesn't need real feet at all." She glanced down at her own feet, safely encased in her work boots. "In which case, his fetish would still need fulfilling and wouldn't interfere with his everyday work – he could still keep the real thing 'for best,' as it were. Just like those into BDSM don't do it every night just because they have a willing partner; it is something to enjoy on occasion, keeping it special." She looked across at the McDonald's wrapper in the well of the passenger's side.

"Like when you have McDonald's occasionally. It tastes really good but if you have it regularly, it loses that feeling of enjoyment. Of course, I'm no doctor. We'd have to double check all that, but it makes sense, don't you think?"

"I guess so. Well, we'll find out a bit more later on. In the meantime, I'm going to do a bit of research and have a chat to the doc, see if she can recommend someone who really does know about fetishism. But you know what, Lacey?"

"What's that?"

"It doesn't matter what he does for a day job, or with whom, because I can't see how it helps our case. And just because he was cautioned for being a bit of a prick with the models doesn't mean he's a hair snatcher. He could be nothing to do with this, merely a coincidence." As soon as he said the word he knew what he'd done. "And yeah, I know what you're going to say."

Amanda heard the deflation in his voice. No, neither one of them believed in coincidence.

Chapter Fifty-Four

꧁❦꧂

His eyes rarely rose to the horizon. What could possibly be more interesting out there than the array of beauty at ground level, right there below him for the taking like jewels scattered on a forest floor? Such elegance, such poise, such visions of wonder. Made by nature itself. And all there in the same room as he.

Hadley Spinks allowed himself the luxury to look in detail only a few times per month, and at today's tradeshow he was in his element. Forget kid-in-a-candy-store. He was sex-addict-in-a-whorehouse, the adult version of the cliché. Hadley chuckled to himself at the analogy, though he'd prefer the whorehouse to be a high-end shoe store.

Or a pedicure spa.

But never a chiropodist. No, beautiful feet were what turned him on, not the calloused feet of old spinsters or the verruca-encrusted feet of teenage swimmers. His passion, his intense interest, had a name − podophilia − but the 'philia' part sounded dirty to him, and dirty was far from what he desired. He desired the beautiful, the cared for, the well-shaped, the elegant. . . His mind wandered as he walked towards the coffee cart, navigating himself via the blue swirly-patterned carpet in the large hall. As long as he kept the bright orange outer circles of the pattern to the top he'd be heading in the right direction. It was one of the gaudiest carpets he'd had the displeasure of navigating in some time.

He'd long ago got used to walking this way – head down, eyes averted – and he knew onlookers might find it, and him, a little odd. They'd assume he lacked confidence, perhaps. That's what it usually meant, didn't it? But he didn't care what the strangers who bustled about him thought, on their own mission to wherever for whatever was important at the time.

No, he was indulging quietly – on the outside, at least.

On the inside? Well, that was a different matter. Parts of him were screaming, wanting, desiring, and he knew he wasn't far off his peak. That's the main reason he was headed in search of the coffee cart.

A distraction.

For now.

But he'd need a proper fix soon, he knew, and that meant making a choice. Who was it going to be? And when? Could he wait, or did he need something now, before the main event, something to tide him over? Oh hell, why had he agreed to meet with the detective later? Why hadn't he left himself some free time to savour his memories of the day, and find release with those? Now he'd have to wait until much later in the day. If he could.

He felt himself salivate involuntarily, and he swallowed hard, licking his lips to dispel the moisture before he ordered his coffee. Talking with lose spittle in one's mouth was not attractive to anyone. He wiped the palms of his hands on his trouser legs to remove some of the clamminess he felt as his pulse picked up, like a greyhound noticing a rabbit.

A glimpse of chrome broke through the melee. The coffee cart was up ahead, and he prepared himself to place an order without making a fool of himself or disgusting anyone. He raised his head to look where he was going, like normal people did when they were about to order coffee. A smile creased his lips at the thought. *Normal people*. Was there such a thing? Who says what normal looks like? Who says humans should be monogamous, and who says some cultures can have multiple wives? And who says it's wrong to drink alcohol at fourteen? And who says it's okay to smoke tobacco but not weed? And who says it's not normal to worship beautiful feet? Who? Who? Who? To Hadley Spinks, normal was what you made it. Did anyone get harmed by his personal desire, a desire he acted on in private? No, never. And while that was part of the rules, even if he didn't do what he did the way he did, he wouldn't want to hurt anyone anyway.

He only wanted to worship them.

He applied his most endearing smile and flashed it to the barista.

"A large capo to go, my darling. Thank you."

Her gaze lingered a second longer than it did on anyone else, but Hadley didn't look or speak like everyone else. He was used to, and indeed revelled in the extra glances and attention he often got.

"I love your neck scarf," she said. "Such a pretty colour and design, and so unusual to see on a male. You wear it well." The pretty young woman smiled her approval, assuring him that she had indeed meant it as a compliment.

Hadley bowed his head for a second, his eyes twinkling before they fell, in acceptance of her kind words. She blushed ever so slightly when he looked back up.

"That's very kind of you, my dear. I try my best," he said, and took two small steps to stand aside and wait for his order. There, he turned to view the room that he'd navigated only moments ago, only this time he kept his head raised, held high, even. His sun-tinged ponytail lay down his back, hanging dead centre of his shoulder blades. It was secured at the very end by a discreet band to keep it from flying out and becoming unkempt. He liked things to be neat and just so, particularly when it came to his own attire. If he demanded beauty, then he had to present the same. He pulled out his starched linen handkerchief and wiped his mouth as he surveyed the room. Such beauty filled it. It wasn't difficult to pick out the heads of the foot models from the heads of the other women. Even though their special body parts, the ones that earned their keep, were at floor level, the women knew the clients demanded the whole package. Many of the women sold multiple body parts to the camera. It wasn't unusual to find a foot model who also had the perfect chin, or nose or wrist. God gave beauty in gift-wrapped packages at creation time, and a very few women were lucky enough to receive one. Those who didn't had to make the best of what they'd got. Some managed, and many didn't.

A tall woman with blonde hair cut tight to her nape caught his eye. He didn't discriminate when it came to type; there wasn't one type of woman he enjoyed, and likewise, there wasn't one type he disliked, either. They were all eligible to be the chosen one. The blonde's head glided evenly along as she walked the length of the stand she was working on, and his eyes travelled down her body, taking her in: narrow shoulders, narrow hips, and long elegant legs. . . but he restrained himself from lowering his gaze any further. He would save that for later. Feeling sure he'd find something special there, he moved his attention to another woman, also obviously one of the models. Only this time, the shining brunette head was travelling towards the coffee cart as though she were walking down the red carpet at the Oscars – slow and steady, allowing the press time to snap her picture. This woman was practiced in her craft and, as she gained on him, he could see she was a little older than the other models, although still stunning visually. And extremely confident. He liked her instantly. Then she was almost next to him.

"Green tea, please."

No milky calories for this woman, he mused. His thoughts were interrupted by someone trying to attract his attention. He was being called.

"Sir? Your coffee, sir."

Turning to the voice, he said, "Why, thank you, my dear." He took the paper cup and took a small sip to test the temperature. He was playing for time, though he didn't need to, really; nobody was likely to move him along, but he felt he needed to have an excuse of some sort to linger a moment longer.

While he browsed what he might have later.

Chapter Fifty-Five

⚜

SHE WAS in a world of her own. Her feet killed, her head hurt and her heart was hammering. Thank goodness for make-up, and lots of it. After another fitful night's sleep, she was hanging on by her nerves and not much else. The skin on her face looked lacklustre and she felt haggard. Not ideal for a model, foot or otherwise, but what could she do? When the headmaster had phoned and asked for a meeting, she'd driven the two hours to the school where Danny boarded and sat in front of the man as he'd described her son's latest sins. Possession of weed. Found in his room. And more fighting. Could it get much more serious than that? Probably not, and all three of them knew it. Dr. Badell had said he wasn't going to involve the police – this time – but since Danny was now firmly on his last warning, he wouldn't hesitate if it happened again, he said, and a note would stay on his file to that effect.

Ellen was grateful for another chance. Danny, though, couldn't have cared less, sulky teenager that he was. She knew he hated the school, but without a father figure in his life at home, she'd hoped the boys-only school would help fill that gap and that he'd eventually settle down. But he hadn't, and Ellen realized now he probably never would. If she took him out of the boarding school now and sent him to the local school, he'd think he'd won, and even he'd acknowledged he wasn't keen on breaking into a new group of friends at the tender, awkward age of fifteen. He didn't want to leave the 'friends' he had at the boarding school, more likely. Better the devil you know and all that, even though she knew he hated them in reality; they were bullies who made him miserable. The headmaster had suggested his behaviour was something akin to Stockholm syndrome, that he didn't want to leave their grasp even though he didn't want to stay, either. He was a mixed-up young man and in truth, neither she nor the headmaster knew what to do. So, the status quo had prevailed. And she knew a good deal more headaches and heartaches would thunder her way.

She needed a drink. In public like this, green tea would have to do in place of vodka, but it was the kick she longed for, then the peace. She had a small bottle in her bag, but there was no way she'd drink whilst working. But it would be there, she knew, taunting her for now, and waiting for her later. On the way home, a couple of mouthfuls in the privacy of her car would be a different matter. She checked her wristwatch; there were still two hours to go.

"Green tea, please," she told the woman at the cart, not really paying attention to anything but her thoughts, and her feet. If she could get through the next couple of hours with a smile stuck hard on her face, she'd make it through another working day without casualty. She didn't notice the man stood to her right, the man with a silk scarf fastened around his neck in a feminine way and a long golden ponytail.

A man in a tailored suit.

A man who was watching her.

Her own world was too consuming to contemplate another being, so she didn't. When her tea had been handed to her, she stopped to take a sip, in no real rush to get back to the trade stand. If only she could slip her shoes off for a moment, let her toes spread leisurely for a while, dip her feet in something cool, even. They throbbed like the pulse in her temple, and she reached up to touch her head absentmindedly, her pale vanilla manicured fingernails on show. She rubbed ever so gently, willing the pain to stop, before reaching into her bag for the paracetamol. It should be another hour before she was officially due another two tablets, but the pain, oh, the pain was distracting. Ellen checked her watch again, expecting an hour to have passed since she'd looked at it only five minutes ago, and wrinkled her nose up in disappointment. It was standing room only at the cart now. There was no point hanging around, so she made her way towards the edge of the hall in search of a chair to rest for a while.

Had she been a little more in tune and aware of her surroundings, she might have noticed the same man fall into step a couple of people behind her and follow her to her final destination of a solitary chair by the wall.

Hadley let her sit and carried on past as though he had intended all along to go that way, she none the wiser to his moves or motive. He stood near the entrance to the gents' room and watched her from less than twenty feet away. It was obvious something was bothering her from her body language, and it wasn't just a hard day at work. Could she be the perfect candidate? His eyes travelled to her ankles again, then lower down to her perfect toes protruding from delicate sandals with thin pins for heels. A little redness was showing, and he wanted to take them in his hands, to soothe them for her, dip them into something cool, like milk, rub them and take care of them. He felt himself harden at the thought of easing her discomfort and stroking those feet leisurely.

For hours at a time. For his own satisfaction.

Chapter Fifty-Six

✿

ONCE INSIDE THE GENTS' toilets, he reached inside his breast pocket and pulled out an ornate pillbox. He held the tiny silver box in his hand like it was the smallest of birds and just as precious. It had been his mother's pillbox, and one she'd used all the time, right up until she'd finally died a rather slow and unpleasant death. Hadley's father, long gone many years before his wife, had looked after the family well. They'd wanted for nothing as the years had rolled by. Old money had kept them all in comfort, and it was that same old money that had enabled Hadley to become a shoe designer. Especially through the early years. There hadn't been a lot of money in the shoe design business back then – still wasn't, unless you were an established name – but it hadn't worried Hadley because there was always the old family money to dip into.

When his mother had finally passed, he'd sold up. Sold the heirlooms, sold the estate, sold everything, and he now had a tidy sum sat in investments and in the bank. His place on Mayfair was extravagant but suiting, as was his holiday home in Guernsey, though he hardly ever frequented the place these days. No, he was happy around London, working, watching and doing his other favourite pastime – anticipating.

He opened the box gently in the privacy of the stall and marvelled at the little grain-like devices. How could something so tiny ultimately bring so much pleasure later on? There were two of them, one green tipped and one amber tipped. The colour indicated what would happen when each one was activated. The amber one, signalling 'look,' meant that a possible individual had been found but the operator needed to do a little digging into their past to find their sweet spot. In other words, what debt they might need settling – and there was always one to be found. Most people had something worth fighting for if you dug deep enough, a skeleton they'd rather not have uncovered. With men, it was usually an indiscretion. With women, well, it was not much different, really: old boyfriends with secret videos and photos, secret babies, or the age-old favourite – secret liaisons. So much of what happened in this particular system was to do with sex of some form from some earlier time.

The other little device, the green one signalling 'go,' informed the operator that an individual had been found and they required immediate surveillance and apprehension as soon as possible. Once the trackers in either case were activated by liquid, such as a drink or stomach contents, there was a 24-hour window to get into that person's life or encourage them into one's own via their sweet spot, the debt that needed settling.

Hadley picked out the amber-tipped grain and held it between the tips of his thumb and forefinger. Closing the little pillbox with his other hand and tucking it away, he knew precisely what to do and how to do it. He was quite the practiced professional after all these years. Keeping the little device firmly in his grasp, he left the stall, left the gents' room and headed back out to where he hoped the woman was still sat. As he rounded the entrance back out into the main hall, he couldn't have been happier. There in the distance, he could see her as she stood with her tea still in her hand and her bag by her chair. She bent to pick it up and leave her resting place – headed back to work, no doubt. Hadley picked up speed as he neared her and, in a practiced move, bumped her right arm with his, hard enough that the tea cup catapulted out of her hand and onto the floor. It was an easy move he'd completed without fault on numerous occasions, and today was no different.

"Oh!" he exclaimed. "My goodness! Please, excuse my clumsiness. Are you okay, madam? I hope you're not hurt?" He looked into the brownest eyes for a split second before he busied himself trying to settle the woman he'd bumped into a moment ago. "I'm so sorry – what an absolute oaf. Look, let me at least replace it. What were you enjoying before I came along?"

He was looking directly at her now, his best gentleman face in place to put her at ease. For his plan to work, she needed to relax a little more. Eventually she spoke. It was more of a loud whisper.

"That's not necessary, thanks. I'm due back on the stand in a moment anyway." She smiled the weakest of smiles he'd ever seen on a woman, and he wondered at her obvious pain. The woman seemed so sad, so beaten.

"Then let me get you something to sip on during the afternoon. Which stand are you on? It's the least I can do, and besides, I insist." He smiled his practiced, gentle smile and to his delight, she returned the same.

"Green tea. Thank you." Such a small voice; it needed cheering up.

Something inside of him glowed warm as she melted for him.

"I'm over there." The woman pointed across the way to her particular stand. He nodded.

"Then you go on ahead. I've detained you long enough. I'll replace your beverage and drop by shortly." His smile was like a full stop to their conversation, and she nodded and turned back on her route towards her work for the afternoon. Hadley stood for a moment and watched her go, the thin grain between his thumb and finger reminding him there was still work to be done. He turned on his heel and made his way back to the drinks cart to order a replacement green tea. When it was safely in his hands, he dropped the tiny grain inside the paper cup and wandered over to her stand. Even if she didn't drink it all, and she probably wouldn't do now, the grain would have been activated and the cogs and wheels would start turning.

In a few short hours, he would know a whole lot more about the delightful mystery woman whose feet he was dying to spend time with.

Chapter Fifty-Seven

※❀※

ACROSS TOWN, the newly activated device appeared on a screen. The flashing amber light was the operator's cue to activate the players within the vicinity and locate the target. Once the target had been confirmed, the next part of the plan would run. That's the part the operator always found the most fun – the digging. Some enjoyed the surveillance, but to him that tended to be boring. What was fun about sitting in a van waiting for a target to move so you could follow them to their next destination, and then sitting in a van and waiting for them to move on again? Monotony was not his forte. He watched the screen as the three players he'd activated made their way towards the glowing amber light that they were following on their own screens. Until they reached the destination, no one knew anything about their target, not even the gender, though from experience, the operator knew they were predominately female.

He didn't have many female clients who used his service. It was only a couple of percent in reality, and over the years he'd been operating, that percentage had stayed about the same. The vast majority of fetish requests – to his own business and to others, he knew – came from the males of the human race. He'd done his research. Fetishists tended to be men, usually with a background of infatuation with a woman – an over-enthusiastic love for their mother or a mother figure – or a dominant woman early in their life. The fetish was something that developed in their teen years, rather than in their later years. Feet, shoes, hair – in fact, any part of the body could be attractive to someone who had developed a fascination with and sexual desire for it. The operator couldn't have cared less. If hair did it for them, then so be it. If fingers did it for them, then fingers it was. The client got what they desired, and in return the giver got their debt paid, even if they never realized it at the time.

But their lives would be better off for it.

There were never victims. Any crime against the giver was mild, maybe burglary or, at a push, assault, but that was a small price to pay for the service he was offering and the better life he was giving. And no one would come to any physical harm. Those were the rules. Hair would grow back, and clients who liked to spend time with certain body parts knew not to overextend their attentions.

Only a handful of those who indulged in his service had ever escalated their desires to another level, but that had never happened on the operator's watch. He knew the temptations his clients faced, so he took precautions of his own. What his clients didn't realize, and would never realize, was that there was a small discreet team assigned to them too, watching out for the giver's safety both during and after the transaction. It only took one overexuberant client to spoil things, and the operator fiercely guarded against it. He had eyes and ears on every transaction at all times. But that was another story. Or service.

Fifteen minutes later, he got the confirmation that the target had been confirmed, and the image of a woman filled his screen. The first thing he noticed about her was her telling face. She looked troubled, but then the client who had activated their device was particularly skilled in seeking out someone with the desired past or problem to be solved, and he'd been doing it long enough.

With a few specific keystrokes to the right places, the operator found her issue almost straight away: her troublesome son. He quickly scanned Danny's school record and saw his previous fighting notes as well as the latest and most disturbing one – possession of cannabis. The operator's first thought was a question: was the cannabis really his? With a history of fighting, was Danny being bullied or had it been planted? He checked the files of the other boys who had been caught fighting with him over the last year and wasn't surprised to find a pattern occurring. Several of them had police records for possession. Those same boys had been active in bullying other students too, students who, on further digging, had since moved away from the school.

He dug a little further into the bullies themselves. Their surnames all rang bells in his head, and he hoped they weren't current clients of his. There was only one way to find out. He tapped his keyboard briskly and, with the information in front of him, relaxed a little. While they weren't clients, he knew who they 'belonged' to. He thought for a moment. This particular problem needed fixing, but it could prove a little more difficult to solve. These people had friends in high places.

He sat back in his chair to think of the best way to handle it. His first plan of attack was invariably the one he went with, but he didn't want to rush this one and risk getting it wrong. The face of the woman on his first screen looked back at him. She really was a beautiful woman, but the strain on her face was evident. It needed removing. He picked up his phone and dialled.

"I need three boys taken out of their posh school for good. And it needs to stick. Can you look after it?"

The voice asked for their names and the school. If the voice was cautious after knowing who their fathers were, he didn't let on.

"I thought you'd find a way. Keep me informed. And it needs doing before the weekend."

The voice confirmed it would be and hung up.

While this particular task would undoubtedly be expensive, it was for a client who had been with him for many years. The operator considered it an investment.

He recalled the three players who were milling around the woman he now knew as Ellen Millar. Their work had been done, and he sent them each a badge of completion as a job well done. The digital leaderboard behind him glowed with their updated tallies. With players back to their regular activities and his current project also being taken care of, he pushed his chair back and headed out of the office for some fresh air.

The stone steps and tiled wall of the stairwell to the street were cool, and the lunchtime sun streamed in through the doorway at the bottom. As he stepped out on to the footpath, diesel fumes hit him full in the face as a double-decker bus chugged past, black poison spewing from its exhaust pipe. Grimacing as he walked and holding his breath until it had passed fully, he slipped to the right and cut through an alleyway heading east towards the sandwich shop and lunch.

Sorting other people's lives out always made him happy, though hungry.

Chapter Fifty-Eight

❦

THE AFTERNOON SUN shone down on Jack and Amanda as they pulled up outside Hadley Spinks' workshop. The red brick building looked, from the outside, like many of the factories that once had been occupied across the south, many of which were now trendy apartments or 'Google office space'–type start-up businesses that someone's daddy was funding, probably in tech. Old dimple-frosted glass filled the small window pane sections that made up giant windows with domed tops. Amanda pointed to one as they walked towards the entrance.

"They remind me of *Play School* – remember that? Always a choice of looking through the square, the round or the arched window. I always picked the arched. How about you?"

Jack turned to Amanda and looked at her like she'd gone mad. "Can't say I watched it when I was little. Was it still around when you were little, then?"

"Yes. Not for long, though. It died sometime in the late eighties. You're the one with the trivia facts, Jack. I'd have thought you'd have known that one."

They had reached the huge metal door and Amanda pressed the bell. A spyhole was visible at eye level just near the old letterbox slot.

Amanda smiled at it like she was Garfield, just for fun. If anyone was indeed watching, they too would have thought she'd gone mad.

"Music trivia is more my thing, and detective stuff – old cases from long ago. Sherlock Holmes, Sweeney Todd. I like the crime shows on the TV too – the real crime ones, not that made-up cop crap."

Male footsteps picked up pace on the other side of the door and the door opened inwards. A well-dressed man wearing a pale lilac shirt and a long ponytail greeted them both pleasantly. Amanda took the lead.

Hello. Mr. Spinks, is it?" The man smiled in answer. "I'm Detective Sergeant Amanda Lacey and this is Detective Constable Jack Rutherford."

"I've been expecting you. Please do come in." Hadley allowed them both to enter then closed the door quietly behind them. "Please, go through," he encouraged them, pointing the way down the corridor, and fell in behind them both. A few steps down and the corridor opened into a brightly lit wide-open space that appeared to encompass several aspects of the business. Natural light filled the room from an almost all-glass roof, and Amanda marvelled at the sky above. Cabinets along the wall housed shoes, clearly designed and created over many years. Sewing machines took up one corner, and desks and chairs another. To their right was a sort of mock-up living room area, complete with velvet-covered chairs, an eighties-style standard lamp and a modern glass coffee table. To Amanda, it looked a bit of a style mish-mash but a comfortable seating area nonetheless.

"Wow, what a great space to work in," she enthused.

An older woman joined them and enquired if they'd each like some tea.

"Thank you – yes, please," Amanda said. Jack shook his head 'no thanks' and the woman left. Hadley invited them both to sit.

"Now, what can I do for you both? It was such a long time ago, I doubt I can be of much help, but we'll see, eh?" He smiled his enigmatic smile at Amanda, and she found herself smiling back.

Hadley had a way with people, mainly women, that instantly put them at ease – which was both his skill and his intention. Amanda noted his silver shirt garters, one on each sleeve. They looked antique and quite lovely. Hadley noticed her glancing at them.

"They were my father's, God rest his soul. And his father's before him. They are quite beautiful, aren't they?" It was a statement rather than a question.

"Yes. I remember my grandfather wearing them, though his were not quite as nice as those ones. Still, not many men wear them now, but they suit you." She knew she was rambling a little off topic, but found herself drawn to the man, drawn to talk. Jack cleared his throat in a hint to get moving.

"If you could take us through the events that led you to be cautioned? Start at the beginning and fill us both in."

It was Hadley's turn to clear his throat before he launched into what had happened the afternoon he had been caught at the agency. When he'd finished telling his story, he looked directly at Amanda intently, perhaps for support.

She went with a question. "So how did you find the place? There's really no signage outside, no note on the door. How did you know it was there?"

"When one has a fetish like you now know I have, you are able to find out these things. And for the record, I'm not embarrassed any more, nor do I hide the fact that I find feet attractive." He was so matter-of-fact about it that Jack raised his eyebrows in surprise. Luckily Hadley didn't notice.

"I'm guessing there are others who appreciate the same things you do," Amanda said. "Are there chat rooms, maybe? Do you take part in online forums?"

"I agreed to chat about the day I was cautioned, not my personal life, Detective Sergeant Lacey. I said I'm not ashamed, but it's really none of your business or relevant to my caution. I was there that day, I tried to speak to some of the girls, and I got reprimanded for it. That really is all I can tell you. I didn't touch anyone and I didn't act inappropriately either. But I realize I upset some of the girls and for that I have apologised. Now, if you don't have any more questions about that particular event, I have work to do." Hadley's voice dropped an octave or two, signalling that this was the end of the discussion.

Jack and Amanda both got up to leave just as the older woman came back with tea for Amanda. The woman's face fell slightly as she realized they were leaving and the tea was no longer needed.

"Just one last thing." Jack stopped abruptly. He was doing his Columbo bit. He even had his first finger extended in thought.

"Do you know a man by the name of Chris Meeks, or maybe Smeeks, by any chance?" He and Amanda both watched for the slightest tell to appear on Hadley Spinks' face – a twitch of the lips, a hard swallow. The room fell into complete silence.

The question did need an answer, though, and eventually Hadley obliged.

"Chris Meeks. . . Smeeks." He rolled the words around his tongue, considering. He looked quite genuine as he replied, "I'm sorry, I don't recall the name. But I do talk to a lot of people. Is it important?"

"Just a name that has come up, a routine question that will probably lead nowhere. If you do recall the name, give me a call, would you?" Jack said. He passed a card to Hadley, who nodded.

"We'll see ourselves out. Thank you for your time," Jack said, and they both walked back down the corridor to the door at the end. When they were back out on the street and headed to the car, Amanda voiced what they both were thinking.

"I'd say he doesn't know of the name. But that doesn't mean he doesn't know of the person. Meeks just might use another name."

Jack slid into the driver's seat and waited for Amanda to get in before responding. She pushed the junk mail newspapers and leaflets to one side with her foot. There must have been at least two weeks' worth in the well.

"I agree, the name didn't light any beacons, but he didn't want to talk about fetish groups or chat rooms either, did he?"

"No, but neither would you if you had one, would you? And particularly if you were talking to the police about something that could be related, at least in subject matter. He's not stupid, but it was worth a try." Jack started the engine and pulled out into the street before adding, "It's still a coincidence, though. And for what it's worth, I'm thinking this Chris character is up to something online with fetishes, but I've no clue what. Just a hunch, but they don't work in a court of law. We need a break, something positive that links all this together besides two women losing their hair, a bloke from way back and a sexual harassment case going away. I can see the DI pulling us off this case and nothing more happening with it. In the meantime, behind our backs, hair is going missing."

Amanda couldn't help but grin.

"What?"

"It just sounds ridiculous when you say it out loud. 'Hair going missing.' How the hell does hair go missing? It wanders off like a cat?"

Jack laughed gently, and then a stab of pain hit him hard in his right side again and he winced as he grabbed at his belly with his hand. There was no way to hide this one.

"Jack? You're in pain, aren't you?" Amanda's voice was sharp with concern. "And that isn't still beef pickle sandwiches, not now."

Even though Jack didn't want to admit it out loud, he'd come to the same conclusion earlier that morning. The pain had stabbed him at regular intervals all through the night and all of today, and it was getting stronger and stronger as the day wore on.

Amanda asked him, "Has that been going on since yesterday, and getting stronger all this time, by any chance?"

"Who are you now, Florence Nightingale?" His lame attempt at humour fell on deaf ears. Then he relented and filled her in. "Yes, as a matter of fact. I'll have to get to the doctors, I know that."

"Give me your phone and I'll call them now, see if someone can see you this evening."

He turned to her, confusion on his face.

"I'm guessing the number is in your phone? Or you can tell me who you go to and I'll use my own." She watched as he pulled the phone from his jacket pocket and handed it over. Sifting through his contacts, she found what she was looking for and made the call. A couple of minutes later, the appointment was set for 5.30 pm.

"You perhaps shouldn't be driving, Jack. Why don't you pull over and I'll drive us back?" She glanced across and noticed Jack's face. It was going an odd colour, like pale processed cheese. Alarmed, Amanda instinctively grabbed hold of the steering wheel just as Jack vomited violently across at the windscreen. Acting quickly, she leaned across him, ignoring the mess, and hauled on his leg, removing his foot from the accelerator. She grabbed the wheel with her free hand and guided the car to the side of the road. Car horns blared as they finally came to a halt in a no-stopping zone.

"Holy fuck, Jack! Are you alright? Speak to me, Jack, speak to me!" She shifted her weight off him and took his face in her hands. A sort of whimper came from his mouth, like a wounded dog.

"I'm calling for help," she said, grabbing her phone from where it had landed in the mess on the floor. "Stay with me, Jack, stay with me," she urged him. She punched in the emergency number and told the operator an officer was down and needed urgent medical attention. She gave their location, hung up and turned back to try and help Jack.

"Hold on, Jack. Help is on its way. Stay with me, Jack." She put the emergency flashers on, then loosened Jack's tie with one hand and undid his seatbelt, holding his hand firmly in her other hand. She found tissues in her bag and wiped his mouth a little to make him more comfortable, and then placed her fingers on his neck, pressing gently into his carotid artery. His pulse was steady but quick and weak. The air was putrid, and she reached across him and opened the driver's side door to get some fresh air to him. Slowly, a bit of colour came back into his cheeks again, though his forehead was hot and sweaty and he was barely coherent.

What the hell had just happened? Amanda wondered. Her beloved friend and colleague looked seriously ill. Amanda hoped he was going to make it.

Chapter Fifty-Nine

AMANDA WATCHED from the curb as Jack was carefully wheeled into the ambulance, still looking very ill but better than he had a few minutes ago. A little colour had come back into his face, and the ambulance team had given him some pain relief. He wasn't talking, though, and Jack always talked. They suspected appendicitis, given the symptoms Amanda had described.

The inside of the car looked like half a dozen carsick children had consumed far too much ice cream, and the smell was already building up in the late afternoon sunshine. Amanda still had specks all over her trousers and dared not pick at it. Dried puke was not something she wanted on her hands or down her fingernails. She smiled encouragingly at Jack as his stretcher was secured, then climbed in alongside him. There was no way she could drive to the hospital in Jack's car as it was; she had already made the call for it to be towed to a valet to get cleaned up. It had needed a good clean anyway; today it would think it was its birthday.

Since Jack's wife had died some years back, there wasn't anyone back at home to notify of his illness, but she dropped Ruth a text to explain what had happened. Jack thought of them both as the daughters he'd never had.

"Need me to grab anything?" her text back read.

"I'll go round later. I have his keys. He'll need toiletries."

"Give him my love and wish him a speedy recovery. I'll see him later."

"Will do. I'll get a lift back. I'm splattered in puke."

"Gross, Ms. Lacey. Love you, though."

Amanda smiled at the last message back. She'd found her soulmate in Ruth, and she couldn't wait until they were married.

"All ready to go in the back here?" enquired one of the paramedics. His colleague was already in the driver's seat, engaging the flashing lights. Amanda nodded and took Jack's hand in hers as the rear doors were finally closed, the driver sounded the sirens and they set off across town towards the emergency unit and a hospital bed. Appendicitis could be deadly if the appendix burst, and time was of the essence. Amanda rocked from side to side in her seat, never taking her eyes off Jack, as the ambulance took left and right turns at speed. Jack seemed more comfortable now that he'd been given painkillers, but he still looked terrible. Wisps of his thinning 'salt and not much pepper' hair stuck to his clammy forehead, and Amanda was tempted to gently push them away.

He turned towards her and tried to speak from under his oxygen mask.

"Sor... f.... messss."

"I think I got that, Jack," she said, smiling at him, still clutching his hand. "Don't try and talk. Save your energy. Your car needed cleaning anyway. How many junk circulars were you trying to collect in there?" She was teasing him, and she smiled to let him know it. Humour was one way to dispel the fear they were both feeling right now.

Ten minutes later, the ambulance was backing into the emergency loading bay. Jack's stretcher was wheeled inside by a waiting team, his vitals were recorded once more and Amanda was ushered to reception to do the paperwork. The intake nurse promised she could go through once he was examined properly, but she needed to wait to be called in the meantime. Swallowing back her worry, Amanda gave Jack's details to the nurse and then sat down to wait it out.

Nearly an hour later, she was able to see him. Behind the curtain screen he was lying peacefully, fast asleep, minus his puke-soaked shirt.

He now wore a hospital gown. A nurse filled in his chart at the foot of his bed.

"Hi, I'm Amanda," she said to the nurse. "I was with Jack when he collapsed. How's he doing?"

The young nurse smiled at her. "Are you next of kin, by chance?"

"Not officially. Jack is a widower and doesn't have children. I've known Jack for some time; I'm a colleague at work. But we're close. There is no one else." The nurse nodded. "It looks like Mr. Rutherford has appendicitis. It's a possibility we may have to operate later if it doesn't settle down."

Amanda frowned. "What can I do or get for him?"

"Nothing in particular, but patients sometimes feel better in their own sleepwear, and with their own toiletries. Are you able to access them?"

"Yes, I have his keys. I'll go straight from here, but I wanted to see him first. I see he's sleeping. Is that normal?"

"It's the pain relief, and he's had a shock to the system so he's tired anyway. He won't be asleep too long, but he's better resting for now. You're welcome to come back later if you want to get off." The nurse motioned at Amanda's own clothes and she realized she was still a mess and probably stank. "If he does go up to surgery, he'll be gone a while."

"In that case, I'll pop off and come back. Will you tell him I was here? I'd hate for him to think no one cares, but I could do with some clean clothes myself."

"Of course. He won't be going anywhere for a little while." The nurse smiled reassuringly, and Amanda felt a little of her worry lift. She took Jack's hand again and said a few words to him, just in case he could hear her in his sleepy state.

"I'll be back shortly, Jack. I'm going to get cleaned up and get you some things, okay? I won't be long. I promise." Then she bent over and lightly planted a kiss on his forehead. While he was still warm, he wasn't clammy anymore and she hoped that was a good sign.

Chapter Sixty

IT WAS JUST after 7 pm when she finally got home and changed, but even though her stomach was moaning its displeasure at being empty, she didn't feel like eating. She dashed upstairs for a quick shower to get rid of the puke smell, then quickly slipped into fresh jeans and a clean T-shirt and was back out the door in jiffy, destination Jack's place. She hit a speed dial number on her phone and Ruth's voice filled the car. The wonders of Bluetooth again.

"How's he doing, hun? And, just as importantly, how are you doing?"

"He's sleeping at the moment. They suspect appendicitis and he may have surgery. I'm on my way over to his place – just grabbed a shower and changed."

"You sound exhausted. Have you eaten?"

"Not yet. Being covered in vomit isn't conducive to eating so I'll grab something later. It won't do me any harm to miss a meal. I've got a wedding dress to squeeze into, remember. I'm headed over to get some toiletries and something for him to sleep in. I'm hoping he has some PJs or else I'm in trouble. Then I'll go and drop them off and see if I can see him awake. I'll get an update, and then I'll be over later. It might be late, though. Will you be up?"

"Of course. Want me to come to the hospital with you?"

"No point until they move him to a ward. You'll only be hanging around. I'll say 'hi' from you. Come tomorrow, maybe?"

"Definitely. Give him my love and I'll see you when you get here. Text me when you leave the hospital and I'll have a mug of hot chocolate waiting."

They said their goodbyes as Amanda pulled up at Jack's place. As with much of the Croydon area, any parking to be had was out the front on the road unless you were lucky enough to have a driveway down the side of your house. Jack's older semi-detached house was one of the lucky ones, and Amanda was grateful not to have to prowl for a space a mile further down.

She let herself in the front door and stood in the hallway to get her bearings. It had been some time since she'd been to his house. There was a fusty smell, a mixture of old stale food and old stale sleep. Wrinkling her nose, she walked straight through to the kitchen and opened the back door to let some fresh air blow through. When Jack had last opened a window Amanda had no idea, but it sure hadn't been recently. She looked under the sink for a plastic bag, something to put a few belongings in. As she pushed old containers of cleaning fluid to the side to look, a mouse ran across the back of the cupboard. An involuntary shriek filled the kitchen.

"Shit. You scared the hell out of me," she said accusingly to the mouse as its tail disappeared through a hole in the failing cupboard wall. Grabbing an old grocery store bag, she left the kitchen and headed upstairs to the bathroom to get his toiletries. The tiny bathroom was standing room only. The walls had once been painted turquoise, and the fixtures had once been white. Now there were rust-coloured stains in the bath and basin where dripping taps had done their damage over time. A brownish tidemark circled the bath. Amanda didn't want to judge, but she was shocked that the man she'd known for so long lived in a place such as this. Sure, he needed his hair trimmed and he sometimes looked a little unkempt, but his home needed some urgent domestic attention.

His shaving gear was on the windowsill and she scooped up what she thought he'd need into the bag, along with some old-looking aftershave, deodorant, toothbrush and paste and his dental floss. With his toiletries collected, she stepped back out of the tiny grubby room and into the hallway.

As she stood at the top of the stairs, she noticed there was a room to her left that she assumed was his bedroom. Old semi-detached houses like this one all had the same footprint inside, or a mirror image of this one if the house was adjacent. From her spot on the landing, she could see by the dull light in the room that the curtains were still closed. Jack hadn't opened them when he'd left for work that morning. She pushed the door open fully and went inside, then stopped dead and gave an involuntary gasp of dismay. Hanging on one of the two wardrobes that had been squeezed into the room was a candlewick ladies' dressing gown and a floral cotton nightdress. On the floor, placed directly underneath, were a pair of ladies' slippers.

They looked like they'd been there for years, and Amanda knew with a dull ache of certainty that, in fact, they had been. She stood transfixed in the doorway in the dying light and scanned the room: pink floral wallpaper densely covered in what looked like huge lilies decorated all four walls and was peeling slightly at the top edges. Pictures of Jack and Janine at the beach, at parties, at gatherings, at lawn bowls tournaments, each frame filled with smiling faces, adorned the chest of drawers. As did a thick layer of dust. The bed was unmade and, judging, by the yellowing once-white sheets, it hadn't been changed for a while. A dark pink eiderdown hung off the edge of the bed; a pair of gents' PJs dangled from a hook behind the door. At least he'd hung them up after he'd taken them off. Figuring they wouldn't be the freshest if the rest of his home was anything to go by, she left them where they hung and pulled out the top drawer to find a clean pair. There were three neatly folded pairs, thankfully, and she selected one. Amanda glanced at the bedside cabinet and saw a couple of books and a spare pair of reading glasses. Not knowing which of the two books he was currently reading, she picked them both up, grabbed the glasses and laid the items with his fresh sleepwear on top of the unmade bed.

In search of a more substantial bag to put all his belongings in, Amanda opened the dated wooden door of a wardrobe that looked like something from before the war. On the top shelf was an old leather bag, and she lifted it down. Quite surprisingly, it was heavy and she dropped it onto the bed before deciding whether to look inside and remove its contents. While she didn't want to pry, she really needed a bag. The thick leather buckle-type fastener on the top unclipped easily and the bag opened slightly, allowing her to put her hand in to open it more. She felt around inside, still uncertain what she might find. She felt wool-like fabric, maybe a sweater, and some other cloth that was much smoother and lighter. And there was something else, something in a hard, leathery box, and when she tried to pick it up with one hand, she found it was too heavy to do so.

"Sorry, Jack, I hope this isn't private stuff but I could do with the bag," she said aloud to the empty room. She began emptying the bag onto the bed, setting each item in turn on the bedspread, and finally pulled out the heavy box.

She smiled then, realizing, and patted the lid.

It was Jack's lawn bowls gear.

Chapter Sixty-One

❧❧❧

"I'M NOT KIDDING YOU, Ruth, the place was like time had stood still – about ten years ago. Even Janine's clothes were hanging on the front of her wardrobe, like a shrine. Slippers too. And it needed a bloody good clean. Jack looks like he could use a little help."

"What are you thinking? Going in and sprucing the place up? He might not appreciate it, you know, proud man and all."

Ruth had a point, Amanda knew. "Well, when I turned up with his things and he saw the leather bag, he looked a little embarrassed." Amanda was thoughtful for a moment then added, "And sad too. And I think I might know why."

"Why? Did he say something?"

"No, he wouldn't but I felt I'd intruded in something sacred. No, change that: I *have* intruded in something sacred. After he thanked me, I put the bag on the floor as instructed and he kept staring at it from time to time, like someone was going to jump out of it. On the set of drawers with all the other pictures were a couple of him with a small group, a team maybe, all dressed in white. Several women and a couple of men. I reckon he and his wife played in lawn bowls tournaments. There was a box of lawn bowls in that bag, and all his bowling clothes, as well as some smooth-soled white shoes. I nearly keeled over when the smell hit me, though. I bet they've been in that bag the whole ten years."

"That's sad, don't you think? Something they both did, and then she died and he probably hasn't played since."

"I know." Amanda fell very quiet in thought. "I put his reaction down to being unwell, but I'm sure there is more to it than that. He misses her terribly, I know that. He probably lies awake in bed at night staring at her nightclothes wishing she was next to him." Amanda felt her eyes well up with tears and blinked them away before they spilled over. "So tidying his place might be a bit intrusive."

"Then let's do the next best thing."

"And what's that do you think?"

"Let's organize for a cleaner to go in once a week. That way, if he doesn't want it, he can cancel and nothing would get disturbed without his say-so. We can get someone in while he's in hospital to do the main things like his bathroom and kitchen and a quick dust of his bedroom. In fact, do you think it would be better if *we* both did it?"

Amanda knew Ruth was trying to be helpful, but she shook her head. "I think that would be worse. Well, having me involved would be, at any rate. He'd hate for his direct boss to have cleaned his loo – as would you or I. No, he'd be annoyed with that idea. Sorry. Nice thought, though."

The two of them sat quietly, their minds busy while they rattled the ideas around, trying to come up with a solution. Finally, Amanda spoke again.

"One thing is for sure: he can't go back to the house as it is, so I say we get someone in to do the main stuff. Call it a get-well present from us. There. That's it, done." Amanda stood with authority as the last words left her mouth and Ruth could only smile and nod her approval. As Jack's work colleague, Amanda knew best. "I'll make the call first thing."

"How long are they keeping him in?"

"Surgery went well. If he carries on with his meds without a hitch, he'll be there for three days so there's not much time to get his house sorted. But right now, I'm off to bed. I'm knackered. You coming?"

Ruth mock-saluted in reply, then gathered their mugs. Without turning the kitchen light on, she placed the mugs on the drainer and, looking up at the window and the dark night sky beyond, she caught her half-reflection looking back at her. After all the talk about Jack and his home being a shrine to his wife, her thoughts drifted sadly to her own father, who had been widowed just over a year ago. He too now rattled around the family home on his own and, while she saw him regularly, at times like this Ruth realized it wasn't enough. Tomorrow, she'd call him and arrange to meet for lunch and give him a hug. She'd not given him nearly enough over the handful of years she'd known him; she'd shown up late in his life, the surprise daughter he had never known he had, and she felt like she was making up for lost time.

Amanda's voice broke into her thoughts, calling her to come to bed.

"Coming," Ruth called back.

Ruth was annoyingly wide awake. She lay in bed thinking about her own family situation and how hers had changed since she'd been a teenager. Her new dad, Gordon, her biological father, had been shocked at her existence but gentle soul that he was, he had warmed to her quickly and they now got on well. Her stepmother, Madeline, on the other hand, hadn't been quite so easy.

Of course, that hadn't all been Madeline's fault, she thought guiltily, not for the first time. When she was younger, Ruth had taken every opportunity to snipe at her, demean her in some way, through subtle digs here and there. Gordon had encouraged her to give Madeline a chance, but Ruth had behaved that way for so long that she'd found it hard to stop.

Until one day, quite by accident, she had discovered Madeline's secret, and had found herself admiring the woman. At last she'd warmed to her, and Madeline had welcomed the blossoming of the affectionate feelings between them, but their new relationship was to be short-lived. Ruth would give her back teeth to have her time over with Madeline again, and if given the chance she knew she'd behave very differently the second time around. But that was never going to be.

She sighed and turned over in bed. Her father was now on his own, and all the talk of Jack being on his own and not coping with his domestic responsibilities too well made her feel maudlin. Amanda lay next to her, little snoring noises coming from her mouth as she navigated through a dream, and Ruth turned to watch her sleep in the slight light of the room. An orange glow from the street lamps outside shone through the crack in the curtain, and it cast an eerie glow that was just enough to get either of them to the bathroom during the night if need be. She hoped both her dad and Jack were peacefully asleep and not lying awake, like her, looking up at the ceiling and thinking about how fragile life was.

One minute the person you love the most in the world is by your side, she thought gloomily, then the next minute, they're gone – forever. Soon Amanda would be her wife. What would the future hold for them both? Would they start a family like Amanda wanted, even though she was in her early forties? If Amanda never came home from work one night, was killed on a job – a very real possibility – how would Ruth cope without her close by and fully in her life?

Ruth had no idea. Sighing heavily, she realized she wasn't going to sleep anytime soon. Rather than sink deeper into 'woe is me' thoughts, she lifted the bedclothes and went back down to the kitchen and her laptop. Griffin had asked her for a favour and she still hadn't done anything about it. Now seemed the perfect time to do something.

Chapter Sixty-Two

DOWNSTAIRS IN THE KITCHEN, Ruth put milk in the microwave to heat up for another mug of hot chocolate. It was about the only thing she used the machine for, even though she bitched about the unhealthy microwaves it emitted into food every time she pressed start. Still, it was quicker than heating milk in a pan. The turntable slowly moved the mug around in a circle, and Ruth followed it with her eyes, transfixed, like it was the most interesting thing in the world. It was almost hypnotizing. The microwave pinged and stopped turning. In the quiet of the kitchen, it sounded like a frantic bicycle bell behind something slow and Ruth mentally 'shushed' it. The last thing Amanda needed was to be woken up after a tough day.

Taking her mug and laptop into the lounge, she curled up on the sofa and sipped at the hot chocolatey liquid in thought. But this time her thoughts were on Griffin's friend's problem rather than the two men in her life. She mused to herself, "So Griffin has a friend, a woman friend in his life. About time, too, young man."

There was no malice in her thoughts but she knew that few people warmed to Griffin, with his eccentric and somewhat OCD ways. To many people, he was just weird, pure and simple. How many folks were as precise as Griffin at everything? How many folks broke routine down into fifteen-minute slots and found new adventures almost impossible to deal with? That was the norm for Griffin. But he'd found someone, it seemed, and Ruth was pleased for him.

She opened the laptop and the screen sprang to life, the bright blue-white light illuminating her face in the near darkness. Opening the TOR browser, she started digging, putting what she thought would bring back results into the crude search box. There were a lot of misconceptions about the dark web, and many newer users confused it with the deep web. In fact, they were two different things entirely. She pulled up the video file and photo Griffin had sent to her, as well as a new window with the software she needed open ready.

Two locations, the results informed her. She clicked on the first link and saw the same video that she already knew to be Griffin's friend. A quick note of the address, a few knowledgeable keystrokes with the other search result and she was about done. She could go no further. The whole idea of the TOR browser was anonymity, and that meant for those on both sides of the screen – the user and the poster. Unless she had elaborate hacking skills or worked in one of the top cybercrime intelligence agencies around the world, she could only look to a point; and she had neither.

The good news was there were only two records of the video – on the dark web, anyway. Next, she did the same search on the ordinary surface web. That threw up a different result altogether, but at least she could do a little more tracking of its origin. Finally, she had twelve results listed in total across the dark and the regular. She knew she could eliminate ten of them reasonably easily without attracting too much attention. The sites that dealt in revenge porn, whether they knew it was such or not, wouldn't notice one video clip going missing; there were plenty more for their visitors to look at and get excited about. She had done what she could and that would have to do. Being a 'grey hat' online, her morals were solid, though she couldn't say the same about her law-breaking antics. Still, who'd be looking and ready to report her?

What had started as a local community online group to help solve petty crimes, watch out for missing cats and the like, had piqued her interest in going deeper. Literally. Now it was long past an interesting pastime. Having used the community site to discover a dog-fighting ring as well as a local sex offender, Ruth knew what the web in general and her little bulletin board in particular had done for the safety of the local community. Since then she'd invested time in learning the ins and outs of the deep and the dark web; she already understood coding with her day job building apps and websites. Hacking, she reasoned, was a natural progression, and doing it all in the name of good was now one of her prime interests. After running, of course.

Reaching for her phone, she tapped out a quick message to Griffin to update him.

"Links to video on reg web all gone. Two on dark I can't get to. Hope that helps a little. Ruth."

She clicked send and it whooshed along the airwaves to Griffin's phone. Hopefully this late it wouldn't wake him up; hopefully he'd see it first thing in the morning. Draining her mug of chocolate, she checked the time on her screen and even though it was past midnight, she knew she still wasn't ready for sleep yet even if she tried. The TOR browser icon glared at her.

"What the hell. Ten more minutes," she said under her breath. "Let's browse a while. Then I'll go."

Then maybe sleep and sweet dreams would take her too.

On the other side of town, Griffin was far from sleep. When his phone pinged with the incoming text and he saw it was from Ruth, he quickly scanned its contents. Relief for Vee filled his veins. Even though the other two links existed, the chances were minimal of anyone on the surface web seeing the video and Vee being embarrassed any further. He tapped a message back.

"Thanks heaps, Ruth. I owe you."

Then he went back to his own search. Finding just what he needed at the right price had proved difficult, but after researching as meticulously as he had, and for as long as he had, he was almost ready to proceed. Soon, his problem would be sorted and he could get some of his lost confidence back again. His next problem was getting the time away to get it done, both from work and from his new friendship. He didn't want Vee thinking the worst of him. The man had said he should allow a couple of weeks, so he'd have to come up with something plausible, and soon.

Griffin certainly couldn't confide in her yet; he couldn't risk the ridicule.

Chapter Sixty-Three

✿❀✿

ELLEN'S HEART sank when the caller identified himself.

"What can I do for you, Dr. Badell?" She was used to his calls by now, knowing he never rang her with any good news. The last time she'd spoken to him had been a week ago, when he'd informed her of the cannabis that had been found in Danny's room. Since then he'd been punished by the loss of extracurricular activities, and he'd suffered for it. She supposed today's message would be no different.

"Actually, Mrs. Millar, I have some news for you I'd like to pass along."

"Oh?" Ellen said wearily. "What's Danny got himself involved in now? What do you need to tell me this time? To come and collect him and his bags?" She couldn't keep the sarcasm from her voice.

"Actually, Mrs. Millar, like I said, I have news, good news for a change. Danny has been cleared of any wrongdoing in regards to the cannabis. Three other young men have admitted they set Danny up, and have also been setting him up with many of the pranks he's been in trouble for over the past months. All three boys have been expelled."

Ellen couldn't believe her ears. Surely she was dreaming? Danny had been set up all along?

"I don't understand, Dr. Badell. You're saying my son is not responsible for all the trouble he's been in, that the incidents were all a set-up to point to him?"

"That's exactly what I'm saying Mrs. Millar, precisely."

Ellen fell silent, thinking. She hadn't been prepared for such news. Part of her brain sang out in elation that her son wasn't a trouble causer after all; he'd simply been a victim of pranks. She was also a little bit suspicious.

"What made the boys decide to fess up and come clean? It seems a little unusual to me that, after all they've put Danny through, they suddenly find their consciences and own up. What happened, exactly?"

The air on the line was deathly quiet. Dr. Badell chose his next words wisely. "I really can't tell you that, I'm afraid. Let's just say the young men involved are no longer at the school, and Danny's record has been updated to show he wasn't involved in any of the incidents. I'll have to leave it at that, Mrs. Millar, except to say I'm deeply sorry for the stress it's undoubtedly caused you and Danny during this time. Please, I hope you can accept my apologies."

Ellen was stunned but grateful. "Of course. And thank you for letting me know. Does Danny know yet?"

"I'm just about to tell him. I wanted to share the news with you first. I'll get him to call you later if you like?"

"Yes, I'd love to speak to him. And thanks again." She hung up and stared at the disconnected phone for a few moments. Thoughts rushed through her head as the news sank in, and her face broke into a grin, something that she'd almost forgotten how to do for the last couple of weeks. Danny had been raised fairly, to be honest and respectful at all times, and she'd found it difficult to comprehend the troubles he'd ended up in at school. Now she knew the answer: it had been other boys all along.

Ellen stood in the lounge where she'd been sat reading when the call had come in. Sun streamed in through the front bay window, and she moved to where the reflection hit the carpet and looked outside. The sky was as blue as a cornflower, and wispy white clouds sauntered slowly across a windless sky. A couple of young children played with a ball on the street, their giggles just audible. So, Danny hadn't been causing stress and havoc; it was some other boys, boys who had then placed the blame on her Danny. Why? For fun? For a bet? What? Her shoulders relaxed as she realized they didn't need to be tense and up around her ears anymore. Danny was innocent of stashing drugs, and innocent of other wrongdoings he had been accused of. She hoped that now the pressure was off him, too, his grades would get back to where they should be, where they had been heading, before it was too late. They'd both suffered with the stress, but it looked like it was all over, thank god. Though in the back of her mind, she wondered why, and how it had all come to an end so rapidly.

Still, she had a foot job to get to. She headed upstairs to get ready.

Thirty minutes later, she checked her Uber app to see where the driver was and, with her prized possessions firmly encased in socks and protective boots, she gathered her bag and went to wait outside on the pavement. Her ride was just turning into her road. She always took a ride rather than her own car or public transport when it came to work. Being a foot model meant that on workdays, walking was almost forbidden. Having a driver pick her up at her door and drop her at the client's door was the most convenient and safest way to arrive in perfect condition. The agency's clients were paying for perfection, after all.

Slipping onto the back seat, Ellen relaxed a little as the driver gave her the quiet she needed. He didn't speak until they arrived at the studio. Stepping out, he opened the rear door and held it wide for her. He smiled at her warmly.

"Thank you," she said. "I'll be a couple of hours or so, so I'll maybe see you on the return journey home?" She smiled brightly, feeling much better than she had in a long time, the weight finally lifted from her shoulders. She hadn't realized just how heavy it had been.

"Thank you, madam," said the driver, "though there are quite a few of us now, so I might not be the one who drives you back home. Have a good day, now, won't you?"

"I will, and you too. Goodbye," she said over her shoulder as she turned towards her destination. And with a lighter step than she'd felt in weeks, she made her way to the huge metal doors and pressed the buzzer, looking into the security peephole. She wondered absentmindedly who might be looking at her right now. And from where.

As she waited, the driver tooted his horn in farewell as he drove past her, headed to his next pick-up.

He knew exactly who would be taking her home later. He would.

Chapter Sixty-Four

THE OPERATOR SAW the 'confirmation of delivery' light pulsing gently on his screen. This particular mission had been one of the easiest and quickest he'd ever had to organize because the client had been specific. He'd found what he wanted and didn't want to wait a moment longer than he had to. And so they'd made it happen for him. 'Baker' had been using the firm's services almost since its inception and was one of the more pleasant people he dealt with. With no unusual needs over and above what he called a 'base desire,' the operator didn't need to monitor all of his transactions like he did other clientele. While 'Baker' was cloaked in anonymity like every other client, it hadn't been hard to figure out just who he was and do the relevant checks. Safety was paramount and Baker was indeed a gentleman, it seemed. He wished all his clients behaved as well as Baker did.

He stared at the pulsing light. In a few minutes, it would begin move as she was transported to a fabulous hotel where his client could appreciate her gift to him in perfect surroundings. And, of course, she would be none the wiser about what had actually happened to her. He'd often wondered what went through the heads of those repaying their debts as they came to, wondering where the hell they were and how they'd arrived there, particularly those who had given their hair or other trophies his clients desired. With this particular client, the operator assumed the woman he had chosen would be a little shaken and perplexed but would otherwise forget the whole thing pretty quickly. He liked that better: nothing obvious would be taken apart from her time. It was the clients who desired more intrusive prizes, like a pint of blood, that he found the hardest to tolerate. He'd even had an enquiry from a man wanting to castrate other men, but he drew the line at causing harm to another and had refused the client. The service he provided was to balance a life problem with a life desire and do it safely, not indulge the whims of sociopaths and criminals.

The tracking device told him she was on the move to the hotel suite where 'Baker' would receive her shortly afterwards. Knowing everything was in hand, the operator relaxed back in his chair to let his team do their thing while he contemplated what to fill his rumbling stomach with for lunch.

Chapter Sixty-Five

✿

BAKER'S PHONE pinged with confirmation that his gift was en route. He'd watched her as she'd arrived at his studio-cum-workshop, peeped at her through the keyhole as she'd waited in the reception area sipping green tea. Of course, he already knew she liked green tea but this tea was different than what she would be used to. It was laced with a mild sedative, which would have the desired effect in only a few minutes. While it wasn't considered the norm to have his reward brought to his premises, for obvious reasons, he'd wanted to savour her being in his territory as long as he could – sitting on his sofa, sipping from his cup and gently falling asleep where she sat. He'd then be able to smell her presence and enjoy her right there in his office.

She'd remember arriving at the studio, of course, but that wouldn't matter because nobody had seen her, and her story, should there be one, would be denied. There would be no evidence of her ever being there; everyone involved would corroborate that. Even the cameras in the street were out of order – temporarily: that was what he paid so handsomely for. She'd be assured that her memory would be playing tricks on her due to recent stress, and when she saw the card later with its very specific instructions not to tell, she wouldn't be foolish enough to ignore them. No one ever was.

Some minutes later, he'd watched her leave through the rear exit, gently taken out to the waiting ambulance, laid out like Sleeping Beauty on a gurney. If anyone had seen anything, it could be explained easily: a model had been taken ill and was being transported to hospital. The plan they created always worked without a hitch, every time; this was also what he paid so handsomely for. All he had to do now was arrive at the appointed time at the designated hotel suite and take his pleasure. The few things he needed to complete his experience were by his side in a small leather bag by his feet, and as he glanced down at it, he felt himself harden in anticipation.

It was time to go. As the ambulance pulled away from the rear exit, Hadley Spinks left by the front door and got into the waiting car. Once he was settled in the back seat, he took out the small bottle of brandy and a glass from his bag and poured himself a drink. It was part of his ritual, part of the pleasure that was about to come, of savouring the moments until she was his. He closed his eyes as the warmth made its way to his stomach. Taking several deep breaths, he tried to relax himself from the inside, working to quiet his now-racing heart. If he didn't slow things down, his experience would be over too soon and that would be disappointing. No, he didn't want that. He wanted long and slow.

It had been some months since he'd last 'treated' himself in this way. In between, and in the privacy of his room, he'd had to be content with watching previous experiences that he'd recorded, the other women he had pleasured in the past. Over and over again he'd watched them, trying to relive the experience and satisfy his craving. But having seen what this young woman had to offer him, he'd known he had to have them. No matter what.

In a few more minutes, he'd have the objects of his desire all to himself.

Chapter Sixty-Six

THROUGH AN UNSPOKEN ASSUMPTION, they'd taken to travelling into London together each day. Griffin had changed his departure time as they'd become closer friends, and he'd kept it that way. Vee was easy to be around and he liked her. A lot. He liked her permanent smile, he liked her easy way and, well, he liked everything about her. Not many people, never mind women, found Griffin easy to be around, but Vee didn't seem to care about his idiosyncrasies, his weird ways. He knew he was different from others but since he couldn't control how he was, he'd given up trying to be someone else and lived his life as he was. It appeared Vee was okay with that.

After Ruth had texted him to say the video file had been removed, he'd pondered how to tell her – and indeed, whether to tell her at all. He wanted her to know she didn't need to worry about it any longer, but if he told her what he'd organized, she might see him as meddling and be pissed at him. And he didn't want that either. So he'd mulled it over and over in is head until he feared there was nothing else in there but the one quandary bouncing off the insides of his skull. But Vee was sensitive and she had known something was bothering him. Being the kind person she was, she had asked him.

"What's bugging you, Griffin? You're too quiet this morning."

He turned to her as they walked to the station and all he could see was her perfect smile, even now as she asked the hardest question, one he knew he had to answer. He wondered how either of his possible responses would change what they had together.

She pushed again. "Come on, you can tell me."

Taking a deep breath, he started to speak, but his mouth had other ideas and he blew empty air out through his wordless lips instead. He waited a beat and tried again. "I've done something for you. But I'm now wondering if I've overstepped the mark. You could be mad at me." The rest of his breath drifted away as he waited, not daring to look at her.

"Then why don't you try me? Unless you've murdered someone on my behalf, I doubt I'd be mad."

He chanced a look her way at the mention of murder and saw that her smile had spread to her eyes. He wished he could feel as confident as she did.

"I haven't murdered anyone on your behalf, no."

"Then I won't be mad. Spit it out, would you?"

There was no going back now; she wanted to know. In a rush, the words tumbled out of his mouth before he could change his mind.

"I've had the video footage of you taken down off the internet. It was on twelve sites but it's gone now. There are still two sites on the dark net that it can't be removed from." Griffin gulped in air, not daring to look at her and waited for her anger. Or a slap. But neither came. He was also aware she was no longer walking by his side. He stopped and turned. She was ten steps behind him, motionless and staring at him. *Oh shit...* Which way would she go? He had no idea. He took a couple of steps towards her, testing the water.

"Have I screwed up? Do you hate me for interfering?"

"Actually, no. The opposite."

Stunned, Griffin prodded for more. "What do you mean? You're not angry with me?"

"No, I'm not angry. I'm touched you would do that for me. And I'm impressed that you know how to do it, and a little scared of that too at the same time."

"Actually, I'm not that talented to do it myself. I know someone who is though. But the file has gone from most people's viewing access so that's a good thing, right?"

Vee walked slowly towards Griffin as she spoke. "Right. And thank you for doing that for me. I really do appreciate it." She was level with him once again. Even though she was a good foot shorter than Griffin, the way she looked up him left him in no doubt what she wanted. She wrapped her arms around his neck and pulled him gently towards her, brushing his lips with a kiss. Like Vee, it was perfect. Whispering, she added, "I've been wanting to do that for a while. Now you've given me a reason."

Griffin was stunned into silence. She liked him? Well, obviously – she'd just said as much.

"So you're okay with me interfering?"

"Yes, and I wouldn't call what you did interfering. More helping a friend in need." She hooked her arm through his and they carried on towards the station entrance. "Come on, we'd better hurry. We don't want to miss the train and be late."

Griffin's stomach was riot of nerves. Now he was back to his original quandary: while he'd wanted to kiss Vee for some time also, what he was hiding made it awkward to get too close to her. How was he now going to keep her at arm's length without offending or concerning her? In his past experience, women either ran a mile at their discovery or ran a mile because he wouldn't move to the next stage. Either way, they didn't hang around for very long after. And he really didn't want Vee to go.

The fact that he'd finally found the solution he'd been looking for meant that the end of all that was in sight, but it also posed another problem: how could he get away for a couple of weeks, minimum, without anyone knowing where he'd gone? Without Vee in the picture, he could have left his job and simply taken off to do what needed doing – Jan would never have given him the time off, of that he was sure. But he knew Vee would never approve of his doing that, and would have been angered and hurt if he vanished suddenly. No, he couldn't think of life without Vee.

Once on the platform, they caught their breath while they waited for the train. It was Vee who spoke first.

"I probably got off lightly."

"You got off lightly?" Griffin said, confused. "What do you mean?"

"Well, when my ex posted that video, we'd just split up. But I never told you why we'd split up."

"Oh? Why did you, then?"

"Because of what I'd inadvertently seen on his laptop. Now, don't get me wrong – everyone has exes, I know. But mine had kept video copies of him and his exes having ... fun ... together, and I didn't like that." She made quotation marks with her fingers in the air around the word 'fun.' "And some of the fun was a long way short of my kind of fun."

Griffin was intrigued. "Go on."

Vee checked for nearby eavesdroppers before she carried on with what she was about to describe. "He had a fetish, and not what I'd call a regular fetish like kissing feet or wearing someone else's undies or something. He liked feces – can you believe that? I'll leave the rest to your imagination." She shuddered involuntarily. "Urgh. Gross."

Griffin couldn't quite believe his ears. He'd heard of people enjoying that kind of thing but he didn't know anyone personally who was into it. He didn't think so anyway, but how could anyone be sure?

"And that's what you saw on his computer?"

"Yep. He'd hinted at us doing it but I'd always resisted. Then he got to be quite uptight about me not getting involved and we argued all the time, so I ended it. I told him he could have his fun without me and that he'd obviously found others to take part with in the past. Finding someone new wouldn't be too hard." Then, almost as an afterthought, she added, "Though I have to say the women in the videos looked almost comatose, like they weren't really present. I wondered if they'd been drugged, or were high maybe."

"And what did he say to that, to finding someone new?" Griffin was all ears.

"He said he'd manage. He'd found an online group of like-minded people. I told him to go forth and multiply with them."

Griffin assumed such a group wouldn't be visible on the surface web, but more likely something a little darker. Particularly if, as Vee said, the women weren't exactly participating fully. His interest was piqued, yet he was disgusted at the same time.

"What was the name of the group? Any idea?"

Chapter Sixty-Seven

"He's had a good night and he's resting. I'm sure he'd appreciate a visitor." The nurse smiled encouragingly at Amanda; she must have assumed Jack was her father, or maybe her uncle. While Amanda didn't exactly look young for her age, Jack looked much older.

"Thanks. He's made of tough stuff, is Jack," she said then headed to his room. When she popped her head around the door, she watched him for a moment before he became aware of her presence. 'The Chase' was firing questions on the TV, though Jack didn't appear to be watching it. He seemed to be daydreaming. Amanda smiled and carried on into the room, taking a seat in the chair by the window.

"And how are you feeling, Jack? You look a lot better than when I saw you last."

"That's because I *feel* a lot better than when you last saw me. And by all accounts, I *am* a lot better than I was yesterday." He smiled appreciatively at her visiting him. "I hope I didn't ruin your suit."

"I was going to buy another one soon anyway. You just brought the day forward."

Amanda told him she had thrown the whole thing in the bin rather than remember it as her 'puke suit.'

"Wasteful woman. There was plenty of life in it yet," he said, but there was no bad feeling in his words. His eyes twinkled a little.

"So you're on the mend, then. That's good to hear. You gave me quite a fright. A bit of notice wouldn't have gone amiss. At least I could have steered the car a bit easier."

"I'll do my best next time my appendix decides to explode on me. Not that I have an appendix anymore. And I thought it was the pickle. Not a very good detective, am I?"

"You're not bad, actually, Jack. And maybe while you're lying here you can solve the case for us, put your brain to good use. I even brought an old laptop for you to play on, do a little surfing."

"Oh? And what am I looking for in particular?"

"I got Ruth to install a TOR browser on it." She opened the laptop bag and pressed the 'on' button. It slowly awakened. "It's a bit slow, but it is an old one." They waited for the old machine to fully awaken. A row of icons popped up along the bottom. "Here, look at the bottom. That's where you'll find the browser you need to use. It makes everything anonymous; no one can see you."

"And back to my previous question: what am I looking for?"

"Fetish groups, I'm thinking. There's no manpower to do this back at the office and since you're not busy, it won't hurt, eh? You might even learn a thing or two." Amanda winked animatedly, though Jack didn't look so amused. He gave her a sideways look. "Start with the ones we know about – hair," Amanda went on, "and see if there is anything related to exchanging it for something. I'm guessing there's a group out there, probably more than one, and Chris Smeeks is involved somehow. He could be the main guy, or he could be the host and nothing more, but he's involved. We just have to figure out how. No coincidences, remember?" Amanda placed the laptop rather roughly on Jack's extended legs and then sat back.

"Hey, watch my stitches!" he yelped.

"Stop crying. Your legs are nowhere near your stitches. And while I'm thinking about it, where's your phone?"

"It's in the bedside drawer. What do you want that for?"

Amanda opened the drawer and took it out. "I'm setting something up for you. What's your pass code?"

"1234. And what are you setting up?"

But Amanda was already busy downloading what she needed. Once it was done, she opened the app and began her search. Jack watched as her face broke out into regular grins, a few seconds apart.

He tried again. "What are you doing, Lacey?"

"Oy! I thought you didn't call me by my surname."

"It's the only way to get your attention."

"Shush, I'm busy. Hang on and I'll tell you."

He watched as she took a set of earphones out of her bag and fiddled with his phone again. A pinprick of a blue light glowed from the screen.

"Okay, here we go." She leaned in, showing him his phone and the green Spotify app. "This is your music," she said, pointing, "and these are your headphones. Put them on." She pressed play on the short playlist she had created. ELO's 'Hold on Tight to Your Dreams' filled his ears, and Amanda watched as a huge grin spread over his face. He needed a shave. Again. His fingers tapped on the bedrail; he was clearly enjoying this. She let him listen for a minute or two then pressed pause. He took the headphones off.

"I thought you'd like a musical accompaniment while you work. And you can add more music in. Let me show you how."

For the next while they sat with their heads together as Amanda showed him how to search for the songs he adored and add them to a list to listen to later. Every so often, he'd say "I used to have that on blue twelve-inch vinyl" or "And that was on purple vinyl" or "I've not heard that in ages!" It made Amanda glad that she'd taken the trouble; now she didn't feel quite so bad about asking him to work while he sat.

When he finally took the headphones off, she broached the subject of his house. "Jack, I have something else for you, something I'm hoping you'll accept in the spirit which it is meant and not be pissed at me. Or Ruth."

"Uh-oh. What else have you done?"

"I couldn't help noticing you need little help around the house. So first of all, I've organized a lady to go in a couple of times a week and keep on top of things for you, give you a hand." Jack opened his mouth to object but Amanda waved it shut. "And she's under strict instructions not to move anything of Janine's or change anything – just take away the inches of dust. And if it doesn't work out after four weeks, you can get rid of her. In the meantime, you've got stitches and recovery to worry about, not dust bunnies and mice." Jack sat quietly. Amanda suspected he knew deep down he needed a hand.

"Four weeks," he said. "I'll let her clean for four weeks, as you suggest. Then I'll decide. Deal?"

"Deal. She might even cook your dinner every once and a while. I wish someone did that for me."

"Well, you're about to get wed, so you two have no excuse between you. You need to get yourselves organized. Living under one roof would be a start. And you've got Wong's if all else fails."

"Too true." The comment about one roof had hit home. "Well, I'm glad that's settled. Now, I've got to go, so let me know if you find anything worth knowing about. If you get stuck, give Ruth a call. She said she'd be happy to be your dark web guide." She added, "Sort of sounds like a tour guide of the seedy. Could be fun." She winked again and stood up to leave.

"Thanks for these," Jack said pointing to his headphones. "I'll report back later with my findings. The dark web will be under my control in your absence." He mock-saluted his captain as she turned to go.

Amanda hoped he found something useful or interesting. Other than porn, that was.

Chapter Sixty-Eight

HER EYES FLUTTERED open in the dusk of the room. Drowsy and disorientated, Ellen lay on the silk comforter trying to comprehend where she was and what time it was. Her eyes searched around the room, the part she could see without moving her head, but nothing she observed looked familiar. Her ears tuned in for sound. Nothing, save for the gentle hum of what sounded like traffic outside, wherever outside was. The light in the room was dwindling; a lamp glowed faintly in the far corner. Slowly she rolled over onto her back, then onto her other side, and scanned the rest of the room, blinking to digest her surroundings. It seemed she was in someone's bedroom.

And alone.

She sat bolt upright, heart pounding with fear now, ears on full alert. Something didn't feel right. Slowly, she lowered her eyes.

Her ankles were bound together.

But not with cord or rope.

They were bound with a distinctive patterned silk scarf, featuring a design Ellen knew well. Hermes. It was tied artfully around her ankles and arranged like it was all part of a window display, in Selfridges perhaps. She looked closer: her toenails, usually painted a neutral shade, were now a deep rouge, the same colour as the border on the silk scarf. They matched perfectly. Instinctively, she wriggled her ankles to see how tightly she had been tied up and was surprised to feel the give. They weren't tight at all.

As her eyes adjusted to the gloom, she noticed that she was surrounded by rose petals that had been delicately sprinkled on the bed, almost the same deep red. She picked one up to test its authenticity, pressed the soft, silky petal to her nose and sniffed. The strength of the perfume surprised her. Was it a natural scent, though, or something from a bottle? She couldn't be sure. Forcing herself to become fully alert, she leaned forward to untie her binding and set her ankles free. Whatever had happened to her, whatever had brought her to this room, she knew she hadn't come here voluntarily.

Shimmying herself off the comforter, she stood on slightly shaky legs and walked around the room as quickly as she could manage. There was a silver teapot and single cup and a small plate of triangle sandwiches, and an envelope was propped up against a milk jug. It had her name on the front. Tentatively, she opened it and took the card out. There was a simple message printed in beautiful handwriting. It read, *"Your debt has been settled. I'd advise you to tell no one. It wouldn't be wise."*

Now even more confused, she went over to the window and peered out. It was dusk. The street below bustled with traffic, lit by the amber glow of streetlamps. Ellen felt the crispness of the card in her hand and re-read the message. It made no sense to her. Her ankles hadn't been bound tightly enough to keep her imprisoned, nor were her hands or mouth restrained, so what was she doing in this room? She walked across to the door and tuned the handle. It wasn't locked. How odd. If someone had taken the trouble to get her into the room and tie her ankles, why not lock her in?

She closed the door and sat on the edge of the bed again, trying to decide what to do. She took stock of the situation: she wasn't a prisoner, but her ankles had been bound while she slept, and not with rope or telephone cord or some such, but a luxury silk scarf. A body scan found nothing else out of order, apart from a splitting headache. She was still fully clothed; her bag was on the small table next to the tea. Though she couldn't see her shoes. The card's message ran through her mind again but she had no clue what it meant or what she was supposed to do, if anything.

Apart from *"Tell no one. It wouldn't be wise."*

At last, instinct took over, and she grabbed her bag, flung open the door and ran barefoot down the corridor as fast as her drugged legs would carry her. The lift was at her floor and she stepped in, resting her head back on the wall. As the doors closed and she descended, she closed her eyes.

The lift took an age to get down to the lobby. Once there, she headed to the main entrance where she stood, barefoot, trying to get her bearings. She shivered. She took a few steps outside; the pavement felt cold to her bare feet. Once again, instinct took control and she bolted off, though in which direction she had no clue. Her heart pounded as did her head, and she pulled up short, panting hard. Looking down, she saw there was blood where she'd come to a halt. She must have run over some glass fragments, maybe from a broken bottle. How could she not have felt it? Maybe she had.

"Can I help you, miss?" a male voice at her side asked. It was the doorman of the hotel. He glanced down at her bare feet and raised his eyebrows, but Ellen was too preoccupied to care.

"Where am I?"

"You're in Knightsbridge, miss. Can I get you a car, perhaps?"

He waited for her reply and seemed about to move away when she said faintly, "Yes, please. I want to go home."

The doorman signalled to a nearby car to pull in and Ellen slipped onto the back seat. He closed her door for her.

"Take care, miss," he added though Ellen barely noticed. Whatever had happened to her that afternoon was going to be a mystery. The last thing she remembered as she wracked her brain was waiting for her car to go to a job earlier on, and that was it. Had she even gone? How had she got into that bedroom? And why? There were too many questions and no answers.

Her phone buzzed with an incoming text and she rummaged in her bag to read it. It was from her agent: *"Are you okay, Ellen? Only you didn't show up for your assignment today. Call me."*

"I didn't show up? I've never done that. Ever. What the hell happened to me?" She glanced down at her perfect feet. Her soles were sore and dirty from being barefoot; there were specks of blood on the floor mat of the car. Going barefoot was something she never did. It was all out of place.

Everything about this day was out of place, including her.

The operator completed the transaction on his screen. Another sale closed, and another happy client. The green light changed to blue and two other smaller lights blinked nearby. They were the lights of remaining players, players in place to monitor what she did next.

I'd advise you to tell no one. It wouldn't be wise.

He knew she wouldn't, but still, he had to make sure.

Chapter Sixty-Nine

✤

AFTER AMANDA HAD LEFT, Jack sat up in his hospital bed. He'd loaded a few more songs onto his playlist and he marvelled at the collection he'd made. While ELO was his life's fuel, he'd gathered Rainbow, Status Quo and other old rockers into one place and they played in his earphones while he worked. He never knew work could be quite such fun.

A self-confessed luddite, he'd been apprehensive about surfing the dark web, not really knowing what he was doing, but sometimes ignorance was bliss. Amanda had given him a brief tutorial, a brief warning about clicking on images and videos, and set the browser up for him. He'd put in search terms that he thought would bring up results that he could dig into. The crude search engine reminded him of back in the day when he'd first started using the web. It had looked very different than it did today. It was like going back in time, a blast from the past. He'd put in 'fetish' and 'hair fetish' specifically and was working his way through, though nothing of interest had revealed itself.

Unless you called other people's kinks interesting.

When he'd found a site for some of the more bizarre fetishes, he'd closed the page as fast as he'd opened it and fought hard to forget what he'd seen. But that was impossible: you couldn't scrub your brain clean or rewind your life like an old movie. No, you couldn't un-ring the bell. The image of a young man drinking from a wine glass filled with blood and masturbating at the same time would take him a while to forget. Determined to not fall into any other places that might scar him for life, he realized he needed a bit more direction to what he was doing.

He dialled Ruth's number and she answered on the second ring.

"Hey, Jack. How are you doing? Feeling any better?"

"I'm a lot better, thanks. Though Amanda has given me a task to do to while away my recovery. No rest for the wicked. And I could do with your help."

"She told me she'd given you an old laptop to surf with. What do you need?"

"Some instruction, if I'm honest. I think she's forgotten I'm a luddite, not a techy like you. I can search and surf, but I don't want to click on shit that's going to stay in my head forever. I've just seen what I can only describe as a vampire having some fun with himself and I nearly puked my guts up again. I swear it's cauterized onto my eyelids. Any advice, O Technologically Savvy One?" Jack could hear her laughing. He smiled despite himself. "It wasn't funny, let me tell you. I'm sure it will stay with me forever, burned right into my eyeballs too. Gross!"

"Then don't click on it, Jack. And keep away from anything with the initials CP on or near it."

"Dare I ask what CP is?" Then it dawned on him. "Ah, no chance of that, let me assure you. Child pornography is the lowest of the low. God only knows how the special units cope with that shit; they must need a shrink on call seven days a week."

"Just keep digging as you are. There's got to be something in there of use for your case. And it's an old computer, so if you do pick up something with a virus, say, it won't matter. But while the boss lady has you working, remember you're supposed to be getting better, not stressing."

Jack smiled into the phone at her thoughtfulness. "In that case, I shall have a nap, then pick this up again later. Thanks for the heads-up, Ruth."

"Good idea. Take care, Jack."

Jack glanced at the disconnected phone. He really could do with a nap, come to think of it. He closed the laptop down and wriggled gingerly down under the covers for a snooze. He smiled wryly: his mid-morning cuppa would probably arrive sometime around then.

Griffin had found Femme Fet-Elle, a group that had interests in things he simply couldn't comprehend. Why would someone be turned on by such seemingly odd experiences? Did these people not enjoy ordinary sex? How could someone get turned on with human excrement in their midst, for example? He shook his head to clear the images.

He remembered what Vee had said about the women in the videos looking out of it, not active or as interested as the males. Were they high of their own accord, then, or had they been drugged? There was no way of knowing, and as Vee wasn't in contact with her ex anymore, getting his hands on the files wasn't an option. And they probably didn't exist anymore anyway, in hard copy at least, though Vee's ex probably had copies in the cloud for safekeeping and private viewing.

He knew there were all types of chat rooms and forums on the dark web, for all types of subject matter – he spent time in them himself, after all – but something about this discovery didn't feel right. His urge to tell someone was getting stronger. What if women were being involved against their will? And what if they were being hurt? And what happened to them after their involvement in the videos: were they passed on to someone else after they'd outlived their useful-ness? He'd heard of victims being 'sold on' after criminals had had their fun with them, usually to someone who would degrade them even further for their own or someone else's personal pleasure, and at a price. But that only happened in the movies – didn't it? He picked up his phone and dialled. He didn't want their misery to be on his conscience.

It was almost two hours later when Jack woke to his phone vibrating on the bedside cabinet.

"I have a name for you to check out," the voice said excitedly. Jack's brain was having trouble coming back into focus after his deeper than usual sleep. But finally, it registered that Ruth was speaking.

"Hang on, let me sit back up," he grunted groggily. "Okay, what is it?"

"Check into a club called Femme Fet-Elle," she said, and spelled it for him.

"And what is that?"

"Quite by chance, a friend's new girlfriend came across some disturbing videos on her ex-boyfriend's computer some time ago. They involved one of the more . . . unpleasant, I'd guess you'd call it. . . fetishes. The ex was apparently trying to coax her into it as well, but she wasn't having anything to do with it and ditched him shortly after. Seems he then posted a revenge sex recording of her to get his own back, and she eventually told this friend of mine, who came to me for help with it. Anyway, long story short, that's the name of the group. Check into it. I've told Amanda, so she'll probably call you later. If there's something in it, she's hoping the DI will pass it up the chain to the cyber unit to deal with."

"Great, because this is out of my league, that's for sure." He rubbed fresh sleep from his eyes and yawned. "Thanks, Ruth. I'm on to it." He hung up and rested his head back to think. They needed something concrete to go on for the cyber unit to take action, and a couple of hair thefts were still not enough. While he didn't wish for a dead body to turn up, he needed a bigger picture, something big enough to warrant more resources and intervention. In the meantime, perhaps he could sniff around a bit more and join the group, pretending he had a fetish that needed fulfilling – though drinking blood had no appeal even in pretend. So, what, then? He glanced at the floor beside his bed. He remembered Amanda coming to see him with the old leather bag from his wardrobe and what she would have had to remove from it. And voila: there was the idea for his own very personal fetish. The question was, would anyone else share it?

Jack got to work, a wide grin fixed on his stubbly face as he typed. He'd have a shave later.

Chapter Seventy

JACK HAD SPENT most of that afternoon creating his fake profile and trying to find a way into the group. There were two aspects to it: first was the chat room, where any member could discuss their interests and ask questions and generally arrange meet-ups. He'd already started chatting and finding his way around in there. So far, so good. But he'd found there was also a premium service on offer. That was the part Jack wanted to look into. Unfortunately, it was available only to those who had been members for at least six months and had a track record of positive activity and respect within the forum. He, however, had neither. Even if he had the prerequisites, he knew the moderators could still refuse to give him premium service for reasons they didn't state. And he expected that, as with any premium service, there would be a handsome price tag attached to it. There had be another way, but what?

The news was playing on the little TV screen over his bed; a local jewellery shop had been turned over and thieves had got away with some key pieces. Security camera footage had luckily supplied reasonable photos of the intruders as they'd fled. One of them had taken his mask off a bit too prematurely. Jack laughed. *Idiot.*

That was when the idea hit him. He laughed again, though this time at its simplicity – and the irony of a cop even contemplating it.

He needed to break in.

He needed a geek. And he knew who might be able to help.

Chapter Seventy-One

❦

"Jack, do you realize what you are asking me?" Ruth sounded incredulous and flattered at the same time. "And what even makes you think that I'd know how to get in? I *build* websites and apps, for heaven's sake, not knock them down. You need qualified hackers like the cyber team, not a self-taught like me who, quite frankly, wouldn't be able to pull it off."

"Ruth, you expect me to believe that you only know 'a certain type of coding'? You're far brainier than that; you've already proven that. And I wouldn't ask unless it was important. Besides, the cyber team are overstretched and not interested, so I'm going it alone."

He heard Ruth swallow a guffaw at the idea of him going it alone on the dark web. Doggedly, he went on. "Shall I get Amanda to chat to you?" He knew mentioning her name would wind Ruth up and away from saying no. Over the last couple of years, he'd got to know her well through their common friend.

"Oh no you don't, Jack Rutherford. Leave her out of this." Jack heard a heavy sigh on her side of the phone. She was tempted. Jack knew what her next words were going to be and he smiled in anticipation. When the confirmation came, he silently punched the air with his fist, then winced as his stitches twinged. A passing nurse glared disapprovingly at him.

"Here's what I'll do," Ruth went on. "I'll set up a profile too and see what I can see from the front end, like you have. Make up an interest and get chatting in the forum. And I'll do a bit of snooping behind scenes where I can, though I'm not sure how much I'll be able to achieve, if anything. Remember, it's all anonymous. That's for a reason. And if they suspect someone is snooping too deeply, and they'll have ways, they may get spooked, close up and move to another address. From what I know of illegal groups and forums, they move about real easy so they don't get caught. But let's see what we can do between us. Is your profile all set?"

"Yes. My username is Rutter, and apparently I'm into women's shoes, the more pungent the better."

"What? That's gross. Where did that idea come from?"

"Actually, Amanda gave it to me. In a roundabout kind of way."

"I won't ask," Ruth said. She went on, "I'll call myself 'Gregory's Girl' – close but not close enough. Look out for me later. What time will you be chatting?"

"After visiting hours tonight until the nurses turn my light out. Even in a private room they make you sleep more than you want to."

"It's called recovery, Jack. That's why you're there."

"Yeah, well, I'm a bit over it now. I prefer my own bed. And mug."

"Well, do as they say and you'll be home soon enough. Look out for me later, then, and keep out of mischief."

Ruth said goodbye and looked at the half-filled-out profile on the screen in front of her. 'Gregory's Girl' liked hair, since that was where it had all started. The longer the better. She saved the information and closed the page down until later. While she didn't mind helping out with the case, she had a business of her own to run, and a client was waiting in the meeting room for her. She doubted the website this particular client was having built would be as fun as the one she was going to dig into later.

New members joined the chat room all the time, each with their own very personal desire, and the operator made it his business to never judge them. It was the more affluent members who went on to become clients of the other side of his business – the premium service, the darker service. They paid big money to have their desires delivered on a silver platter, and many of them were repeat business to him.

There were six new requests to join in the last 24 hours, and he looked at their interests. He'd seen and heard it all before, and pungent ladies' shoes were no exception. He allocated the access level for the new member and did the same for the other five. Then he did some basic digging with the information he had. As usual, there was nothing to see: all anonymous users with anonymous backgrounds. Still, occasionally he got lucky with someone's stupidity and ended up with information he could use somehow. But not today. Hopefully a couple of them had money.

Chapter Seventy-Two

❦

ELLEN HAD BEEN SENT PACKING. And the client wasn't happy. She knew her feet weren't looking their best after she'd run barefoot from the hotel; they hadn't had time enough to recover. In reality, she should have pulled a sicky and not gone to the job in the first place, but school fees didn't pay themselves. Now Jules was going to be pissed at her when the client phoned to complain, which they'd inevitably do. What was Ellen going to say? What was her excuse going to be? She'd worked with Jules for many years and they had a good relationship. Ellen was one of her top earners, so why hadn't she just said no to the job?

She knew why: when you fall off a horse, you have to get back on. After waking up in a strange hotel room, with her ankles bound and smelling of expensive perfume, she'd realized she hadn't got herself there – she'd been taken. Somehow. She'd turned up at the studio for work, but everything after that was a blank. And now she was letting Jules down for a second time.

It was as if there had to always be stress in her life. At least Danny was feeling better; his stress had gone, and that had taken a weight off her shoulders too. But now it had been replaced with another one, a different type. Instead of Danny being miserable and Ellen trying to sort it out, it was now Jules's turn.

She smiled as she thought about her son; she had spoken to Danny several times on the phone, and the transformation in his voice was incredible. He sounded almost back to himself, almost happy again, and it was good to hear. Whatever had happened, whatever the story was, she was pleased for him.

The driver pulled up back outside her house. She thanked him, stepped out, and walked up her front path. Once inside, she closed the door and leaned back on it, gazing up at the ceiling for the answer that wasn't there. Still, she was home now. She untied the laces of her protective walking shoes and slipped her socked feet into the waiting slippers. The phone in her bag rang. Probably Jules. She let it go to voicemail.

"I'll call you and explain when I've had some tea, okay?" she mumbled to herself, and the phone, as though hearing her, went silent. Ellen walked through to the kitchen and turned the kettle on, staring out of the kitchen window to the small patio outside. The few planters were filled with low-maintenance greenery; just enough to add some style to the little space without needing any work. A small link of irrigation hose joined them up; it jumped into life on a timer in the evening during the warm months. A water feature gurgled in the centre; a simple bronze pipe recirculating water into a large concrete basin completed the oasis. The sound always soothed her. It was all she needed: a little space of green tranquillity to appreciate and relax in. She took her mug of tea outside and sat in the recliner to listen and think.

Ellen hated lies. But she and Jules went back many years. Should she tell her the truth? It was unheard of for Ellen to not have the best feet at all times, and she couldn't think of an excuse to give Jules as to why they were in such bad shape now. Sure, she could say she'd been mugged and had run off, but that was a lie. Jules would want to know why she hadn't informed the police, for starters. Yet the truth, whatever that was exactly, was far more sinister.

Tell no one. It wouldn't be wise.

And the debt being paid? What was that about? She didn't owe anybody anything, so how could a debt have been paid? Has someone got identities mixed up, confused her with someone else, maybe? She was unharmed, apart from her feet, though that had been her own doing in running from the room that she hadn't actually been held captive in. But she'd bolted, been scared out of her mind, and hadn't cared as she'd fled barefoot down the pavement.

She sipped her tea and listened to the soothing sound of water trickling into the pool. Finally, she knew what she needed to do.

Tell the truth to Jules, but don't tell anyone else.

Before she had a chance to change her mind, she retrieved her phone from where she'd left it inside and listened to the voicemail message. While Jules didn't sound angry, she did sound concerned. Ellen dialled and waited.

"Hi, Ellen. You got my message, then?"

"I did, and let me first apologise. I should have said something sooner and let someone else do the job rather than hope the client didn't notice. I'm really sorry, Jules. It won't happen again."

There was a long pause before Jules spoke again. "Apology accepted. And what happened with the no-show? You say you went; they say you didn't. Why would they lie? What's going on with you, Ellen? This is not like you."

What indeed, wondered Ellen. Suddenly it came to her: she hadn't lied. *The client had lied.*

She took a deep breath. "Jules. I need to tell you something. Something a little odd, in fact, and also the reason my feet are looking the way they are. But first, I need you to tell me you won't tell a living soul. Can you do that?"

There was a pause. "Sounds ominous," Jules said at last. "Ellen, whatever is it?"

"Tell me you can keep a secret, Jules. This is important."

"Okay, I get it. Cross my heart and all that. Now what is it?"

Ellen took another deep breath and began to speak, the words rushing out of her mouth in a tumble, figuring the faster she explained, the less painful it would be.

"I think I was drugged, abducted, taken to a hotel. Someone tied my ankles together and left me to wake up in a room in Knightsbridge.

When I awoke, the bedroom door was unlocked and I legged it bare-foot." Her voice caught. "That's how my feet got damaged. I had no shoes to get home in. And yes, it sounds ridiculous, but you couldn't make that up, could you?" She gasped for breath as the experience came back to her vividly. Tears filled her eyes. "What the hell happened to me, Jules? And why?" Ellen began to sob down the phone, partly from distress but mostly from the relief of confiding in some-one, someone who'd said she wouldn't tell a soul, someone who had known and trusted her for so many years.

"Hey, come on, Ellen," Jules said soothingly. "Steady on. Slow your-self down. It won't help to get so upset. Breathe, my love. Breathe."

Ellen took a deep breath and it did soothe her nerves, just like Jules said. She was beginning to feel better for having let it all out. She took another long breath and felt the stress beginning to drain from her system. She slowed her sobs and blew her nose.

"Feel a bit better now?"

"Yes, thanks. Sorry about blurting it out, but the note they left told me to tell no one, that it wouldn't be wise, but I knew I owed you an explanation. Can you forgive me, Jules?"

"Of course I can, and don't you be worrying about that now. Look, take some time to get yourself back together and your feet back in shape. I won't tell a soul what you've told me. Your secret is safe – though god only knows what that was all for. But the main thing is you're unharmed and in one piece. Let's keep it that way."

Ellen sniffed and blew her nose again. A problem shared was a problem halved, as her mum had always said. Ellen felt better for having apologized to Jules and told her the truth, and she was confi-dent Jules would keep to her word.

"Thanks, Jules. I knew you'd understand."

She finished the call and rested her head back. It was now begin-ning to ache from crying. With the fountain tinkling in the back-ground, yet another question entered her head.

Why hadn't Jules sounded surprised?

After calming Ellen down and thanking her for being honest, Jules finished the call. And found she was once again in a quandary: Ellen was not the first of her models to have told her such a story in confidence. The bigger details were the same in each one: the mention of a hotel room and of having been drugged. It was only the smaller details that changed: the items that had been given or taken.

And Ellen had mentioned a note. What on earth was that about?

Since the break-in, since that day her database had been hacked into, Jules had been wondering why. And now she knew, almost for certain.

Someone was using her girls to fulfil the desires of others.

Jules tapped her teeth with her finger, thinking; it had to be an elaborate set-up for it to have been going on for so long and on such a grand scale. Whoever was behind it must be charging a small fortune to ensure the girls kept quiet and their clients were kept happy. Perhaps she should have mentioned all this when the police had visited her office but she hadn't, not wanting to betray the women who had fallen victim and go back on her word.

But now whoever this was had targeted Ellen, and for Jules, that was the last straw: for one thing, Ellen was far too valuable to her, and their friendship went back way too long. But more importantly, it meant that this person still had access to her database. He was still watching, and she needed to find him and put a stop to this.

Picking up her phone again, she searched through her contacts for Chris Smeeks, then pressed send. He answered on the third ring.

"Jules! What a pleasant surprise. To what do I owe this honour?"

"I urgently need your help. And I don't think what I have in mind is quite legal."

"Not quite legal is my specialty. Tell me more."

Chapter Seventy-Three

JULES SAT NERVOUSLY on the park bench waiting for the investigator to show. He had asked to meet her in person to hear the rest of the story, not trusting digital eavesdroppers. In his line of work, he couldn't be too careful. She wrung her hands and tapped her fingers restlessly as she waited. She couldn't understand why she felt so wound up. She'd done nothing wrong.

In the distance, she saw him approaching, his figure cutting a fine image as he jogged to a nearby bench and fastened a shoelace that didn't need fastening. When he was satisfied there was no one in the immediate vicinity, he strolled over, wiping his face on the bottom of his running shirt. Sweat trickled down his tanned neck as he sat at the end of the same bench she was sitting on. His name was Valance.

"Nice afternoon for a run," Jules said.

"It surely is. Are you running much these days?"

Jules made a scoffing sound. "Pilates is more my thing now. It's easier on my body."

Valance smiled, casting a subtle appreciative glance at her stylish and slender frame.

"Have you found him yet?"

"Patience, Jules. These things take time. But that aside, I will have something for you later on today. From what I've learned so far, he has a lot going on with various shell companies and complicated set-ups, and it's not been easy to unravel things. But we're not far off. Why aren't you involving the police?"

"I can't involve the police. Too many of my girls have been threatened and I'm loyal to them all. They've told me their experiences in confidence and I have to respect that."

"I've set things in motion," he said. "That's all you need to concern yourself with – trust me. Though when I find him, what's the plan from there?"

"I'm a big believer in taking your own medicine," Jules said, a sly grin on her face as she turned to him. "I think he should be made to appreciate his own skills. I want him to become the victim of his own success."

Valance grinned in reply. "I see you've not lost your touch where fairness is concerned. A nice trait to have if I may say so. What are you thinking?"

"I don't want him just found, I want him taught a lesson. And I want to be there to watch. I'm still working out the details, but let's say I'm quite looking forward to it."

"Understood." He grinned. "I'll keep you updated. Sit tight." Then he stood and ran off in the same direction he'd originally been heading before he'd stopped. Jules watched his strong legs push him forward as he ran off into the distance and wondered what the penance might be for Chris Smeeks when they got him. Whatever it was, it was going to be satisfying to administer.

Jack smiled as he replied to another member of the forum, someone with the handle of 'Looby' who he'd since learned had a real love for Christian Louboutin shoes. It seemed he – Jack assumed it was a 'he' – was wealthy enough to be able to afford such items in quantity and had been cautioned for loitering outside several of their London stores. Not deterred, he'd found the same group as Jack to share his experiences with other like-minded people and post evidence of his astonishing collection. What Jack had found surprising was the set-up he'd created for each pair in order to appreciate them. The room looked like a showroom, carefully constructed and filled with glass cabinets that were filled with the objects of his desire. It looked like a shop itself, but with only one customer.

"Frigging weirdo," he'd muttered as he'd looked at the images the man had shared. But he was supposed to be working, not entertaining himself with things he didn't understand.

"Impressive collection. Are they all unused or do you like them to have been worn? I prefer the sweet scent of a woman's foot myself." Jack nearly balked as he typed.

Looby replied almost instantly. *"A mixture, though it's a lot easier to find new ones."*

"You ever taken them without permission, lost in lust as it were? That's what I enjoy the most. The gym is a great place for me – so many to choose from."

"Not taken them, no. I love to watch them, touch them if I can. The theatre is my candy store equivalent – all the ladies out for the evening in their finery. Then I go home to my collection."

Jack wrinkled his nose at the weird conversation he was having, and then gave his head a shake: this was research, he reminded himself. All in a day's work. But he'd had enough for one night and 'Looby' wasn't being much help; he didn't fit the profile, whatever that was. He bid Looby good night and looked at the other threads that were taking place. He was about to sign off when a conversation caught his eye: 'Gregory's Girl' was having an in-depth conversation about hair, long hair specifically, and Jack paused to watch. He was becoming quite the voyeur, not to mention something of a reluctant expert on the subject.

From his research during his hospital stay, he'd found out a great deal about the fetish community and the behaviour of men with fetishes. And yes, they were mainly men: women made up only a very small percentage of the fetish community. It seemed very few men took their fetish to another level and went on to do real harm. California's Jerry Brudos and Canada's Russell Williams were two of the more horrifying examples he'd read about.

On the other hand, the women involved in fetishes were usually into masochism. Many of them enjoyed doling out pain and pleasure to those who liked to receive, and he'd seen far too many photos lately of women in black leather holding whips. Jack squirmed a little in his bed. He had enough trouble removing sticking plaster from a hairy forearm, and these people did pain for pleasure. Holy freakin' moly!

At any rate, he had deduced from his research that even though, statistically, half of Croydon's male population might have a penchant for black lacy ladies' undies or spike-heeled shoes, they were unlikely to turn it into anything more sinister. He and Amanda would need to go at this another way.

A yawn forced its way out of his mouth at the same time as the night nurse passed by his door. She popped her head in.

"It's probably time you got some rest, Mr. Rutherford. You can do that in the morning, I'm sure." She nodded at his laptop and gave him a look that said 'I'm in charge.' He had a sudden image of Hattie Jacques dressed as a nurse in *Carry On Matron*. No one messed with her.

"Right, yes. I'll just log off."

"Good move. I'll be back in a moment to make sure that you're resting."

Jack didn't doubt she would be. He absentmindedly wondered about those who had a thing for nurses. Being in hospital must be a candy shop experience for them too – if they felt well enough, that was.

He slipped down under the covers and closed his eyes, a broad smile on his face. Janine's smelly white lawn bowls shoes filled his mind for a very different reason.

Chapter Seventy-Four

❧

JACK HAD ALWAYS BEEN an early riser. Spending so much time lying in a hospital bed had thrown his normal routine into turmoil, and that meant he'd been awake since 4 am. Unfortunately, that then meant he'd be fast asleep at 4 pm, taking a nap like an old man.

He *was* old. Who was he kidding?

Neither the sun nor the birds were up yet. And at 4 am in hospital, there wasn't a fat lot else going on there either. Breakfast was another three or four hours away. He was parched and needed a cup of tea desperately. Gingerly, he pushed the covers back and steadied himself as his feet touched the floor. If anyone saw him and asked, he needed the loo. If they didn't, he might make it down the quiet corridor to the visitors' room and make himself a cup. He hoped the night nurse had her head in a good romance and wouldn't pay him any attention.

Unfortunately for him, however, she knew every sound in her ward, and his creeping down the corridor was one of them. He'd been rumbled. She looked at him sternly over her reading glasses, her chin nearly touching her chest as she glared. Or was that chins?

"Mr. Rutherford, are you all right?"

"Yes, just thirsty and couldn't sleep. Thought there might be some tea going somewhere."

She closed her book. It mustn't have been that enthralling, thought Jack. Either that or her ears were incredibly well tuned in.

"You only needed to have rung your bell. I'll go and make you one, but you go on back to bed. Do you take sugar?" She smiled as sweet as two spoons full.

"Thanks – one, please. Don't suppose there's a biscuit to go with it perhaps? I didn't eat much dinner last night. Or earlier on, at any rate. My body clock is all out of whack." He tried to match her smile with one of his own, but he didn't have the same effect. Her sideways look told him there were no biscuits.

"I'll bring it to you," she said again. "Now go back to bed, please, and be careful as you go."

He swore he heard her tut-tutting like Hattie Jacques. Not wanting to test her patience any longer, he did as she suggested and headed back to his bed, managing to get his tartan pyjama–clad body back under the covers without mishap.

Ten minutes later, the nurse appeared at the door, cup and saucer in hand. He was pleased to see a Digestive biscuit balancing on the edge of it. He beamed at her.

"Oh, what a woman. Thank you very much." Pleasantries always went a long way, he knew. He watched as she placed the cup on the table that half straddled his bed, moving his newspaper and laptop to the side a little to make room.

"There you go, and you're welcome. Just push your buzzer next time. There's only a small staff on at night, and I don't want to be worrying about you falling while I'm seeing to another patient." She tucked his bedclothes in like his mother had done when he was a little boy. He found it strangely comforting. Maybe that was half of the appeal of nurses: someone to take care of you and make your decisions for you.

"I'll be good, I promise," he said, trying on a little-boy pout. The nurse returned a curious smile. Before he could stop himself, he said, "You know, we've got a case at the moment involving fetishes." *Now where on earth did that come from?* he wondered.

She stopped in her tracks, her expression even more curious now. She was quick with his meaning. "And you think because I'm a nurse, I get randy old men leering at my behind in a uniform, enjoying me being bossy to them?"

"Something like that. Do you? Get many, I mean?"

"A few, but we handle them. Remember, most people are in here because they're sick, so getting amorous is not right up there on their list of activities. Why do you ask?"

"Research, really. I've been doing a lot while I've been lying here and it's been both fascinating and weird. You wouldn't believe some of the fetishes I've come across."

She quickly checked her watch, which was pinned upside down over her left breast, and then wandered back towards his bed. Curiosity.

"What's the case?"

Jack told her what he could without divulging details. When he'd finished, she said, "Nothing surprises me anymore. I expect in your research you've been to some of the clubs in town?"

"Not yet, no. I've kind of been laid up." He grinned. "Why? Any in particular I should visit when I get out of this bed?"

"Do you have a partner, female maybe?"

"Amanda, yes. Why?"

"She got a good body?"

"Eh? Well, she's not my type, but no, nothing stunning. She's a sensible Doc-Martens-wearing type of woman. And very talented."

"I think I've seen her here. Visiting." She looked thoughtful for a moment. "Then you need to find a woman who would look knockout in PVC and send her in undercover. If she's clever, she'll be let in right away. Women always get in, as long as they're dressed appropriately, if you understand my meaning. It would be easier to do that than have you go in, I expect. You'd stick out like a sore thumb." She smiled. "I'd start with the most well-known club first if I were you. It's extremely popular with the kinksters."

"Oh? And what's it called?"

"Femme Fet-Elle. It's in Islington."

Jack had seen the name in his research. He nodded. "Okay. Thank you."

She turned to leave and Jack called to her retreating back.

"And what's wrong with me going in? I'm in reasonable shape, aren't I?" Despite himself, he felt slightly miffed. She turned to answer but changed her mind and rolled her eyes instead.

"Thanks for nothing!" he said, trying not to sound huffy. "And I won't ask how you know so much."

Over her shoulder, she said "You never know what goes on behind closed doors." She gave him a wink before walking from his room, leaving Jack feeling like he was the only one in the world who didn't have the appetite for something other than vanilla. You never know, indeed, he thought wryly. He checked his phone for the time. It was still too early to chat to Amanda, but he sent her a text anyway. If Ruth was up and out running, she might be sipping her first coffee of the day.

He was correct.

Chapter Seventy-Five

IT HADN'T TAKEN much to find out where he lived. Now all they had
to do was find out how he was connected to the two cases they had so
far. And Amanda was damn sure he was. Between herself, Jack and
their DI, they'd come up with a plan. They would monitor him for a
time to avoid spooking him before they could get hard evidence that
he was involved. And that meant surveillance, watching his house and
following his every movement.

The main problem they faced was that an internet-based business
could be operated from anywhere that had internet access. Did he
have a home office, then, or run it from someplace else?

Amanda sat outside in her car. Chris Smeeks' house was about 100
metres up ahead, tucked firmly behind a tall, thick red brick wall with
large black wrought-iron security gates. Leafy green bushes protruded
over the top of the wall. The place had the air of an extremely private
property, the type owned only by a select few – successful business
people, actors, premier league footballers. Other homes along the
street were of a similar style – private, secluded and glamorously large.
There wasn't a barking dog or pounding stereo to be heard. This neigh-
bourhood was renowned for wealthy inhabitants. It was rumoured that
a couple of A-listers had property along the row and threw legendary

parties for those lucky enough to get an invite. It was obvious these folks worked hard, earned hard and then partied hard.

On her first drive-by of Smeeks' place, she'd noticed through the gates two cars parked up on the driveway, a shiny black Porsche and a shiny black Mercedes. Husband and wife, then? There hadn't been any mention of a partner from her intel but that didn't mean he didn't have a live-in lady. Or maybe he just liked a weekend car for entertaining himself and went to work in the Merc, wherever work was. There was no record of an office leased to or owned by him, but again that didn't mean it didn't exist: it could mean they simply hadn't found it yet.

Amanda sipped on her coffee. Being on a stakeout was particularly boring and something that was normally done in twos. Keeping tabs on movement was hard for one person; boredom and drifting off were real risks. But there was no one else. Since Jack was still in hospital, she was it. No one else had been quick to offer their time this evening, even with her promise of a burger. Who could blame them? Her colleagues were probably sipping cocoa in the comfort of their own homes right now. She sighed and took another sip of coffee.

A moment later her phone buzzed with a text from Jack, a welcome distraction.

"Any movement? any anything?"

"No, nothing. Bored already."

"How long you staying put?"

"Until 10 pm then heading home. I'll come back tomorrow. No resources to sit 24/7 so doing what I can."

"I'm hopeful of release tomorrow, and then I can help."

She smiled at the word 'release.' Had Nurse Bossy-Pants detained him? Jack had mentioned his rather friendly and knowledgeable nurse and her suggestion. While she couldn't see herself in a PVC dress, she had thought, not for the first time, that Ruth would indeed look knockout in one. As outstanding figures went, Ruth had been first in line for the best of everything when she'd been born, and all the time she spent pounding the pavement running kept her in shape.

"Excellent news," she said, yanking her thoughts back to the task at hand. "It'll be good to have you back when you're fit. And only then."

Now who sounded the bossy one?

It was then that she saw movement up ahead: the big electric gates opening wide. Which car would drive out and who would be driving it, she wondered?

"Gotta go, Jack. Movement up ahead. Talk later."

She rang off, threw her phone on to the passenger seat and gave the driveway up ahead her full attention. The black Mercedes nosed its way to the curb, then turned right out of the gate towards her. She slithered down in her seat to be less noticeable. Why hadn't she brought a cap with her, a bit of disguise for her bright blond hair? She reprimanded herself for being so dumb; it was Stakeout 101, and any rookie would have known to do that.

As the large black car cruised by, she managed to get her arm out the window and snap the registration plate with her phone. The driver, unfortunately, was hidden behind tinted windows.

"Let's see who owns the big car," she said to no one. The Mercedes carried on down the road as she watched in her rear-view mirror, then turned right at the bottom, towards the M25. And that meant whoever was driving could be headed anywhere. She cursed herself again for not having worn a cap; with her hair covered, she could have risked trying for a better look.

She leaned forward to switch on her engine and noticed another car crawling along the quiet road at a snail's pace, its headlights off. As she watched, the driver switched the lights on. Odd, she thought: in the gathering dusk, they should have been on earlier. She left her engine off and watched as the car passed her. She reached for her phone again and snapped the registration plate, then watched in her rear-view mirror as, just like the Mercedes before it, turned right at the end of the road.

Satisfied that there were no more vehicles coming her way, she turned her engine on, pulled out of the spot she'd been closeted in and set off, turning right at the end of the road. If the Mercedes and the second vehicle were headed to the M25, she could follow at a distance fairly easily for as long as the fading light lasted. If they weren't, she'd have to give it up for the night and have a word with the DI tomorrow.

She activated the speed dial. The sound of a phone ringing came through the car speakers, closely followed by Ruth's voice.

"Hey."

"Hey yourself. I'm letting you know I've left my spot, but I'm not headed back just yet. I'm following a car following a car to see where they take me."

"Be careful. You're on your own, hun. That's not good."

"I'm only following, I won't get out, and if they don't go on the M25, I'll be straight home."

"Okay, I'll be up. Let me know when you know. See you later."

Amanda hung up and concentrated on following the taillights ahead in the failing light.

They turned on to the M25.

Chapter Seventy-Six

SHE'D HAD to give up for the night. Amanda had followed both cars until they'd turned off the M25 again and headed towards London itself, and she knew she couldn't do a proper job on her own. She pulled over at a petrol station to phone the cars' registration numbers through. Once she'd done that, her plan was to head home. She was knackered.

"Hang on, Amanda. I'll punch them in," the uniform back at the station said. Amanda waited, listening to the sound of keystrokes. A moment later, the officer said, "Here you go. Got a pen?"

"Yup." Amanda balanced her notebook in her lap.

"The first is a black Mercedes, registered to a company in the name of 'Mild Holdings,' so that might need some extra digging to see who's behind that. And the other is registered to a Jules Monroe. Mean anything?"

"Well, now, that's interesting."

"Which one?"

"The woman. Jules Monroe. Not what I expected to pop up at all. Funny how these things come about, isn't it? Looks like I'll be seeing Ms. Monroe again tomorrow. Thanks again."

She hung up and sat back to think. What on God's earth was Jules Monroe doing hanging about outside Chris Smeeks' house?

At night?

And why was she following him?

The data breach had been a long time ago – had she been in contact with him all along? Or had she, too, found him again only recently? Regardless, what was she doing outside his home and following his car?

She dialled Ruth. "I'm on my way back now. I'll be about forty minutes, so don't bother waiting up. I'll see you when I scramble under the covers. I'll try not to wake you."

"I'll be awake. I'm just playing on my laptop propped up in bed. You drive carefully."

Amanda blew her a kiss down the line and then headed back on the M25 in the opposite direction. Even though she'd been sipping coffee for the last couple of hours outside Smeeks' place and should by rights have been wired, she felt surprisingly sleepy. She cracked the driver's-side window open and let the cool night air fill the car. The taillights of the cars in front dazzled her, but not as much as the bright white headlights of the oncoming traffic, three lanes wide. Six lights appeared to be heading straight for her, and another six directly behind them. And another six behind them. Did the M25 ever slow down or thin out to a trickle?

Her thoughts drifted slightly as she drove, and she made a mental checklist of things to do tomorrow: talk to Jack about Jules first thing, find out who 'Mild Holdings' were, and find out where the Mercedes had been headed and whether it had been Smeeks at the wheel. CCTV cameras could help with that one, hopefully, though the tinted windows didn't help. Maybe they would get lucky and get a full face-on windscreen shot.

Her thoughts drifted again. What did Jules know? She'd need to speak to her again. And would Jack be out tomorrow? She hoped so. She also hoped he was going to be happy with her choice of housekeeper. Maybe she could straighten him up a bit too.

Jules kept her distance from the black Mercedes, but it was proving difficult. To the uninitiated, tailing another car was not as simple as it looked, and she hoped she hadn't been spotted. She had no idea where he was going, or what she was going to do when they got there, but she had taken off after him anyway. On the seat next to her was a camera with a powerful lens attached to it that she'd borrowed from a photographer friend. He'd assured her she could point and shoot easily and wouldn't be detected in the darkness as long as she didn't ram it in his face and kept back discreetly. Hopefully he was right.

The Mercedes pulled into a narrow London side street and she cruised past, stopping just past the entrance he'd gone down. It was far too risky to follow him; she'd be found out for sure if she hadn't been already. Turning her lights off, she put the camera into her bag and slipped out of the car. She set off back towards the dimly lit street, pulling into a dank doorway in the semi-darkness. It smelled of urine and puke. There were people milling about, as there were in most of London's streets at night, some already the worse for wear, staggering and generally being loud. The majority of the revellers here were wearing thin coats, like raincoats, she noticed, and long ones at that. That was odd, she thought; it was a cool summer evening, but it definitely wasn't raining, so why the need? It was curious.

She watched as men and women slipped down the side street towards an opened door, manned by a bouncer of enormous proportions, and filtered in. There was no velvet rope like many nightclubs used to manage the queue outside, and there was no queue.

Whatever went on in there, it was no ordinary club.

She couldn't see Chris any longer. He'd been lost in the throng, but she assumed he'd headed into the same door as the others. What to do now, she wondered? Approach the door and ask the bouncer what the place was? Google the address and see what popped up? A woman in unusually high heels picked her way delicately towards the street entrance and Jules watched her fishnet-clad ankles, mesmerized, as the woman made her way towards her in the darkness. She too had a long coat on. From her hiding place, Jules noticed the woman's make-up as she passed under a street lamp: it was both theatrical and stunning. Jules resisted the urge to ask her where she was headed; she figured the woman needed to concentrate on her walking so she didn't break an ankle, rather than having Jules emerge from the shadows and scare the hell out of her.

She picked her phone out of her bag and did a search for the street name. As it was a small narrow street, there wouldn't be too many businesses listed to choose from, she was sure. And she was right. Four names came up and she scanned them individually, knocking out the first three. It was the last result that made all the sense in the world.

Femme Fet-Elle was a fetish club. That's where Chris Smeeks had headed.

Chapter Seventy-Seven

❧

SHE'D BEEN at work a couple of hours when Jack texted her.

"Any chance of a lift home? Out at 10 am."

He'd been given the all-clear to leave, then. That was good news, though she knew he wouldn't be back at work for a couple more days, but going home at least was a step in the right direction. She texted back:

"Great! I'll come get you. Lots to fill you in on."

What would he make of Jules following Chris Smeeks last night? She wondered if Jules had found anything out. They could do with a break. Amanda then dialled Mrs Stewart, the housekeeper she'd organized for Jack a couple of days per week.

"Hi, Mrs. Stewart, it's Amanda Lacey here."

"Nice to hear from you Amanda. How's the patient?"

"Coming home today, apparently. I'll pick him up at ten and bring him round. Are you able to be there, by any chance?"

"Yes, not a problem. Everything is set. Maybe I'll bake a pie?"

Amanda smiled at her thoughtfulness. This was going to work out well. She hoped so, anyway. "Oh, that sounds lovely. He'd like that. How thoughtful of you."

"Good. I'll see you later, then."

Amanda rang off and smiled at the phone. She and Jack had both met Mrs. Stewart briefly during a case when her boss, James, had died suddenly in his bed after taking a Viagra on top of his heart medication. Mrs. Stewart, his long-time housekeeper, had been the one to find him and she and Ruth had helped her through the worst of the investigation. She was a lovely woman, and she'd been the obvious choice when Amanda had thought about getting Jack some help.

Amanda felt someone approach her desk and, looking up, saw it was Raj, the DC who'd been on duty last night. He had a sheet of paper in his hand.

"What you got, Raj?"

"The background on Mild Holdings. It seems, after a bit of jiggery-pokery, that the person behind the company is one Chris Meeks, or Smeeks as he's known by us. He owns a black Mercedes – the one you saw last night – a black Porsche and a couple of other vehicles including an old ambulance, of all things. What he would be doing with that I've no idea, but you might."

"Meeks – of course, that explains the 'Mild' in the company name."

"Eh?"

"As in 'meek and mild,' not arrogant, can be submissive. Gentle. I guess it's his idea of being amusing, though I don't think what he does is particularly non-arrogant or gentle. I wonder what he owns an ambulance for, though. Thanks, Raj."

She wasn't at all surprised to hear his name connected with their case. This was more fuel for the fire they were stoking. She fancied another coffee, so she picked her mug up and took it to the sink to rinse it out. Jack's dirty mug was still on the drainer; nobody had bothered to wash it for him in his absence, so she filled the sink with soapy water and cleaned them both properly. She'd hate him to think nobody had cared while he'd been ill.

Her DI, Laurence Dupin, walked in to make himself a cup.

"I'm picking Jack up at ten," Amanda told him, "then dropping him home. He's on the mend. I guess he'll be back in a couple of days, knowing him."

"Good. We could use the extra resource. How's the hair case going?

Close to wrapping it up yet? We may need to move you soon. Other cases could do with the resource."

She took his dirty mug from him and washed it before handing it back to him. Maybe the gesture would be noticed. And score her a Brownie point, though probably not. They didn't refer to him as 'Dopey Dupin' behind his back for nothing.

"Getting there," she said. "It seems there are others with an interest in our target. I followed a vehicle that was tailing him last night. I'll go and speak to the driver later, but I need to get some other stuff in place first so I don't spook her. A bit of a surprise turn-up, actually. I'm concerned she's got a vigilante plan going. We'll see."

The *plop plop whoosh* of the coffee machine made Dupin raise his voice in reply. "Right. Keep me informed. Say hello to Jack for me." Taking his filled mug, he left the small kitchen area and Amanda turned her attention to making one for herself. The aroma of fresh coffee filled the space, a smell that always delighted her nostrils. As it filled her mug, she thought about what he'd hinted at. Damn resources. Is that all she and Jack were? It frustrated the hell out of her sometimes.

Jack was waiting in his room. He was sitting on the bed, old leather bag at his feet, when Amanda walked in.

"All set?"

"All set. It will be good to get back home. Thanks for picking me up."

"No problem. You'll feel a little better once you get back to your own bed. And I've got a surprise for you."

"Oh?"

"Wait and see. I'm not telling."

"Come on, Lacey. You know I don't like surprises. What is it?"

"Wait and see." She picked his bag up and they slowly walked to the entrance. Her car was parked nearby in the no-parking zone. She caught his look.

"I'm a detective, on urgent police business."

The car beeped as it unlocked. Jack got in the passenger seat and

Amanda put his bag on the backseat. As they pulled away Jack asked, "So what's new, then? Where's the case at?"

"It seems Jules has an interest in Smeeks too. I followed her following him last night, but I couldn't see it through. I plan on having a chat with her after I've dropped you home. And Smeeks owns Mild Industries, as in meek and mild. What an arse."

Jack chuckled at her annoyance.

"We should check out this Femme Fet-Elle club," he said. "It's the most popular one. Or so says my nurse." Jack winked as she turned to him for clarification. "Info comes at you from all sorts of places. I guess nurses are entitled to relax in the same surroundings as accountants and builders. Or anyone else that has a particular fancy, for that matter. I just don't get it, myself."

"*I'll* do the checking out. You do the recovery. And a bit of research if you feel up to it."

"Now look who's being the dominant – though I guess you are the woman here."

"And the boss, if I have to pull rank," she said with a sideways smile. "And not one that's into masochism."

A few minutes later Amanda pulled up outside Jack's house.

"Whose is that car on my drive?"

Amanda got out and helped Jack to the door, ignoring his question. She hoped this wasn't going to go down as well as a cold sore at an orgy. It opened before they arrived. An older woman stood waiting, a pretty floral apron tied around her middle, a smile on her friendly face.

"Why does she look vaguely familiar, Lacey, and what's she doing wearing an apron in my house?" Jack said, stopping halfway up the path.

"This is Mrs. Stewart. She's helping you out a couple of days a week, and she looks familiar because you met her once. The book club chap that died – James. Remember him?"

"How could I forget? He really was a stiff, wasn't he?"

Amanda shushed him and marched him to the door.

"Hello again, Mr. Rutherford," said Mrs. Stewart, "or do I call you Detective?" Her eyes twinkled as she spoke and she held her hand out to shake.

Jack took it. "Nice to see you again. And Jack will do." As he spoke, he caught the smell of something savoury on the air and wrinkled his nose like a dog to take it in.

Amanda was right behind him with his bag. "Let's go inside," she said and ushered him into the living room. The curtains were open; a breeze entered through the open windows and the room looked a whole lot more inviting than it had a week ago. Photo frames gleamed, a clock on the wall ticked, yet nothing had been moved.

"Wow. Looks like someone has been busy," Jack said, clearly impressed. "And what's that glorious smell – a pie, by chance?"

The women smiled at each other and Mrs. Stewart spoke up.

"It's a meat and potato pie. I believe you're partial to those. It will be ready in fifteen minutes. Why don't you wash your hands and get ready?"

Jack turned to Amanda with a mixture of amusement and delight on his face, his eyes twinkling too at the prospect of pie.

"Need a hand upstairs?" Amanda asked him.

"I'll manage."

Amanda waited as he climbed the stairs slowly, knowing his first port of call would be his bedroom. If he was going to be pissed off with this new arrangement, it would be round about now. The floorboards told her he had entered the room, the shrine to Janine, then there was silence. Amanda had given strict instructions to Mrs. Stewart to clean but not move a thing. They heard him exit again, his footsteps calm and quiet, and knew she'd done just the right amount to freshen his room. The two women collectively breathed out as Jack slowly made his way back downstairs.

"Is there gravy with the pie by chance?" he enquired.

Chapter Seventy-Eight

❧

AMANDA DIDN'T STAY for pie, though it did smell damn good. She was extremely pleased that Jack was okay with her well-intended interference. The man needed some care and attention, and the bit of company would do him good, too. Mrs. Stewart had jumped at the chance of a bit of extra income, and Amanda had a feeling they were going to get on fine. The pie had been a great peace offering – who didn't like a homemade meat pie? Her mouth watered a little at the thought of it. She herself was stuck with her wilted ham sandwich from a nearby garage, but there was work to be done. Jack had asked to tag along, of course, but since he'd only left hospital a few hours earlier, she wasn't taking any chances. Detectives leapt out of hospital beds and back onto the job in movies, not in South Croydon.

Up ahead, she could see the door for Body-licious and pulled up outside. To her right was the car she'd seen last night, the one that had followed Chris Smeeks to wherever he'd gone. Perhaps Jules would tell her where that was exactly. Amanda hoped she was in a receptive mood. She opened the door and climbed the stairs to the main office. Another striking receptionist greeted her warmly. Perhaps the models took turns doing the job.

"Good afternoon. How can I help?" Long eyelashes fluttered like a butterfly kiss. Amanda was mesmerized for a moment by the length of them and then caught herself.

Don't stare.

"I'd like to speak to Jules Monroe, please. DS Amanda Lacey." Amanda flashed her credentials and the woman took a closer look.

"I'll see if she's available. I won't be a moment."

"She'd better be," Amanda muttered to her retreating back. Standing alone in the reception area gave her the opportunity to look again at the perfect images of body parts that adorned the walls. They made her feel frumpy stood there in her sensible work boots and trousers, though she'd never been the feminine type, not even as a child; always the tomboy. Ruth was the gorgeous one, the one who could have been in any one of the pictures on display. Still, not everyone could be perfect.

The incoming stilettos sounded on the floor, and Amanda noted they didn't seem quite as angry as they had on her and Jack's first visit. Chanel No. 5 filled the room, and Jules appeared. Amanda smiled warmly, hoping the woman-to-woman thing would work this time too. She stretched her hand out to shake and Jules took it.

"Nice to see you again, Ms. Monroe." Start as you mean to go on. "I have a couple more questions for you, if I may. Is there somewhere we can talk privately?"

By Jules' face, it wasn't going to be a problem. Maybe she'd had the right amount of coffee or happy beans so far today.

"Hello again. Yes, come through this way," she said, and turned to lead the way back through the door she'd entered only a moment ago. So far so good. "Can I get you a coffee, or water?"

"Water, thanks." Amanda watched as Jules filled a glass from a nearby water cooler and then handed her the glass. She took a sip. If Jack had been with her now, he'd have been chomping to get going with the questions, but Amanda waited a moment until Jules was seated. Amanda's first question was going to be a surprise to her.

"Where did Chris Smeeks go to last night? Where did you follow him to?" She watched as the colour drained from Jules's face and she started to stutter a response. She'd clearly been caught totally unaware. Jules took a breath in exasperation.

"You were following me?" Incredulous.

"No. I was sat outside his home and as he left, you pulled out too. Want to tell me why, when you'd told us you hadn't been in touch since the hacking?" Amanda sipped at her water for something to do while she waited for a reply. The one who spoke first was the loser here.

Jules lost the standoff. With an air of exasperation, she said, "I guess you'll find out anyway. I followed him to a fetish club, actually. In Islington. I didn't go in."

"Why were you following him?"

"Because I've reason to believe he's still gaining access to my database."

"Oh? What makes you think that?"

"I have my reasons. I can't say any more. Apart from the fact that I know some of the girls have been approached."

"Approached?" This was like pulling teeth. "Come on Jules, you're not telling me the full story. I can't help if I don't know."

"I can't say. You'll just have to take my word for it."

"How did you find him after all this time? And a name change?"

"Hired someone cleverer than me. He gave me the address and I've been watching."

"And anything to report, apart from the club visit?"

"No. But that's enough, isn't it? He's obviously a part of something. Some of my girls have been involved in unpleasantness, and what with the old guy who was cautioned, it's all fetish related. Maybe the club is a front for something?"

Unpleasantness? And more than one of her models? Amanda frowned. Was this getting bigger by the minute? A thought was percolating like coffee on a stove. Had Jules's girls been treated to a nice hotel room and discovered something missing after the fact? Like Stephanie, and like Taylor? Like maybe a bunch of others? Well, she thought, in for a penny, in for a pound.

"So, some of your girls have received notes encouraging them not to tell, am I right?"

The colour that had drained and returned to Jules's face drained for a second time. Amanda hoped she wasn't going to pass out.

"How do you know about those?"

That was all the confirmation Amanda needed.

"So now we have that straight, let's hear the whole story. What you know so far. All of it."

Jules could only nod.

"When was the first one reported to you?"

"About ten years ago. There were only a couple back then, but since the hack, they've increased quite a bit. The girls who have been targeted were terrified and begged me not to tell, so I haven't. I only found out by accident – girls missing jobs and odd out-of-character things going on.

"After the first couple, it was easy for me to ask them, and they trusted me. It was a huge relief for them to get it off their chest and tell someone they could trust, explain their behaviour. There could be many others I don't know about, of course, but it's been steady over the years. And because of the mention of a debt being paid, they've been loath to take it any further with the official authorities. Some have figured out which debts the notes refer to; others haven't."

"Who is the latest that you know of?"

Jules sighed heavily again, not wanting to break confidences. She'd told Ellen she wouldn't report what she'd said, and she'd meant it.

Amanda could see the conflict in her eyes. "It's going to be out in the open soon," she said, more gently now. "There are too many women having these horrific experiences, and it's gone on too long. It's time it was stopped. Whoever this latest victim is, we need to hear her side of the story to figure out exactly *how* this thing operates. It's distressing, I know, but he needs to be stopped so that no one else has to go through it."

"I know. I won't give you her name just yet, but I will tell you what she told me. Then perhaps I can persuade her to talk to you."

"Tell me what you know."

And Jules did: that her employee had gone to an address, but the story didn't pan out as she remembered it. The driver denied taking her, the client denied seeing her, and she'd awoken in a hotel room in Knightsbridge with a scarf tied around her ankles and a note on the side table.

Amanda scribbled furiously in her notepad. When she had all that

Jules was offering to give, she asked, "And what's your plan now, then? I'm assuming you have some sort of revenge organized?"

Jules looked a little sheepish. "I do, actually. And while you might not like it, I think it's a good plan. Maybe you can help?"

"Why don't you tell me what it is first? Then we'll see."

When Jules was finished speaking, Amanda had to admit it could work, though there were elements that concerned her. She'd need help to pull it off. Someone strong, someone intelligent and someone with a knockout body. And she knew just the right woman to step in.

Ruth.

Chapter Seventy-Nine

"WELL, first off I think you're mad, and probably a bit desperate if you're asking me, but it does sound like fun." Ruth was pulling out a few stray dandelions from around the rhubarb in the small garden at the back of her house while Amanda watched. Gardening and Amanda were like nails and cheese: not two things that went together. She preferred others to grow food for her.

"I'll be there in the background, and it's only to see what goes on there, nothing more. You won't be in any danger."

"Like I said, it sounds like fun. I get to dress up." Thinking, she added, "I might wear a sort of mask too, so nobody can see all of my face. Wouldn't want to see a client in there. Them see me, I mean. That could be a tad embarrassing."

"Jules Monroe will be there with you. She's the woman who runs the body part model agency. I'll introduce the two of you beforehand. She had a vigilante plan that hopefully I've stomped out now, but we did agree a snoop-around would be useful, and she's game to go in. There's no point me doing it though," she said, fanning her hand dismissively across her body.

"And why not? You'd look great in a pair of tight leather pants and a plunging top."

Amanda smiled at Ruth's attempt at a compliment. "Who are you kidding? Me in tight leather? I'd look like a Cumberland sausage squashed in all the wrong places. I don't have the figure to draw attention. I'd be a laughingstock."

Ruth got to her feet and put her arms around Amanda's shoulders, careful not to get dirt on her. "You wouldn't, actually. You have a low estimation of yourself. But I said I'd be happy to help and I will. Now stop with the crappy body image talk. You'll look knockout in your wedding dress because you're you. We both will." Ruth pecked her on the cheek and pulled her in tight for a hug. When she released her, she asked, "When are we doing it? I need to get a suitable outfit organized because, funnily enough, I'm right out of PVC or leather dresses."

"Tomorrow evening. The club opens at ten pm, so we'll leave here about thirty minutes before. It fills up pretty quickly from what Jules has seen, and I want to make sure we get in – that you both get in."

"I'll be ready. It will be fun to go shopping for a bit of fetish gear. Maybe *we'll* use it afterwards?" Ruth winked at Amanda, who rolled her eyes in return.

"Let's see what you come back with first. I'm not wearing a gimp mask for anyone. Nor a rubber suit. How do you even get into one of those things?"

"Talcum powder, I guess," said Ruth, winking. They both laughed.

"Right, I'm off to make dinner," Amanda said, and headed back up the path to the house.

Inside the kitchen, Amanda put water on for the rice and stirred the pot of chilli, tasting it gingerly from the wooden spoon. Chilli was one thing she could cook well. While she waited for the water to boil, she called Jack to see how he was settling in back at home and ask whether he needed anything.

"How are you feeling?"

"Tired, but glad to be home. I've had a nap in my chair this afternoon – fell asleep with my headphones on listening to The Style Council, of all things." His gentle chuckle made her smile at the phone.

"Glad you're resting. I thought I'd see how you were doing and let you know about my meeting with Jules Monroe."

"How'd it go?"

"She couldn't deny anything. I'd seen her following him, so she fessed up pretty quickly and told me the whole story. She's very protective of the girls, and while she thought the hack was all over many moons ago, she was shocked and upset to learn Smeeks was still getting access as and when he needed something. It seems it's been going on for at least ten years that she's aware of, and a considerable number of her girls have been targeted over the years. The latest one was only a few days ago."

Jack grunted he was still listening.

"I'm hoping she'll speak to me – the latest victim, I mean – though she didn't have hair stolen. Get this – she was left in a hotel like the other one but with her ankles bound in a silk Hermes scarf and rose petals scattered all round her. My bet is a bit of foot worship went on. Creepy, eh?"

"Damn right."

"Anyway, Smeeks owns a company called Mild Industries, which owns the club and a few other properties around London, as well as a collection of vehicles. I told you he owned an ambulance, didn't I?"

"You did mention it. That in itself is creepy. Wonder what he'd want it for?"

"Transportation, I'm guessing. Who would query an ambulance turning up? My big question is how he can have so many people involved. You'd need rent-a-crowd to pull some of the stunts off without anyone knowing. Just think about it. How do you get a doped woman in and out of a hotel suite without her knowing, or anyone suspecting anything? And how do they ensure the victims don't tell? Asking them by note is pretty risky, yet none of them do. There must be some dirt going on in their backgrounds for them to keep quiet, like Stephanie with the sexual harassment case suddenly going away."

"I hear you, Lacey. And the answer is I've no idea. But do you remember a movie called *The Game* back in the late nineties? It starred Michael Douglas and Sean Penn. It sounds a little like the same concept: a rent-a-crowd pulling off something big that goes on in the background of someone's life. Might be worth looking it up. Maybe it could shed some light on how this fits together?"

Amanda wasn't convinced. "What makes you think it's a game? Because if it is, it's not a nice one."

"No, that's not what I meant, but the organization of it sounds the same. They were actors and actresses, if I remember correctly, on a big movie set. Look it up and watch it."

Amanda grunted in response, not convinced. "Anyway, Jules is going to go inside the club and have a look around. I can't stop her doing that anyway as a member of the public. I've asked Ruth to keep her company, and she's happy to. I'll be in the background, preferably outside or in the cloak room, perhaps, and listen in from there."

"How are you going to do that?"

"Just by keeping the phone line open, her phone to mine. If the music is too loud I may not hear everything, but we'll see. There shouldn't be any danger, since it's a public place of sorts, and I won't be far away."

"It goes without saying to be careful though, eh? Was does the DI say?"

There was a pause in the conversation as Jack realized she hadn't told him. "Lacey? You've got to tell him. He'll go nuts if things don't go to plan. Cover your arse."

"I know. I'll mention it tomorrow. But it's only a look-see, anyway. No need to concern him yet." Amanda heard Jack's heavy sigh. "Don't you be worrying too." Changing the subject, she asked, "How was the pie?"

Chapter Eighty

IT WAS LATE. But the beauty of having a business on the web was that you could work whenever you wanted, from wherever you wanted, as long as you had an internet connection. Just as writers worked from coffee shops and libraries, nocturnal forum owners could work from bars and clubs, and he had a couple to choose from. Chris had his favourites, depending on his mood and what he was doing. Simple background checks for premium required some degree of quiet, while new member authorizations for the chatroom required nothing more than a tick box. His venue for tick boxing this evening was his small but perfectly formed fetish club, Femme Fet-Elle, one of his favourite places. He had a permanent space at the end of the bar, a space from which he could do his work and observe what went on in the club at the same time, and that was where he was sat now. Not much raised his eyebrows any longer. He'd seen and heard it all, and as a provider to the kinksters and in particular the wealthy ones, he'd filled many fantasies spanning many years.

The strong pulse of the dance music reverberated through his laptop and up his wrists as his fingers worked the keypad, and he found himself moving slightly to the beat as he typed. He looked up from his screen for a moment to take in the ambience around him. The electronic music was almost deafening, but he found it invigorating. PVC-clad clientele of all genders gyrated to the music, unashamedly rubbing themselves and others with gloved hands or peering out from behind leather masks, making suggestive gestures with their mouths and tongues. Later on, the dance floor would empty out as people found willing partners and separated off to get their own personal high together.

He felt good tonight, wired even, and judging by the swell in his trousers he thought he might get a little action himself later. He caught the eye of a woman stood a couple of paces further along the bar, hips moving to the beat ever so slightly, trying to attract the busy bartender's eye to order her poison. Her hair was shoulder length and looked silky soft, as did the skin she had on display. She smiled seductively at Chris then turned away in an instant, her drink order more important than his company. He perused her body while she was preoccupied. She was encased in black leather from her chest to just below her buttocks; her shapely legs disappeared into the tops of thigh-length fire-engine-red boots. They had the highest heels he thought he'd ever seen. Around her neck was a studded black dog collar, with two rows of spikes running around the length of it. It looked lethal to the uninitiated. A moment later, another woman, dressed in a similar fashion though her dress was electric blue leather, joined her. Her buttocks were more visible than her friend's, the soft flesh just begging to be touched.

The first woman passed a drink to her and caught Chris's eye again as she did so, lowering her chin in silent acknowledgment, encouraging him. He smiled back, slipped off his stool and walked towards them both, leaving his laptop where it was. He sauntered over slowly, keeping eye contact with the lady in black, hoping he was reading the signals correctly. A stirring in his trousers reminded him of how he was feeling, what he might take later on. Standing beside her now, did he imagine her eyes twinkling in excitement as the strobe lighting flashed across her face? Was she feeling game too? He hoped so, and there was only one way to find out. He reached out his hand and gently ran the back of it down her leather-clad back. The woman responded like a cat being stroked, the telltale arch greeting him in response, and he heard her murmur something, though he had no idea what. Perhaps she was purring. . .

She turned her head towards him slightly, and he could see that she was smiling. Yes, she was encouraging him, enjoying the feeling, the attention. But her friend in blue wanted her turn, and she took his hand now and encouraged him to run it down her back, except this time she led the way with her own to guide him, guiding him all the way down, stroking the rise of her nearly exposed buttocks and then moving down, down to the flesh itself, the part that had caught his attention. She closed her eyes, enjoying herself, but she clearly wanted more.

She placed his hand directly on the bare flesh of her left buttock and then moved it lightly backwards and forward, moaning her pleasure into her friend's ear. Her friend turned and stroked her other buttock seductively, nibbling on the earlobe of the lady in blue. Chris watched, mesmerized. He'd seen two women having fun on numerous occasions and it never failed to excite him. The woman in blue pulled away first, turned to Chris and fixed him with a smouldering gaze. This was all the confirmation he needed that she was ready to play, that *they* wanted to play. Taking the lead, the lady in blue led him through the crowd towards a set of swing doors at the rear of the club. Behind him, the friend followed, drinks in hand.

Once through the doors, the atmosphere immediately changed. The heavy, throbbing music was replaced by a quieter soundtrack, and under that he could hear languid moaning and groaning. Had he turned around, he would have noticed that the lady in black was having trouble not to stare as she walked and was doing her best to look as though she was a regular, came every month, knew her way around. Inside she was gasping with astonishment. In one corner, a man wearing a full leather gimp mask was tied naked to a bench face down and a woman with a leather riding crop was flicking his reddened backside with the tongue of it. In the centre of the room, a woman on all fours was being periodically slapped on the buttocks by a mystery bare hand and, judging by her cries, was enjoying every sting of it. But Chris was intent on the lady in black, just ahead of him, who carried on leading the way.

He knew where they were leading him: there was only one destination in the direction they were headed – the private rooms, where willing participants got their kicks together. As the woman in blue led him through the door of a dimly lit room, she winked to her friend and then turned to lock the door to make sure they wouldn't be disturbed. She then approached him, drink in hand, and encouraged him to sip from the glass, which he dutifully did. Then between them, and taking their time, they seductively stripped him down to his underpants.

The lady in blue was playing her part perfectly, and Ruth let her take the lead. It was her show, after all. Only Chris was unaware of what was about to happen next. The lady in blue again offered her cocktail glass to his lips. He took two large gulps to refresh his mouth and reached out to kiss her as she rubbed herself up and down his naked thigh encouragingly, sensuously.

Inside the top of the fire-engine-red boots, Ruth's phone line was open, and Amanda listened in from where she was hidden between Mackintosh coats in the cloakroom.

A striking woman, Chris had thought when he'd first seen her at the bar. He could see now that she had short-cropped dark hair with a white flick at the temple. And now he was in a private room with her and a friend and was about to have some kinky fun with them both.

And that's about all he remembered as he passed out on the bed.

Chapter Eighty-One

"WHAT THE HELL?" Ruth's voice sounded strained.

Amanda pressed her ear buds more tightly into her ears. So far, things had been going well but now she wasn't so sure. Ruth's familiar voice didn't sound happy.

"What the hell have you done, Jules? I thought we just wanted to chat when we got close, not knock him out."

"It was." Jules was speaking now. "But I thought in for a penny, in for a pound. We've got the bastard now and we can do one of a couple of things."

Amanda couldn't believe her ears. What the hell was going on in there?

"Oh? And what are the two choices, eh? Kidnap I'm guessing is one, like he did to the others, and what's the other?" Ruth had raised her voice a couple of octaves. "Amanda, are you getting this?" Her voice came clearly to Amanda now as Ruth reached into her boots to retrieve the phone.

Amanda was livid. "Where the hell are you both? What have you done?"

"Head through the dance floor and keep walking to the rear. We're in the room on the right. I think it had a shoe on the door rather than a number or name. It's locked, so knock and I'll let you in."

Amanda grabbed her identification badge, flashed it at the gorilla on the desk and made her way towards the back of the club. Heads turned at the strange vision of a woman wearing regular street clothes wrestling her way through the gyrating bodies on the dance floor as best she could. When an anonymous hand reached out for her backside and squeezed, she shrieked but pressed forward undeterred. It was like cutting her way through dense forest with a butter knife. Nobody wanted to move; everyone wanted to party. Except for her. Strobe lighting played havoc with her sight, but she pressed on and finally came to the entrance of a much quieter space. Quieter save for the cries of those deep in their own individual pleasure zone. She didn't hang around to watch as she headed for the door to the right. A stiletto platform shoe so tall that it could never be worn signalled the right door. Amanda knocked, Ruth opened, Amanda entered. Jules was sat on the edge of the bed. Smeeks was out cold.

"I'll let you sort her out," Ruth said through gritted teeth. "I'm going to see if I can at least salvage this operation and go and get his laptop off the bar. Hopefully, it's still there." Muttering, she pushed past Amanda and stomped back out into pleasure land.

Speechless, Amanda closed and locked the door behind her, then turned to Jules. It took all her self-control not to scream at her.

"I thought we had a plan, Jules? Did you have a different version to work from?"

Jules sat quietly as though realizing she'd gone too far.

"Speak to me. What have you done? What have you given him?"

"It's only a roofy, nothing more. He'll be awake in an hour or so."

"Oh, well, that's okay, then. A roofy. Bloody perfect!" She paused and drew in her breath. "And where the hell did you get a sodding roofy from?" she screamed. "You just happened to have one on you, did you? Do you realize what you've done? How this could royally screw things up? What is your plan from here then, eh? Do tell, because I'm struggling here." Amanda sizzled like a sausage in a hot pan. "What will happen when he wakes up and realizes?"

"We'll be long gone. He'll be none the wiser. He doesn't know we're on to him, remember?"

"I'm a sodding detective, for heaven's sake," Amanda yelped. She could feel a vein pulsing in her forehead. "I can't be a part of drugging a suspect, and he is *only* a suspect – remember? We have no actual proof of anything yet."

A knock at the door brought her screaming to a halt, and she took the opportunity to catch her breath. From the other side of the door came, "It's me, Ruth. Let me in."

Amanda opened the door and Ruth strode past her, a laptop wedged under her arm.

"Oh great," groaned Amanda, staring at the laptop. "Now I'm involved with theft as well as drugging and possible kidnapping. What else have you two got planned? Because I hope it involves finding me another career. I'm going to need it, since this one is over."

Ruth spoke quietly as she opened the laptop and started tapping. "I'm a civilian and so is Jules, and you had nothing to do with this. Give me a minute to see if I can get in and take a look around, then we'll talk, okay?" Ruth was doing her best to defuse the fireworks going off inside Amanda's chest. "Give me ten minutes then we'll talk."

Amanda flopped down on the corner of the bed, exasperated and also more than a bit concerned. This had been a shit idea. Smeeks' bare feet hung over the bed and were level to her knees. She moved away a little, not wanting to be part of this stupid plan gone wrong.

Ruth said, "It's password protected, as you'd imagine. I'm going to need some help."

"You can't take it out of here, Ruth!"

"Then we won't take it out. I'll get help to come here."

Jules spoke up now. "I know someone, a person to help if you don't have one. Shall I call him?"

Ruth frowned at the laptop. "If you have someone in cyber intelligence someplace, then yes, go ahead."

Both women looked at Amanda for confirmation. Amanda threw her hands in the air.

"Oh, what the hell. I'm screwed anyway. May as well solve the case while I get my arse kicked from high above to hell and back. But tell them to hurry. That laptop isn't leaving this building, understand?"

Jules nodded and dialled. A brief conversation ensued and then she hung up.

"He's on his way. I have to take it to his car, though. He'll never get in here. I'll slip out the fire exit out the back and bring it back as soon as he's done."

Amanda ran her hands through her blond hair. She felt like tearing it right out, clump by frustrated clump. What choice did she have with the laptop now?

"Well, while we wait, can I suggest you put his clothes back on? He doesn't need to know you stripped him. Whatever the reason, the plan – I don't want to know what it was. So much for a simple look-see." Looking around the room and up at the ceiling she added, "I hope there are no cameras in this room."

No one had thought of that.

Chapter Eighty-Two

WHAT A COMPLETE SCREW-UP. This was not how she ran an operation. Why the hell had she thought involving a couple of civilians was a good idea? Yes, Ruth was smart and resourceful, but she was probably also in big trouble along with Jules though not as much as she herself was. She'd be lucky if she were put on traffic duty with new recruits, if she even had a job anymore. The whole mess needed salvaging somehow, so at least she could get the culprit in the shambles. At least that might appease the DI a little. She checked her phone for the time. Jules's contact would be here any minute.

"So how do you know this guy, Jules, and does he have a name?"

They'd been sat in contemplative silence since Amanda's outburst.

"Valance Douglas. He's a private investigator who deals in cyber intelligence – off the books."

"Great – he's a hacker! Just when I thought it couldn't get any worse."

"He prefers to call himself a forensic PI. He runs a legitimate business. He was the one I turned to see if this louse was still getting access." She flicked her thumb over her shoulder to Smeeks, who was still out cold on the bed. Thank god. Jules's phone buzzed with a text and she looked at the screen. "He's out the back now."

Ruth stood up. "I'll go with you in case you have any problems. You might need a hand. And he needs to know what he's looking for."

Amanda stood by and watched, pretending she had no part in what was about to happen. In her mind she had her hands over her ears like a child, saying *La la la* out loud. It had always worked back then and she hoped it would now.

"We'll be back shortly. He shouldn't wake up yet," Jules said, and the two women left the room, leaving Amanda and a comatose Smeeks alone. *Shouldn't?* Amanda hadn't thought about what she'd do if he did wake up in their absence, but since he was now fully dressed again, she supposed she could badge him and tell him he'd fainted. Since she was a police officer, he might believe her lie.

She looked around the room again for possible hidden cameras but couldn't see anything. The key, of course, was the word 'hidden.' She sighed. Passing the time in the room was painful and she was tempted to ring Jack, but it was nearly midnight and he'd be fast asleep. And what could he do, apart from berate her and ask if she'd lost her marbles? There was no point. He'd get his chance tomorrow when this all came out and he was looking for a new work partner. Amanda squeezed her eyes tightly to get rid of the image. A knock on the door brought her back to the present situation and she got up and opened it.

Two leather-clad women rushed back in and it took Amanda a moment to realize it was Ruth and Jules. No, she'd never get used to this. Both were breathless with excitement.

Ruth spoke first. "We've got him! It's all on there. His client list, a list of operators and a nice bit of software where he watches the whole thing unfold. And video recordings of events. Obviously, we couldn't look too deep because we only had a few minutes, but yes, Amanda, you've got him!"

She and Jules beamed at Amanda, who stood dumbfounded. "And the list goes back more than fifteen years – that's how long he's been supplying victims to high rollers who could afford it. Oh, and this room and the others are recorded so we did delete that little file." She grinned self-consciously.

Amanda groaned and closed her eyes, then opened them again.

Nope, she was still inside the room. No magic fairy had intervened and whisked her away.

Ruth carried on. "There are going to be some embarrassed individuals when this all comes out."

Amanda thought about that for a second. "Why would they be embarrassed? Why would *their* names be made public?" What was she missing?

"That's the only way to get Smeeks without you getting into bother with all this mess. It was Valance's idea, actually, and it makes total sense. We leak it. Remember WikiLeaks? We'll do the same here and find a reporter, too. That way, you're in the clear. It just means a couple of embarrassed faces, but that can be their punishment for their purchase."

Amanda had to agree: on the surface it made sense and would keep the sticky mess away from her front door. She'd need to percolate the idea first, though, to be sure. "What's the plan from here, then? I'm assuming you've got one."

"First off, we get the hell out of here, and leave Smeeks where he is. He'll have a sore head when he wakes, but that's tough. I'll slip his laptop back where I found it. Valance has what we need on a drive, so we can look at it when it suits. I suggest you and I meet him tomorrow first thing and hatch out a plan properly." She stopped for a moment to collect her thoughts. "Or I can do it on my own, now that I think about it. That way, you can truly deny all knowledge and involvement. And don't tell Jack. He doesn't need to be a part of this, and no one else needs to know." Ruth beamed from ear to ear, as did Jules. Amanda looked from one to the other. It sounded so easy, so simple. Jules went on,

"That should work, and none of us will get into bother. It will have to stay our secret, though, so if any of us is thinking of coming clean, don't bother. I shall deny all knowledge of my part. And I suspect you two will as well. Let's keep this quiet."

"Perhaps we should do the pinkie thing like when we were kids?" said Ruth, holding up her hand.

Amanda groaned and rolled her eyes at Jules. Ruth said the dumbest things sometimes for such a bright woman.

"What?" said Ruth, putting out her lip like a child. Her expression looked ridiculous with her outfit, and suddenly Amanda started to giggle. Really, dressed in tight leather and wearing 'don't-fuck-with-me' boots, they both looked stunning, and Amanda was suddenly helpless with laughter.

Ruth and Jules looked at each other, confused.

"Sorry," Amanda said, wiping her eyes, "but looking at you both reminded me of Charlie's Angels. They would have got into a mess like this, and happily dressed up like you too. Apart from Sabrina that is – she's got to be me, hasn't she, in a roll-neck sweater?"

Jules spluttered as she caught the joke, and they both joined in the laughter, leaning on each other's shoulders, tears streaming down their faces.

A groan from the bed startled them into action, and all three ran for the door at once as though a firework had gone off, scrambling through it together. They looked, thought Amanda, less like Charlie's Angels and more like the gang from Scooby Doo.

Chapter Eighty-Three

✿❦✿

THE STORY BROKE two days after their visit to the nightclub. Ruth, Jack and Amanda were having a casual breakfast together at Ruth's place, each reading from their own copy of the same newspaper that Ruth had bought on her way back in from her run. A pot of tea stood steeping in the centre of the table; a rack filled with toast went untouched. Never before had the kitchen table seen so much interest in a local newspaper story. Three sets of eyes frantically read the copy, the odd murmur of appreciation or surprise the only occasional sound in the room.

The story covered both the front page and a two-page spread in the centre and went into great detail of what had been happening to women all over London, and maybe beyond. There were photographs of several unfortunate clients who had been caught up in it as well as a mug shot of the alleged organizer of the service, one Chris Smeeks. The words 'whistle-blower' and 'dark web' and 'hackers' fairly leapt off the pages. The reporter's anonymous source had provided ample evidence – video files, photos, and client lists – and the reporter had handed everything over to the police.

It was estimated that the service had been going on for more than fifteen years, but thanks to a couple of victims who were willing to tell their story and to the anonymous source, it was being shut down. The police had asked the reporter to hold off printing the story until their suspect was in custody for questioning, and the man was now helping CID with their enquiries.

Believed to have started the service for a bet, he'd gone on to find a surprisingly lucrative market and had convinced the many people needed to pull it off that it was all a game and they were vital players. These players had even been even rewarded with virtual badges when they reached certain levels. It was virtual gaming in real life. A list of the players' names was also in the source's possession but since they had had no idea what they were involved in, the source didn't see the need to divulge it.

Amanda was silent when she'd finished reading it all, as was Ruth.

Jack, on the other hand, smelled a rat. "Wow, that is a twist, isn't it?" Jack looked at both women like they were two children hiding the fact they'd taken the biscuit jar to their room and eaten the contents. And he didn't believe that was all they'd been up to. He detected some chocolatey fingers somewhere. Ruth answered first.

"It really is, though I'm glad he's been caught. It must be terrible to wake up with your hair missing one day, to know that someone has been in your room while you slept and touched you. Horrendous, actually. I'm glad he's in custody. A bit of excellent work." She quickly put her head back inside the newspaper and pretended to be reading another story.

Jack pursed his lips and turned to Amanda. "Tell me again how all of this came to light."

"Not much to tell, except Jules Monroe followed Smeeks to his club and confronted him. He denied her accusations, as he would, but another man overheard her shouting at him. He was intrigued by her looks and took a photo of her without her knowing. She's quite distinctive, as you know, with that white streak of hair. Anyway, he found her name by doing a reverse image search on Google, then found her model agency, put two and two together and handed over what he had. Then he went to ground."

Amanda hated lying to her friend, but she was anxious to keep him out of her screw-up, for his own good. Jack wasn't long off retirement and she'd never forgive herself if she jeopardized it for him. This way was a much better bet. She smiled sweetly at him and added, "Couldn't have come at a better time, eh?"

All Jack could do was agree. "One other thing though. How come it was a sports reporter who broke the story and not a mainstream journalist? And a friend of Ruth's, at that?" He turned to her again. "Griffin Stokes is a friend of yours, isn't he, Ruth?"

"He is, yes. He's been spending heaps of time surfing the dark web looking for an alternative surgeon to remove his excess skin after his dramatic weight loss. He's got such a lot of it, and it's embarrassing for him as a young man. It's a really big job to get it taken away, and a long recovery time, and he was looking for a cheaper and quicker way than a UK hospital. The waiting list here is over two years and he didn't want to wait any longer.

"He met his source in an online group, though I'm not sure which one or what the topic was, but it's on its way to being sorted now. It's a bit of luck and a coincidence, though, I agree."

Jack looked across at Amanda again, and she shrugged her shoulders. Judging by the look on his face, he wasn't convinced.

Ruth stood quickly to forestall any further questions and said, "Well, I fancy a proper breakfast someplace else. Maybe some bacon and scrambled eggs. Who's joining me? Jack? Do you fancy bacon and sausages to go with your eggs? Amanda, can I tempt you?"

Amanda stood and scraped her chair back noisily.

"That's a great idea," she said, a bit too eagerly. "I'm in. Come on, Jack. Toast was never your thing anyway. I'll buy."

Jack knew when he was on the road to nowhere and the conversation was over. Still, they had a suspect helping with enquiries and the cyber boys were now heavily involved working through the mess. It seemed they'd found the time to take it seriously now.

He stood and reluctantly said, "Well, if you're buying, I'm having a full English. I've got some making up to do on the eating front after my hospital stay."

Behind his back, Ruth smiled knowingly to Amanda, who returned the look, but neither woman said a word. Amanda took up the rear as they filed through the house to the front door. The word 'coincidence' entered her head again. "But we don't believe in them, do we, Jack?" she mumbled.

Nothing missed Jack's ears. "What was that, Lacey?"

"I said I'll drive. You choose the music."

Chapter Eighty-Four

"WHO'D HAVE THOUGHT IT, eh? A right turn-up for the books."

Griffin and Vee were sat on a bench in the park with a vanilla cone each, frantically licking their rapidly melting ice creams. It was a gloriously warm evening as they sat; dog walkers and families strolled past, enjoying the fresh air.

Griffin carried on "And your experience helped the police nail the guy, so well done, you, for dropping that piece of info into the conversation. Otherwise they might still be hard at nothing." He took another long lick as a rivulet of ice cream made its way down to his hand. He made a slurping sound as he tried to suck it away.

"So, what's the plan with the story, then, Clarke Kent?" Vee was being cheeky but Griffin wasn't bothered. He liked her cheek.

"She wanted me to hand it over to one of the other more experienced reporters but since it was my source, the story is mine." They both smiled at the word 'source,' knowing full well there wasn't really one, and that Ruth was behind it somewhere. In order to disguise what had really happened, he was happy just to get the story and the notoriety that went with it. And there was a lot more story to come, he suspected.

Vee took a long lick of her ice cream then threw the remainder of the cone to the birds. Turning to Griffin she said, "I want to ask you something." Griffin picked up on her serious tone and stopped licking.

"Oh?"

"Can I ask you why you spend so much time on the dark web? What do you do, or what are you looking for?"

Griffin was not in the habit of lying, but he couldn't think of an alternative answer to the truth quick enough. He froze, saying nothing. Ice cream dripped down his hand.

"Whatever it is," Vee said, "I know it's important to you and I'm fine with it. It's just that, after my experiences with the last boyfriend and the videos and so on, I'm wondering what I might be getting myself into again." She took his free hand in hers. "I really quite like you, Griffin, but in order to go on, I need to know what it is that interests you so much. And I know it's not the sport and drugs article. Call it a woman's intuition."

Griffin's shoulders sagged and he tossed his remaining ice cream across to where Vee's had landed. Birds settled into the extra cornet. Taking his handkerchief out and wiping his hands, he knew he was playing for time. At last he turned towards her and looked straight into her dark hazel eyes. She sure was pretty. The time had come to tell her.

"Okay, here goes nothing. But before I tell you, it's nothing sordid, though it is extremely personal. But you are right: I need to get it out of the way, though in my experience, this is where the girls run a mile. I'm telling you this so that when you get the urge, you can just go." Griffin dropped his shoulders and stared at his rather interesting knees as he began. Once he'd finished, he raised his head and looked across at Vee, expecting to see disgust and revolt on her face, followed by her hastily retreating body. But what he saw instead gave him hope. A tear slid down her cheek and even though it wasn't a tear of joy, she was beginning to smile through it. Then she flung her arms around his neck and pulled him in close, albeit rather awkwardly. Somewhat taken aback, Griffin ended up falling into her lap and Vee burst out laughing. Had it not been for her words as she laughed, he would have thought she was taking the mickey.

"I think I might love you, Griffin Stokes. Is that okay?"

Shocked and a little surprised but incredibly happy, Griffin said, "I think that's very much okay, Vee Dobbs, because I think I might love you too. Is that alright?"

The return smile was all he needed.

"Will you come with me for support, to Thailand?"

"Try and stop me," she said. "My bag is almost packed."

Also by Linda Coles

THE CONTROLLER - BOOK I IN THE SERIES

One man's courage could save man's best friend...

Pete is trying his best to get on the right side of the tracks. Dog-napping spoiled pets for ransom money seems harmless, and he could really use the cash. All he has to do is locate targets with his drone and tell the gang where to find them. It's easy money, until Pete learns what's really happening to the dogs...

When the gang starts to sell the canine captives as bait for an underground fight ring, Pete changes sides in a hurry. With help from local detective Amanda Lacey, they have one chance to hatch a daring rescue. But will they be in time to save the kidnapped dogs from torment and certain death?

Get The Controller

Also by Linda Coles

HOT TO KILL - BOOK 2 IN THE SERIES

She's literally getting away with murder... Madeline Simpson is hot, sticky, and stressed to the max. She's had it up to here with people treating her like dirt, and the hot flashes certainly aren't helping. When her temper causes her to accidentally murder her landscaper, she expects to live out the rest of her menopause in prison. But the police have their hands full with a series of sexual assaults... Feeling above the law, Madeline aims to teach her biggest offenders a lesson. While her pranks take a dark and dangerous turn, Madeline begins to suspect the true identity of the serial sex offender. To catch the culprit, Madeline will have to go it alone... or risk unburying her deadly secrets.

Get Hot To Kill

Also by Linda Coles

The Hunted - Book 3 in the series

They kill wild animals for sport. She's about to return the favour…

Philippa is fed up with the big-game hunter posts clogging up her newsfeed. The passionate veterinarian can no longer sit back and do nothing when hunters brag about the exotic animals they've murdered and the followers they've gained along the way…

To stop the killings, Philippa creates her own endangered list of hunters. By stalking their profiles and infiltrating their inner circles, she vows to take them out one-by-one…

There's no telling how far Philippa will go to add the guilty to her own trophy collection. And she won't stop until their kind is extinct…

The Hunted is a suspenseful mystery set in the Detective Amanda Lacey series. If you like eclectic characters, untamed adventures, and revenge stories fit for the technological age, then you'll love this thrilling tale.

Get The Hunted

Published by Blue Banana

About the Author

Hi, I'm Linda Coles. Thanks for choosing this book, I really hope you enjoyed it and collect the following ones in the series. Great characters make a great read and I hope I've managed to create that for you.

Originally from the UK, I now live and work in beautiful New Zealand along with my hubby, 2 cats and 5 goats. My office sits by the edge of my vegetable garden, my very favourite authors are Harlan Coben and Karin Slaughter and apart from reading and writing, I get to run by the beach for pleasure.

If you find a moment, please do write an honest online review, they really do make such a difference to those choosing what book to buy next.

Enjoy! And tell your friends.

Thanks, Linda

Keep in touch:
lindacoles.com
linda@lindacoles.com

16581320R00187

Printed in Great Britain
by Amazon